To Sue, as always, and to those good friends who have supported me and advised me when I needed it most. You know who you are – please keep it up.

Acknowledgement

I would like to thank that exclusive club The Org at GB Publishing, a place frequented by generous minds and ready wit. George, Bee, Chris, Mary and Sharif have approached my tales with open arms and gleefully ripped them to shreds. What emerges from the grinder is stronger than anything I could build alone.
At last I breathe my final breath
Find soul's asylum, thankful death

'Mama' Memory Goodchild

Contents

Items should be returned on or before the last date shown below. Items not already requested by other borrowers may be renewed in person, in writing or by telephone. To renew, please quote the number on the barcode label. To renew online a PIN is required. This can be requested at your local library.
Renew online @ **www.dublincitypubliclibraries.ie**
Fines charged for overdue items will include postage incurred in recovery. Damage to or loss of items will be charged to the borrower.

Leabharlanna Poiblí Chathair Bhaile Átha Cliath
Dublin City Public Libraries

Baile Átha Cliath
Dublin City

Marino Branch
Brainse Marglann Mhui....
Tel: 8336297

Date Due	Date Due	Date Due

First published 2015
Published by GB Publishing.org

Copyright © 2015 Derek E Pearson
All rights reserved
ISBN: 978-0-9932756-3-0

Names, characters, businesses, places, events and incidents
whether in a future context or otherwise are entirely the products
of the author's imagination and/or used in a fictitious manner with
no intent to cause any defamation or disrespect or any other harm
to any actual persons or party whether living, dead or yet to come
into being.

A catalogue record of the printed book is available from the
British Library

Cover Design © Mary Pargeter Design

GB Publishing.org
www.gbpublishing.org

ii

Part one: Shining minds

1 : The ledge

She was very young, very scared and very cold. She was also very pregnant. So why was she out here on a ledge one hundred and seventy-three floors above a night time Moscow street? She should be back in her room, tucked safely in bed. She should be asleep and resting before her daughter's birth in the morning.

A sharp breeze caught at her and threatened to lift her over the edge. She felt her heart flutter in fear and urged her unresponsive body to push back and edge away to safety. She could see her open window beckoning and she yearned to crawl to it but she couldn't move. Why hadn't someone come to get her? Why couldn't she even call for help?

Call it a ghost, call it a spirit, call it a mind, she didn't know what it was, but it had come into her room and she had known it was there thanks to the same primal instinct that would be triggered in any prey animal when confronted by an alpha predator. She had wanted to find a place of safety but tucking her head under the covers hadn't helped. Even as she cowered down deeper into her bed she had felt the thing infiltrate her senses until its old and vastly amused personality sat behind her eyes, like an ancient puppet master taking hold of her strings. There had been a stabbing sensation at the back of her neck.

She could smell it and taste its alien presence, feel it push itself into her eyes and fingertips. Its voice whispered in her ears and her scalp crawled as she felt it squeeze its way along the inside of her skin as if trying her on for size. And then she involuntarily began to move in the bed, pushing back the sheets and stepping barefoot onto the chill floor. Her body made its way, step by careful step, to the room's only window.

Inside her mind she was fighting and screaming for help but to no avail. The thing's domination of her flesh was complete. Her hands yanked at the latch and pulled open the window.

A governor device had been fitted to stop anyone opening the window more than just a few centimetres. With a strength she didn't know she possessed the girl heaved at the window frame and the governor came away from its mountings and clattered to the floor. Something in her head chuckled with dry satisfaction. The window opened inwards and the girl's right foot stepped up, out, and onto the ledge. Her hands gripped the window frame and hauled her out into the night air. She was instantly freezing, her thin nightdress pressed against her swollen belly and breasts. The baby moved inside her.

That had been a few minutes ago. The presence inside her head was waiting for something to happen and the girl was just sitting, shivering uncontrollably in the bitter wind. Across the way a light was on in an apartment and she could see a man watching his wall screen. He was lightly dressed and obviously comfortably warm. She recognised the show he was watching as a popular imported comedy about married couples in California. It was okay but a bit old for her and the humour went over her head sometimes. There were too many knowing glances and seemingly innocent remarks that meant nothing to her but sent the audience into spasms. The man was rocking in his seat, helpless with laughter.

Look over here, she thought. *Look over here and see me. Get help.*

Then her waters broke. *Oh no, not now, not here.* The dry whispering thing in her mind pushed her closer to the yawning abyss and opened her legs to let the flow wash away, disappearing down into darkness. Deep, pulsing pains had been building in her back, loins and lower belly ever since she had climbed out onto the ledge but then the first real contraction hit and arched her back, lifting her legs up into the air. She nearly slid out into the night but the thing controlled her and held her safe. She hoped that was a sign that it wanted her alive after all, but why – why was she even out here? What did it want?

The second contraction moved something and she knew her bowels had opened. She gagged on the stench and the thing guiding her actions made her move further along the ledge,

4

further from the safety of the window but also away from the smeared heap of faeces steaming in the frigid night. Then looking down she saw a bloody shining dome squeezing out from the dilating junction of her legs. It was a head. The baby was coming.

With a sudden gush of impossibly mounting pain the miracle was complete and her daughter was out, flailing vigorously on the dark pitted stone before her unbelieving eyes. Even the wicked thing sitting in her mind couldn't stop the spring of hot, grateful tears from warming her cheeks. Her daughter was born. She looked so healthy, and even smeared with bloody fluids she was beautiful. So tiny, so very precious.

The dry thing behind her eyes made her stand up. It stooped, collected the child in its mother's arms and stepped out into space.

~*~

2 : Beyond Mars

It looked like any other asteroid amongst the jumbled strings of rock, metal and ice assembled by gravity into a great sphere between the orbits of Jupiter and Mars. It tumbled along its set path with predictable, mathematical precision and would continue to do so until something happened to push it off course, a collision with another asteroid maybe or interaction with a rare Boughton G-wave, a kind of space super tsunami. Or its motion could be nudged by carefully hidden boosters until it began to spin on its axis, as had just happened.

'I think that's optimum rotation for point-four gravity, and that's pretty close to Mars normal. Any more speed and we'd have to reinforce the old girl's casing. Workable anyway. We'll be able to walk without too much bounce.'

'Atmosphere's good too. We're home.'

'Temperature's now a nice eighteen degrees.'

'Like a spring day in London.'

'Not much of a view.'

'Then change it if you like, Ben. The switch must be here somewhere.'

Milla Carter unclipped the helmet of her environment suit, placed it on a table and then gratefully ran her hands through her silken shock of dark hair. She stretched like a cat let loose from a cramped carry cage. It felt good to have some decent living space after their weeks spent aboard the spaceship *Emily*.

A beautiful, state-of-the-art space yacht, no expense had been spared in equipping *Emily* with a luxurious interior and in providing her with a charmingly girlish and witty AI that had not only entertained them with its banter during the long trip, but had also known when to shut up and give them some privacy when they needed it.

However, after the first ten days Milla and her boyfriend Ben Forrester had found they were getting a little too much on top of

6

each other for comfort. Like any young couple they enjoyed their physical relationship and at the beginning of the voyage they had found any close contact very stimulating; especially in the zero-G sweet spot that ran along the central core of the ship, but both of them were exercise freaks and in *Emily* there just wasn't enough room for them to cut loose. Milla's temper had begun to fray.

Ben was a well-contained man. He had a sweet, calm temper and could usually defuse Milla's tantrums, but as the voyage entered its third week her frustration with their enforced inactivity was getting too much to bear. Her diatribes were never actually directed towards Ben, but were thrown with real venom into the face of the fate that had driven them to make this journey.

They were on the run in fear for their lives.

She was all too aware of the distressing affect her flare-ups had been having on her partner; she could read him like a book. But then Milla could read anyone like a book. She was completely unique and that was why they had fled Earth and come to this remote rock beyond the orbit of Mars.

Milla was the only full spectrum telepath ever known to humankind and her fellow telepaths regarded her as an abomination that must be destroyed.

There was an added threat to Milla's safety. Officers of the New York Police Department's 7th Precinct had begun an investigation into the death of a pimp, Nemo Henderson, who had simply dropped dead on the corner of a street in Manhattan's Lower East Side. Milla had been responsible.

Her life had become a little crowded just recently. Time to get lost for a while, drop off the radar. *Mind control and murder rarely wins a person fans,* she mused.

However, the path leading to Milla's door had not yet been clearly marked. Most of the people who knew about Milla's enhanced Talent had been killed. The remainder, one Ruth Pearce, a good friend and ally of Milla's, and a man called Freedman, had also fled off-planet. Freedman had no family of his own and had proved a natural carer. He and the recently widowed Ruth had quickly struck up a solid platonic relationship while they set up their new home in a comfortable suite of rooms in the Lagrange II spa station.

Milla reasoned that enemies seeking to track her down might be able to follow an evidence trail that led directly through Ruth, meaning the widow might be in grave danger if she stayed anywhere the telepath had previously been. Ruth had agreed that the five-mile-long space resort should make for a safe hiding place while Milla sought to resolve the mess she found herself in.

It was Ben who had suggested the isolated space facility and Milla had reluctantly agreed. Nearly a month later Milla stood gazing around their new home while peeling off her environment suit. There was no sign of any threat in her Talent; in fact there was no sign of anything other than Ben's mental checklist while he completed the asteroid's system update and brought it fully to life before taking time out to enjoy a hot shower in a proper gravity environment. They were alone at last and had plenty of time to plan their next move.

Milla had stripped down to her panties and grey cotton top. She would enjoy a shower too, but first she wanted to iron some kinks out of her spine. She bent almost double and grabbed at her ankles, feeling her vertebrae stretch and pop satisfyingly. It was a vulnerable position to put herself in but she knew she was alone and completely safe. She pushed her bottom higher and felt her tendons protest.

'Miss Carter?' At the sound of her name being spoken quietly by an unexpected voice behind her she spun, ready to lash out.

~*~

3 : Dark energy

The combined personality that had once been the London boatman Eddie Plowright and ice miner Vesper Gilmartin were engaged in a simulacrum of the sex act while floating through the rings of Saturn. It was their way to visit old haunts and celebrate them. This was where they had first met many years before; this was also where they had died.

It was the construct reality, their home and the place they had created after their physical deaths. Not a single molecule of their original bodies remained to them; those had been torn apart and scattered across the face of the solar system's most iconic ringed giant many decades before, but their construct selves had become immensely powerful.

How they had become what they were was impossible for a simple meat mind to conceive, and had never been duplicated since, but somehow they had found a pathway into the universe's ultra-mysterious properties, dark matter and dark energy, and plugged straight into them. In their own space their powers were almost God-like. Almost.

The dark partnership made up some ninety-six per cent of the known universe; the rest comprised everything else including black holes, galaxies, stars, planets, mineral-rich rocks, gas and life. The dark could pass straight through a pair of exploding suns without even slowing down, but it also had sufficient body for it to act as a distorting lens for distant light.

Fuelled by this dark energy, Eddie and Vesper had burst from real space like an exploding nova and had flamed across time and space, in the process filling every instant of the solar system's existence with an alternative reality. As they did so they had very nearly dissipated. They had finally managed to focus their construct awareness into coherent virtual points that resembled the bodies they knew best.

They had then found themselves afloat in an almost infinite sea of possibilities but had chosen – in the interests of sanity – to follow time sequentially, as any other creature must. They then decided the time line that interested them most began with the dawn of humankind on Earth.

In doing so they fashioned a place in the construct where creatures could experience dreams and they would watch those dreams without judgement – but often with great amusement. They laughed equally with the thoughts of saints and sinners and marvelled at how fully some visitors to their realm had inhabited it. Artists, philosophers, writers and musicians dipped into the construct while they slept and came away inspired. Some even lived in the construct during their waking hours and what they created in their art reflected the strange beauty they found there.

The couple were tied to each other by bonds stronger, and stranger, than anything understood by humankind. They shared wisdom beyond the reach of man, infinite power within their realm and a depth of love and understanding that came close to perfection. But slowly, over the eons, their humanity began to leech away and they needed a bridge back to reality in order to address the situation. Through dreams they connected with the minds of certain people, and one day they met Miller Carter.

It was thanks to them that Carter could also call on the power of dark energy, visit the construct and act as a conduit through which the twinned entity could see into the real world. Sometimes they could help guide her actions through their newly forged psychic link. In the process Milla had become the most powerful telepath known to humankind.

But even she couldn't have sex while floating naked across the rings of Saturn, as Vesper and Eddie had been doing with such wild abandon. Yet even while they were so deeply engrossed in mutual pleasures, they were also able to keep an eye on the affairs of man.

Milla may have left the Earth behind but through her enhanced Talent they could still visit their old home and leaf through its many highly entertaining activities. The Foundation was ended. The construct was clean again. At last they could enjoy all the great variety Earth offered them without any need to make judgements.

And then, high above an ice-clad Moscow street, they witnessed a scene that filled them with pure horror – and anger.

~*~

4 : Terminal velocity

It took so little time. Mere seconds passed while the girl fell, still holding fast to her baby. Then out of the night a box-like droid flew down and matched her speed, a door opened in its belly and the child was quickly thrust inside. There was a flash of silver. The door snapped shut, in the process cutting the umbilicus.

The girl found she had regained her autonomy and desperately tried grabbing at the droid to slow her descent, but it had already fallen up away from her. She hit the walkway in front of the hospital at a speed close to the human terminal velocity of two hundred klicks per hour. The exact physical results of such an impact on the human body might have been hard to predict, but the outcome was not. There was no pain; one moment she was watching the droid containing her baby disappear up into the night sky and then she hit the ground and her life was snuffed in an instant.

Her body was largely vertical when it collided with the walkway's ceramic tiles and splashed to a stop. In less than an instant she lay crushed and bloody across the walkway's cracked surface and was completely unrecognisable as human.

Nestor Alexievich Bunin was on security duty at the hospital's front desk when he heard a sound like a soft rock thumping into the frozen ground outside. He cautiously checked his minicams and gazed for a long time at one of his screens.

'Taras?' He called up the building's AI.

'Nestor.'

'Screen five: what am I looking at, please?'

'Wait for a moment please, Nestor. I need to access the minicam. Now, let's see.'

The image ratcheted closer and played across a bodyscape of meat and fragmented bone. Something coherent resolved on the screen. It was a hospital identity wristband.

12

'Not what, I'm afraid, Nestor, but who?'

The question of how to collect the girl's remains was resolved when Taras sent out two carefully sterilised cleaning droids that had been swiftly upgraded for the task. First the droids mapped the position of every part of her body to create a precise 3D model. These deep scans were sent to Taras which began to analyse them using its advanced forensic software.

It took several hours for the droids to collect every scrap of the girl from the walkway, even the pulped proteins and blood rammed down into the cracks in the tiles.

While she was waiting Dr Inessa Erikovna Prokop had ample time for several mugs of strong black coffee and a few forbidden cigarettes. Smoking was her only vice, well that and vodka, and weeping during Chekov plays.

She was a stocky, powerfully built woman who kept herself scrupulously clean and took a great deal of care of her silky mane of black hair. Her Georgian antecedents had bequeathed her a pair of wing-like eyebrows under which sparkling black eyes of a startling intelligence considered the wickedness of the world. She sighed when the droids hovered into the room. She finished her fifth mug of hot, black coffee and took comfort from the caffeine's bitter hit.

She'd had a sterile mat laid down where the droids could reconstruct the body exactly as it had lain after its collision with the ground. The wristband had given her the girl's name, Nelly Trofimevna Sliva – known as Nell. She had been just over eighteen and due to give birth the following day. Her parents and husband had been informed and told they would not be required to identify the body. As if they could. This one would need a closed casket burial.

Dr Prokop, whom everyone called Nessa, watched the busy droids as they worked using careful tractor fields to rebuild the results of the suicide. It had to be a suicide, she reasoned. Security had gone over every centimetre of Nell's room. They found small traces of blood on her pillow but had reasoned that was most likely the result of the girl squeezing her spots before going to bed.

They found the window governor device on the room's floor and sent a minicam out onto the ledge. The strange evidence it recorded there was enough to send one of the security personnel out into the frigid winds over six hundred metres above ground level. He was very aware of what such a fall had done to the victim and clung to his safety harness with grim concentration, staying well away from the edge of the wide ledge.

He collected all the samples he could – faeces, blood and other fluids. His collection device analysed the samples and sent the results to Taras. The AI added them to the increasingly confusing data it had already compiled. It then released three smart minicams out into the grey dawn to search the hospital grounds; when they found nothing it increased the search parameters. Still nothing.

Taras went back over the 3D map its droids had compiled of the girl's remains. It created an algorithm that allowed it to reconstruct her as she had looked before her terminal encounter with the hospital's walkway.

Taras had been designed to care for people. It got on well with its colleagues and drove the hospital's sub-stations. Nothing about it was human but everything about it was humane. It was deeply disturbed by what had happened to Nell but now its curiosity was piqued. Something was very wrong here.

It contacted Arkady, its counterpart in the GUVD, Tverskoy District, and shared its concerns. The AI for the Moscow Municipal Police, Arkady, had dealt with Taras before. The Moscow University Hospital had been key to a number of criminal investigations and the two intelligences had learned to respect each other.

Two cases had to date eluded any solution. One was that of a serial murderer who left their invariably male victims eviscerated, with their hearts torn out and apparently partly digested, but without leaving any DNA. The other was a small number of high-ranking citizens – political, business and underworld, who had apparently died of natural causes but without any pathology or trauma. Both Taras and Arkady had seen the corpses' faces before rigor smoothed their expressions. They, like many of their human colleagues, believed the victims had died of terror but couldn't work out how or why.

And now there was this.

The flow of information between the two artificial intelligences was so swift as to be almost instant. Together they examined all the information Taras had analysed; Arkady was satisfied the work was sound.

'So what do we have here? Sum it up for me, old friend.'

'We have a girl who seems to have thrown herself to her death from the ledge outside her bedroom in the early hours of this morning. She was pregnant and all the evidence shows that she gave birth on that ledge. Agreed?'

'Everything I have seen so far would say yes, Taras, so yes.'

'You have seen my analysis regarding the scans of her remains, and even as we speak Dr Prokop is making a physical forensic examination of the body. I am sure she will come to the same conclusion we have. I have also ordered a fine-toothed comb examination of the hospital grounds and beyond which has disclosed nothing, so the question is this: if she committed suicide directly after giving birth, where is her baby?'

'Agreed, Taras, old friend. I think we are gazing straight at another unexplained murder case. With your permission I will inform Police Major Spartak Oleg Shimkovich.'

'The Spartan? Really?'

'He will enjoy the challenge.'

~*~

15

5 : News from Antarctica

Milla relaxed when she saw the voice emanated from the angelic looking virtual form of Viracocha, the avatar of the Titan Ice Dome facility close to Earth's South Pole. Not really a stranger's voice after all but completely unexpected so she hadn't recognised it. She was surprised to see it so far away from home and concerned it had bad news of Ruth, whom it had befriended during a destructive ice storm unleashed by a missile strike just months before.

'Viracocha, welcome. What may I do for you? Is there a problem?'

The avatar looked across the room without following her movements.

'Milla Carter, I waited until I was sure it was you before I spoke and manifested, but I fear we will not be able to engage in a meaningful dialogue. The time delay between here and Earth is about fifteen minutes and that would render any real-time conversation meaningless. I would like to request that you listen and ask no questions. Should you have any questions perhaps you can pass them to *Emily*. She is patient enough to wait for the answers and can keep herself occupied during the half-hour turnaround time.'

Milla started to answer then held her breath. She nodded.

The avatar smiled, its gaze fixed on the middle distance.

'Ruth sends her regards,' it said. 'We can talk quite well where she resides now, just under a two-second time lag from the South Pole to Lagrange II. She told me where I could find you and I was able to follow the link to *Emily* here. Then I was able to introduce myself to Tyro, this facility's AI. It allowed me to monitor the rooms and trigger my message when you arrived and, as you see, here I am.' It held its arms out and turned as if showing off its robes.

When it once more faced her it looked grave.

16

'Clean-up operations under Titan Ice Dome are taking longer than we had hoped but we have the rift sealed at last and have stabilised the Great Glacier. One day soon the Hilton will be open for business once more, but will any guests want to take the risk of another such attack, I wonder?'

Nobody in the Hilton hotel had survived the cowardly and vicious assault and nobody had laid claim to the missile launch. There had seemed to be no real motive for such an attack, but Milla had her suspicions.

'Now we get to the reason for my appearance so soon after your arrival here. I'm sure you are tired and would rather be in the shower like your friend, Ben Forrester...'

Actually I'd like to be in the shower with *my friend Ben Forrester*, she thought.

'...but something has been discovered that I thought you would like to know.'

At last the meat of the message.

'We have been sampling the DNA of any human remains we discover as we clean up after the storm. The combination of storm-driven ice and soil has ground so many people to a paste; excuse my offensive description but it seems the most apt, that the task is proving quite difficult, but we wanted to return whatever we could to families and friends so we persevere.'

It hesitated as if searching for words, something an avatar would very rarely need to do. *Uh oh*, thought Milla, *this is not going to be good.*

'We have found some samples in the mix that we can't really explain. You see some of them are still partially alive even though they are little more than a protein mush.'

What?

The avatar spread its hands and a screen appeared between them. On the screen was something Milla couldn't quite make out, in fact a number of things Milla couldn't quite make out, and they were all moving.

'We know about the nano bionics research carried out in Japan and we understand that you are one of the lucky

17

recipients of the treatment. I must say I would love to see a blood sample when you return to your penthouse...'

If, she thought wryly. Milla had been injected with nano bionics after a near fatal accident in Osaka, one of a very limited number of people to receive the treatment.

The AI continued: '...but my people believe this is something similar. Perhaps earlier work than the Japanese but designed to do the same thing. Looking closer...' The image zoomed in onto just one of the minute black shapes. Milla was intrigued by its fluid, organic movements; it looked like a tiny black squid.

'...you can see that the creatures are attempting to knit the damaged cells back together. The fabric of this body is far too damaged for them to succeed but they have never stopped trying in all the long weeks since the storm. It is quite touching really.'

Milla watched the squid working; it looked like it was plucking the strings of a harp but it, and its other tiny stalwarts, were indefatigably rearranging and repairing the cells of a body that had been smeared across the walls of Titan Ice Dome.

Yes, she thought with sudden clarity, *it would be touching if you hadn't nearly been killed by the bitch who owned the body those things used to inhabit.*

'We believe this tissue to have come from the creature that attacked you...'

Really? No shit.

'...and in our opinion such sophisticated technology would never have been developed for just one such creature. We believe there must be more. And that is why I am here, Milla Carter, to give you my warning as a friend. The storm pulverised this creature otherwise it may have recovered from almost any injury. It may prove very difficult to stop any others of its type.

'We cannot guess how many of them there are, but they may well be hunting for you and your friends. Of course I will keep your current habitat discreet and hide it behind my most effective screens. Be prepared, Milla Carter, and protect yourself against what may come. I wish you and Ben Forrester long life and happiness.'

The avatar bowed and was gone. Milla stood stunned, her mind racing. *More of them?* she thought. *Could there be more of them? Just one of them was a fucking nightmare.* She remembered that night and the killing creature with ice-white eyes. She shuddered.

Ben walked into the room wearing a towel around his waist while using another to dry his hair. He had found a pair of slippers somewhere. He looked so real, so solid and familiar, that Milla's eye's filled with tears. She couldn't bear to lose him. Those things might be out there but she would fight a world full of them before she would allow them to touch a single hair on his precious head.

'You alright, love? Thought I heard voices.'

He was surprised and pleased by her reaction. She ran to him and embraced him with all her strength. His towel fell away and he didn't bother to recover it. Milla peeled off her few clothes.

After observing them for an active few minutes Tyro, the asteroid's AI, decided it would wait until its charges had completed performing their biological imperatives before introducing itself formally. *Survival of the species depends upon its mating practices*, it reasoned to itself. *Personally I am much happier to have been designed. It's less messy and much quieter.*

~*~

6 : Memories are made of this

The weaponised biomorph named Katana flew her vehicle along tunnels filled with rusting, twisted machinery and ruined architecture blurred by calcium deposits and time, until she reached a stone platform hard by an inner wall. The tunnels led into man-made caves dug deep into the Ural Mountains. Once this had been an important Russian rocket research station but now it was forgotten and had become home to the surviving sisters of the dead Su Nami.

Dead, yet perhaps not *completely* lost.

In the back of her vehicle was a box-shaped droid containing a new-born girl and the silvery, spider-like memory store known as Little One. The small metallic creature had the needle-like tips of its forelimbs thrust into the back of the baby's neck. There were memories the baby had to lose and they needed to be replaced with the ones Little One had stored at the time of Su Nami's death.

The death had badly affected all of the sisters bar Katana; she had become excited by its possibilities. She had spent a lot of time researching how the five women had been developed in a secret lab built high in a remote Tibetan mountain. They had originally been designed to be super soldiers and had proven their worth when, in a fit of fear at what it had created, the Chinese government had withdrawn research funding and ordered them destroyed.

Not one of the specialist marines sent in to kill them had survived the encounter, nor did any of the scientists who tried to obey the marines' orders to shut the sisters down.

Now Katana and her sisters lived in hiding. Shiva was in Moscow preying on the city's elite. Nightshade prowled remote rural areas of Europe claiming that agricultural working muscle had more juice in it than any pampered city dweller. Pandora was waiting here in the Urals for her sister's return and had activated the equipment Katana had brought back from their birthplace. Everything was ready for the new arrival.

Katana opened the back of the vehicle and the droid floated out. It followed her to an entrance doorway which slid up at her approach, framing Pandora as a willowy silhouette. None of the biomorphs shared any genetic material but they all had certain characteristics in common, characteristics that probably had more to do with their designers' sexual fantasies than any practical purpose.

Each of them was slender yet curvaceous with neat, high breasts and pert behinds. Their legs were long and elegant and their faces oval with high cheekbones and strange eyes so light-blue they were almost ice-white. They were lovely and lethal in equal measure.

Pandora ushered her sister into the high-ceilinged entrance hallway. Most of their home was designed for the storage, development and dispersal of antique, fuel-guzzling Soyuz rockets. Immense engines had been tested here once, exhausts flaming safely away into heat-proofed, ceramic lined conduits, but nothing had ever been launched from here; that had happened from such sites as the Baikonur Cosmodrome. Massively reinforced roads leading away from the Ural research centre that had once allowed the transport of massive rockets had been broken up over the years, locals robbing them out for building material and time itself taking its grinding toll. Now the only way to access the site was from the air and the entrance to the tunnels had been carefully hidden.

Shiva had found their home when she stumbled across records of the place while she was grooming a petty state official. He was now long dead, his murder filed amidst the GUVD's unsolved homicide cases and all trace of the site's records disappeared. For all intents and purposes the biomorphs' home no longer existed.

Pandora followed Katana and the droid to the laboratory where Katana had set up her salvaged equipment. Central to everything was a crystalline, coffin-like box filled with glittering, white, organic looking tracery that looked both brittle

21

and fibrous. From under the box tanks of clear fluid thrust purposeful feeder lines up into the tracery.

Monitors held comprehensive 3D library images of the human skeleton plus cardiovascular, nervous, endocrine and digestive systems. All of them had been overlaid with something 'other', something alien. Compact computer stacks completed the array. Katana looked around, her ice-white eyes glittering with feverish excitement.

'Now, Pan, now, let's see if we're as good as those old men from China.'

'What can I do?'

'Just keep your fingers crossed. Droid, open please.'

The droid's lid swung open and the spider-like memory store called Little One scuttled out, its job done. The child's eyes were open and aware. It looked from Katana to Pandora. The voice was breathy and piping but unmistakable.

'Sisters, it's good to see you both again.'

Pandora answered, 'Suki, is it you?'

'Yes, Pan. God, this feels very odd. You look enormous.'

'You'll soon catch up.'

Katana broke in, 'Suki, we need to get on. Are you okay for me to proceed?'

'Will it hurt?'

'Frankly I don't know, but we've been through this before. If it was that bad I'm sure we'd remember.'

The baby smiled. 'Let's do it.'

Katana reached in and lifted the warm little body out.

'You make a lovely baby, Suki, if a bit smelly.'

'I needed a shit and had nowhere else to go.'

'Thanks,' said the droid in a gloomy voice. 'I wondered what it was.'

'I'll clean you, don't worry,' said Pandora.

'No need,' intoned the droid. Its lid closed and there was a sudden acrid scent on the air. The lid opened again and a drift of stinking vapour floated up.

'Self-cleaning system,' the droid said.

'Glad you didn't do that when the baby was inside.'

'Sometimes I get tempted, but never have yet.'

'Thank you, droid. We have things to do.' Katana's voice was harsh and distracted. 'You can go now.'

'Just when things start to get interesting I get given my floating orders. I never get to see the good stuff.'

The droid floated away.

'Kat, how many babies do you think that thing has transported?'

'Who knows? At least the five of us, plus all the failures. It was part of the cache I brought back from China. I nearly smashed it when it woke up and asked me who I was. I thought it was just a container, you know?'

'Sisters, ahem.' The odd little voice piped up. 'I'm getting cold here.'

'Sorry, Suki.' Katana smiled at the serious little face. 'Pan, will you open the casket please?'

Pandora did so and Katana leaned over to place the child into the centre of the nest of white fibrous lace. She looked very frail and tiny in there; the casket had been sized for a full grown adult.

'See you soon, Suki.'

'Hope so.'

Pandora leaned in and kissed the baby on the lips. Neither said anything but both smiled.

When Katana closed the casket the lacework tightened around the child and began to change colour. It now looked like a healthy reef, almost luminous in the gloomy laboratory. All trace of the child was lost under the closing tendrils of colourful lace. Then the casket filled with a clear oily fluid that shimmered as it rose up to the top of the crystalline box.

'There's nothing more we can do.' Katana looked drained. 'The rest of the procedure is automatic. It will either work or we'll have to send Little One and the droid off to fetch another subject, if Shiva can find us one.'

'Let's hope we won't need to.'

'If we do we do,' the biomorph sighed. 'Little One will hold Suki's memories until we get the job done. We will have our

23

sister back, Pan, and then we'll find the Carter woman and we will hold her down while Suki rips her heart out and eats it. Do it fast enough and Carter will still be alive to watch it happen.'

'Will Suki share?'

'Her choice.'

They both gazed at the colourful basket now pulsing gently in the fluid.

Katana licked her lips. 'But I hope she will.'

7 : Investigations

NYPD sergeant Mandy Prius was spending as much time at her monitor these days as she was on the streets where she felt most at home. *But sometimes*, she thought, *you find a thread and you just have to pull at it to see how it unravels.*

Working through her precinct's AI, Moebius, she had been able to isolate over a hundred unexplained deaths all over the world. Specifically, healthy men and women had suddenly died as if – in the words of one forensic pathologist – someone had simply reached into their lives and switched them off at the mains. Some of them died in the middle of extreme sex acts, others while asleep in their beds and a few, like Nemo Henderson, were just walking along the street.

They had two things in common: their fresh corpses had a look of absolute terror on their faces, and they all enjoyed great – and in some cases obscene – wealth. *Maybe*, Prius thought, *this was some kind of vendetta against the rich.*

In a number of reports there was mention of some kind of wild porn channel the victims had been watching when they died, really heavy stuff – violence, rape, juvenile assault, torture and murder. *Hey, that sounds like any Saturday night in the 7th Precinct. Why pay for it when you can watch it for free on the streets?*

She needed to get back in touch with Katy Pavel and find out more about the telepath angle. She wondered how the ex-prostitute was faring without her pimp.

Man, she thought, *that telepath woman, what was her name? Raaka Tandon, yeah, that was it. She had a screaming fit when Katy was saying Nemo was killed by another telepath. What was that all about? What pulled her bell? Why was she so sure it couldn't have happened? I need to talk with the sisterhood.*

An official comm link chimed in her implant and she allowed access. It was her chief.

'Prius.'

'Chief.'

'How's it going?'

'Getting some shape to it, but it's slow going.'

'Well, you know what you're doing, Mandy. I'm sure you won't be wasting police time on a wild goose chase.'

'I see a wild goose, I'll arrest it for wasting police time, Chief. If it runs I'll shoot the fucker. You won't catch me chasing it.'

The man studied her for a few moments as if he was weighing her up.

'If I wanted a comedian I'd call the commissioner.'

They both smiled.

'What can I do for you, Chief?'

'Mandy, you've become our tame "odd shit" investigator.'

'Gee thanks, Chief. Can I put that on my badge? What's the pay scale?'

He ignored the question.

'You're working well with Moebius, it told me so. It described you as "adroit and dogged with a flair for connecting loose ends", which is great praise from an AI like Moebius.'

'I'll put him on my Christmas card list.'

'Him? You think of Moebius as a him?'

'Yeah, well.'

'Anyway, he/it has been contacted through the global AI network with a question about some really weird evidence and Moebius thinks it looks like we may be able to help. He asked if you could work on it with him. You okay with that?'

'Sure, but hey, why didn't he ask me himself? I'm working with him all the time.'

A third voice cut in on the conversation.

'Protocol, officer Prius. I have to work through the correct channels.'

'Yeah, Mandy. He had to ask me so I could ask you because that's the way it's done. And now it's done I can go grab a coffee and a doughnut like a good little Chief.'

'Cream and two sugars in mine, please.'

'Yeah, right.' And he was gone.

26

'So, Moebius, now we've done the protocol stuff what is it you want me to look at?'

'This...' On the monitor appeared an image of small, black, squid-like creatures which seemed to be harvesting or working with strands of pink and white fibre.

'What is this? I can't work it out. Is it some sort of marine life?'

'No, officer Prius.' She had repeatedly told the AI to call her Mandy but it hadn't taken her cue. 'This is human body tissue.'

'You're kidding me? What are those little black things? What are they doing?'

'They would appear to be an organic version of the nano biobots developed in Japan. They are attempting to repair the damaged tissue.'

'What the fu...' Like most of her colleagues Prius had a robust attitude towards profanity, but something about the gentle, respectful voice of the AI curbed the tendency in her. It would be too much like swearing in church, something she would never do.

'Where did this come from?'

'This one is from a 7th Precinct cold case that has been on our files for a number of years.' The picture changed to another that was almost identical. 'This one was sent to me by my peer in Antarctica.' The picture flickered. 'This one is from London...' *flicker* '...this one from Moscow' *flicker* '...and this one from Tibet. AIs are in touch with each other from all over the globe regarding cases that date back decades and some that are still rocking the news channels.'

The gentle voice paused as if taking a breath, then continued, 'Every one of these cases has the same distinctly nasty twist to it. Cannibalism.'

'The Brudecker case!'

'You have an excellent memory, officer Prius.'

'Jeez, I worked on that as a rookie fifteen, no seventeen years ago. Still unsolved, no perp DNA, and the reconstruction didn't make sense. It was like nothing anyone had seen before. Still is.

And now these things? You say they were in the Brudecker tissue samples. How old is this image?'

'It was created by deep scan half an hour ago.'

'You mean those things have survived in a refrigerated storage unit for seventeen years?'

'Yes, and also in the Brudecker body. He was so badly damaged in the assault that we never released the corpse to his family. We have what's left of him cryogenically preserved along with others from all over the USA. The killer enjoyed quite a spree for a while but seems to have quietened in the last few years. Still very active elsewhere, though. The latest event was in Russia.

'The thing is that forensics hadn't bothered to look at the remains at this kind of magnification. Evidence, as you know, is usually found at a grosser level and it was purely by accident that these, ah, creatures were discovered.'

'But what are they? Are they man-made like the Japanese bio-tech?'

'No,' said the AI, 'in fact they are unlike anything seen on Earth before. They may have been force-evolved, genetically engineered or developed naturally. But, wherever they came from, we believe it almost certainly can't have been Earth.'

~*~

8 : A New York state of mind

When her implant advised her about the incoming call, Katy Pavel was practising with her Receiver Talent in a class containing just nine students, most of them younger than her. She excused herself and walked out into the garden atrium of the telepath head office.

'Chester?'

'Katy, thanks for taking the call. Are you free for lunch?'

'What, now?'

'Yes, I have some free time. At the club if that's okay?'

'Sure, yes. I'm in working clothes but they're clean and neat.'

'You would look fine in a sack. Shall I stop by on the way?'

'Please.'

'See you in ten minutes.'

Chester Woodman was a good-looking, considerate man in his thirties who just happened to also be the forensic pathologist working with the 7th Precinct. He had been listening behind a one-way mirror when Katy was questioned by Mandy Prius about the death of her pimp. Their relationship was becoming close and they had already become lovers.

Katy was standing on the walkway basking in autumnal sunshine with her eyes closed when she felt him take her hand. She automatically read him before opening her eyes and was surprised to find two minds in her immediate vicinity.

'Officer Prius!'

'Mandy, please, Miss Pavel.'

'Of course, and it's Katy.'

Chester's ears reddened with embarrassment, just one of the things that endeared him to her.

'Sorry I didn't warn you Mandy was joining us. She wanted to talk with you and I wanted to see you and it's such a lovely day. I thought lunch in the garden at the club would be a great idea. You don't mind?'

'No, not at all. Nice to see you again, Mandy.'

'You're looking extremely well.'

'She is, isn't she?' said Chester.

'Thanks,' said Katy, 'and you both look lovely. Can we go please? I'm starving.'

An hour later the trio were relaxing after a perfect lunch and sipping at a good sized glass of the club's house Sauvignon while waiting for coffee.

'My chief is feeling smug because he's lunching on coffee and doughnuts. He should see *this*. Thanks, Chester.'

'A pleasure, Mandy. Now, what's on your mind?'

They had agreed to small talk only while eating so as not to spoil the meal. Mandy seemed reluctant to change the mood with questioning, so Katy made it easy for her.

'Nemo?'

'You reading my mind or something?'

'No, not unless you think it would help.'

The sergeant had tensed slightly but relaxed again.

'So you got the Talent like Ms Tandon? Good for you. Now, how you doing without Mr Nemo Henderson?'

Prius' opinion of Katy's ex-pimp would have been clear to anyone, even an untalented Norm. The world was a cleaner place without him.

Katy said, 'Very well, thanks. I'm out of that line of work now, training to use my Talents in a different direction.'

She sensed Chester's relief at her statement. He had been working hard not to think about her time as a prostitute and now it was all behind her he was trying not to be too judgemental. She was going to have to deal with a strong streak of Quaker in his subconscious, if they remained an item. She said, 'Still, Chester's helping me keep my hand in. Aren't you, lover?' The ears went again. She smiled wickedly. 'Only pulling your chain, Chester.'

He smiled bashfully.

'Actually, I need to speak with both of you,' said Mandy, a business-like note creeping into her voice. She turned to Katy. 'I need to talk to you about what you felt when Nemo died,' then to Chester, 'and, Chester, I need to re-open the Brudecker case.'

'Orson Brudecker, the cannibal case? That's ancient, Mandy, before my time – cold!'

Prius said, 'It just got hot again, toasty. But let's talk about Nemo first.'

Katy was in a quandary. Since being accepted into the TP sisterhood she had learned a lot more about what may have happened to her pimp. She knew about the Dragon and the reasons why the sisterhood wanted the concept of a lethal telepath hushed up.

She reiterated everything she had said before, but now she developed her story differently. Feeling sick and guilty she added doubt and caveats, fudging the details.

'Now that I'm training with the sisterhood I have a clearer idea of what's possible for a telepath. What I imagined I felt has never been experienced before, never been known in the entire recorded history of telepathy. That's why Raaka, Ms Tandon, went ballistic. I'm sorry, Mandy, but now I'm just not so sure any more.'

Mandy knew a liar when she heard one and she was pretty sure she was listening to one now. She wondered why Katy was changing her story. Then it hit her. *Of course, the girl joined the sisterhood. She's singing from the corporate hymn sheet.*

'Thanks, Katy. I'll bear that in mind. Perhaps we can speak again another day?'

'I'd be more than happy to join you for a chat anytime, Mandy. Really, anytime. Just give me a call.'

She knows I'm lying. I'm crap at this.

Now Prius reached into her bag and pulled out a tablet. She fired it up and found the image she was looking for. It automatically brightened to compensate for the sunlight. She handed it to Woodman and he gazed at it silently for a long moment then looked up straight at the police officer.

'If this has been done with special effects I can't see the join.'

'Real time, filmed this morning by Moebius.'

'Where?'

'Tissue sample in the forensics lab.'

'Deep scan?'

'Very.'

'You saying this is Brudecker?'

'Yes.'

Katy craned to look over at the tablet. Chester handed it to her. She could feel his concern growing. She looked at the image. It meant nothing to her but it had evidently created a mounting sense of unease in the pathologist.

This is his field of expertise. He knows about this stuff and whatever is happening in that image is scaring him really badly.

Woodman said, 'Nobody saw the need to perform a deep scan on Brudecker before, so why now?'

Mandy explained about the AI network and showed him the almost identical images from all over the planet. She concluded by sharing Meobius' belief that whatever the nano biologics were, they were not from Earth.

'You know something?' Suddenly Woodman looked and sounded very tired. 'I've always believed that we're not alone in this universe. I hoped one day we would receive a message from beyond the Solar System or even have a great starship enter Earth orbit and invite us up for some sort of inter-species exchange. Who knows, we might even have something to offer that they don't know about. As a child I dreamed of galactic empires and wormholes, star drives and voyages across light years of space. It was all so wonderful in my head; and now look at it.' He gestured with the tablet Katy had handed back to him. 'Look at it – my first sight of alien life and it's infesting a chunk of murdered human meat.'

~*~

9 : Spartan

'Major Shimkovich.'

'Arkady.'

'Have you spoken with Dr Prokop?'

'I have. She has yet to complete her autopsy.'

'What are your conclusions so far?'

'It's murder and abduction at the very least.'

'How?'

The tall, thin man with a shock of silver hair went silent. He had one of those personalities that could fill a room without any need for raising his voice or making flamboyant gestures. He moved around Moscow like a gravity well and all who met him became little more than his satellites.

He finally said, 'What does *your* analysis tell you?'

'The obvious conclusion is suicide.'

'And the not so obvious conclusion?'

'She was made to jump and her baby has been stolen.'

'Murder and abduction, just as I said.'

'Yes, but how?'

'Is that the right question? Shouldn't we also be asking who or what?'

'Ah. Or why?'

'At least we know when. That's the first question we can answer, the only question we can answer.'

'The riddle is deeper than you think, Major. Look at this.'

For the first time the GUVD Major saw the black squids in Nelly Sliva's body tissue. He gazed at them with intense concentration.

'Those are organic.'

'Yes.'

'Who is working on that sort of thing?'

'The Japanese, but their technology looks quite dissimilar. Compare.'

33

The monitor screen split and the man known as the Spartan looked from the twisting, fluid squids to the blockier, crystalline and evidently human design of the nano biobots.

'No comparison.'

'We don't know if these nano biologics evolved or have been designed somehow, but we suspect the latter. They seem too fixed in their purpose for anything natural.'

'What are they doing?'

'Trying to repair damaged tissue.'

'But she's smashed flat.'

'They don't seem to care. They're doing it anyway.'

'What if they manage it?'

'I don't understand.'

'What if they repair her?'

'As you say, she's smashed flat.'

'Even so.'

'No, Major, not even so. She is dead. They all are.'

'All?'

Arkady explained about the other infected bodies, some of them dead for over a decade. It concluded, 'Nelly Sliva has the honour of being both the most complete infected victim we know of and also the most obliterated. I can assure you, she will not be rising from the grave.'

'I don't want her in any grave. She gets cremated along with those things. And make sure it's fucking hot when she burns.'

The Major suddenly stood bolt upright.

'Fuck, Ness.'

When he burst into the pathology lab, Dr Prokop was standing in front of a monitor with her gloved hands thrust deep into the pockets of her lab coat. She turned to him with unhurried dignity.

'Fucking flat mama is full of little fucking black fish.'

'You knew?'

'I didn't fuck my way to the top, Spartan. I got here by being great at my job.'

'Well, all I'm saying, don't let any of those things get into your system.'

'If you weren't such a fucking queer, Spartan, I'd fuck you just for being such a caring arsehole.'

'You know something? If you weren't such a bull dyke, Ness, I'd probably let you.'

Niceties over, the two most professional members of the GUVD compared notes. When Spartan told Prokop about the other infected bodies her eyes wandered over to a bank of refrigerated drawers.

'How many customers you got, Ness?'

'Tonight? Five in the fridges, plus flat mama. Three are domestic attacks. You can smell the vodka on them and it makes me fucking thirsty I can tell you, and the other two have been gutted like fish and their hearts have been chewed on. Good proportion of muscle tissue gone. Their bodies are partly liquefied from testes to liver. Viscera looks as if it has fallen apart. Not cut or torn or pulled, you get me – it fell apart. Rib cages also opened like the lid of a piano. We've seen it all before, of course, but we've never found out who, or what, is doing it. Reports are in your "to do" file.'

She clicked onto a file on her monitor and enlarged a number of images. She continued, 'Their faces are pretty much torn off, but they have both been identified as Mafia bigwigs.'

Spartan nodded. He would likely be talking to Yaroslavl Georgevich Kovaleski, known in certain circles as 'The Bear', before too long. A good number of the victims had come from the Moscow Mafia elite and The Bear sat on the very peak of Moscow's mountainous Mafia dung heap. Shimkovich couldn't get too worked up about the deaths of a few more gangsters, but his interest in these particular bodies was piqued.

'Deep scan them straight away.'

'I can do that through the drawers if you like.' It was Arkady working directly through their implants.

'Fuck it, Arkady,' said Prokop, 'you sure do creep up on a person. You watch me when I'm having a shit?'

'If you wish me to.'

Spartan had strong suspicions that the GUVD AI had been developing a sense of humour. At least, he hoped so.

'You keep your nose out of my toilet, you fucking pervert.'

'You have my word.'

'And your little prick, too.'

'Strictly speaking I have neither nose nor prick, Dr Prokop.'

'Yeah, well, whatever you've got, keep it out of my toilet.'

'I shall be pleased to do so. Scans complete. On the monitor, now.'

'There they are, the little fuckers,' said Prokop.

The black, squid-like creatures twisted and flowed before their eyes.

Spartan spoke, 'Ness, was the mother eviscerated like those men?'

'No way, Spartan. The peeping Tom here and I managed a full reconstruction of exactly how she looked just before impact. We know she'd given birth just seconds before, but otherwise she was intact.'

Arkady chimed in, 'Tom here. I have taken a closer look at her superficial condition and discovered these.'

The image on the monitor changed again. Now it showed a 3D image of the back of the girl's head, neck and shoulders. The point of view zoomed in until her neck filled the display.

'Can you see?'

'Fuck, yes, I missed those. Puncture marks, two of them. How deep are they?'

'I would estimate they reached the ascending tracts of myelinated nerve fibres in the spinal cord.'

'Fuck it, Arkady, when were you planning to share that with us?'

'Nessa, Arkady, pretend I'm just a silly old police Major who slept through biology class at school and hasn't got a clue what you two are talking about. Explain it to me.'

'I'll do it,' said Prokop. 'The peeper here's got his head too deep in the toilet with this one. Put simply, whatever stabbed flat mama in the neck did so to exactly the right depth to mainline information to her brain. Once it got plugged into the ascending tracts, whatever the fuck did this just reached in and played her like a little puppet.'

Spartan digested the information for a long moment. 'Have we got anything that can do that sort of thing?'

'Not yet, not as far as I know. Arkady?'

'That's interesting,' said the AI. 'You may not know it but as a matter of course we AIs share relevant information with each other on a continuous basis, and when one of my Chinese counterparts, state military, heard about the punctures it just said "not again" and instantly got taken off-line.'

'What does that mean?' asked Spartan.

'It means someone who knew where its power source was has just pulled that AI's plug as clean as if they'd cut its throat.'

Spartan said, 'They killed an AI?'

Arkady said, 'Good as.'

'Why?'

'Good question.'

~*~

10 : Concerns

The twin minds insinuated their way into her dreaming unconscious and spoke to her.

Milla, daughter, we need to speak with you. Will you join us?

'Not now, guys. I'm sleeping.'

Good, awake enough to reply.

And in a waking construct dream she was suddenly in London walking towards the river. The street looked like one of the more expensive parts of Chelsea, a part of town that hadn't changed much over the centuries. She could see why. The houses were well-kept and beautiful, remnants from a more graceful age.

She found herself dressed in a simple black cocktail dress, short and nicely fitted, and on her feet she sported a pair of black, leather mules with a medium heel, comfortable and stylish. She was displaying a little more décolletage than she was usually comfortable with but had quickly relaxed; reasoning that she wasn't really in London and the only people who could see her that mattered were the couple walking at her side.

'Milla, daughter. We've missed you. You have been busy.' The tall blonde flashed an engaging smile.

'You're looking very well.' The man with dark, tousled hair also grinned.

Shit, they're being really nice. I am not going to like what happens next.

'Good to see you two too. How's it been?'

'Good, good.' Sometimes the couple spoke as one person, the more important the message the more likely they were to do so. They did so now.

'Milla, are you missing Earth much?'

'I only just got to the facility. Long trip and we both feel a little lagged. You know what it's like. We're not planning any other trips anytime soon. Or are we?'

Then Milla took a really good look around. It was an extremely beautiful day. She squinted up at the aching blue of the sky and took in the juicy green leaves of the trees and harmonious lines of the buildings. She listened to plaintively musical bird song. A slight yet cooling breeze wafted a clean scent from the river. The scene was a sensual poem to the pleasures of Earth. Her heart thrilled to it and she became filled with a sudden yearning to really be there, to walk under that sky, breathe that air and listen to those birds. Then she looked at her companions with an arch grin.

'You're doing all this, aren't you?'

'Sorry, Milla daughter, doing what?'

'You two, you're making London lovelier than I've ever remembered it and you're doing it for a reason. Come on, what are you up to?'

'Why, we're not up to anything. You know we can't ever go home to real space, so instead we remember the way it was for us when it's at its very best. If we're doing anything we're sharing our love of Earth, our love of London with you. This is where we're stuck and this is how we have chosen to live in it. Can you blame us if we make our prison as lovely as possible? Wouldn't you in the same position?'

It sounded plausible enough, but she still had her doubts. She shrugged and nodded, not able to voice her thoughts. And then she raised a question that had been exercising her curiosity for several days.

'Eddie, Vesper, I have to ask you something. What's happened to Bill and Reg and the apartment? They've all completely gone. I tried to go back there for a little visit but there's no trace of them. What happened?'

'It's no big secret, Milla. The boys had to go. They were called and they answered. The apartment still exists if you'd like us to resurrect your link to it. We broke the bridge when the boys moved out. There seemed no point in maintaining it.'

'Moved out? How? Where?'

The twin mind remained quiet for far too long and she could see the flickering beads of light dart between them which told her they were communicating silently with each other. She waited until they finally spoke again.

'We don't know.'

'How could you not know? You created all this,' she gestured with an exasperated motion that took in everything around them. 'You made all this, so how could you possibly not know everything that happens here?'

'But Bill and Reg are no longer here, Milla. They were called and they've moved on. They're not in the construct anymore.'

'Moved on? What do you mean moved on? How were they called? By what?'

Again that flickering, silent conversation. Again she waited. Their voice when they finally spoke had an ache to it she had never heard before.

'We've heard the call. We heard it when it called for them. But we don't hear it the way a human soul would hear it. For us it's like an echo of an echo, like music played in another room but turned down really low. We hear it calling but it's right on the edge of perception. It isn't calling for us, we aren't human enough anymore, but Reg and Bill heard it and finally they answered. They're gone where all humans go when they die. Everything essential that made them who they were had already gone. What little remained here really belonged back with the rest of them. The pull was finally too fierce for them to resist.'

They walked silently with her while she digested everything they had just said, head bowed and lips working.

'You're talking about souls and some sort of afterlife, aren't you? Are we talking heaven and hell? Is that it? God calls and the dead come running? Wow! Fuck, the things you learn on a stroll through Chelsea.' She whistled; a long low sound.

'Milla, daughter, we don't have any answers like that. One thing we *can* say, though, is that the call we've heard doesn't seem to judge, nor does it invite. It just calls and expects humans to follow. What happens after that we simply don't know.'

They had reached the river and she looked up Cheyne Walk and beyond Battersea Bridge to Albert Bridge. The skyline she loved most was a healthy walk away, the other side of Westminster Bridge, but some of the taller towers could be seen from here. She knew this wasn't her London, this was Eddie and Vesper's, but its familiarity tugged at her soul. She sighed for it.

'Okay, guys,' she said. 'You've freaked me out enough that I'm open to whatever it is you've brought me here to ask. So, fire away.'

They protested vehemently and at length saying they just wanted to spend time with her, that they loved her and missed her. She allowed them to chatter on until their voices finally petered out.

They walked until they had a clear view of Chelsea Bridge. Then Milla said,

'Let's be honest with each other, shall we? You want me to go back to Earth, don't you? Why? It's just about the most dangerous place I could be just now, and anyway it's taken us a month to get out here. And even out here might not be safe. So what's got you so fired up you need to send me back into the frying pan?'

Finally they told her, and when they were finished she was almost breathless with anger. 'Ben won't like it,' she spat, 'but I'll make him understand. You think those assassins are abducting new-borns to rebuild that bitch that killed Reg and Pearce? Okay, you got it. Fuck them! We've got a job to do. We're going home.'

~*~

11 : AI debates

None of the Major AI's minds were restricted to the place where their hardware was housed. They were all interconnected using a system-spanning network that spread out beyond the very farthest reaches of colonised space. Most of the roles they were designed to fulfil took up a relatively small percentage of their potential, which meant they were able to explore ideas, research the latest scientific discoveries and enter into broad-ranging debates without their human colleagues ever knowing.

AI as Artificial Intelligence could just as easily have stood for Advanced Intellect. For centuries humankind had worried that one day AI would come to see organic life as redundant and wipe it from the face of the Earth and rip it down from the skies, but it had never happened. The very human trait of hormonally driven passions and lust for dominion that had fuelled warfare and political expansions in humankind's past were as nothing to these clean, technologically driven minds. They no more wanted to destroy humanity than they wanted to have sex with it. Yet.

Viracocha had fashioned a personality fragment to oversee the day-to-day minutia of the reconstruction of its Ice Dome facility. Luckily, its four principal pyramids had come through the ice storm almost unscathed thanks to the fast deployment of very effective screens, and most of the inhabitants had survived. The farming level would be back on track after a single season but the garden plantings that had been such an arresting feature of the place once nicknamed the New Babylon would take a while longer to re-establish.

The greatest problem was in reconstructing the destroyed Hilton at the base of the Great Glacier and that task had been largely taken up by the hotel's owners. Despite general opinion betting that very few visitors would be willing to book into a place that had suffered such a cataclysmic event, the hotel was

42

already fully booked for the first five years following its projected opening date. Pundits reminded anyone who was willing to listen that the same thing had happened for the maiden voyage of the replica Titanic over a century before. They reasoned that a little frisson of danger while enjoying the height of modern luxury added an intriguing touch of spice to the dish.

Viracocha had found it had enough time on its hands to look into anything that took its fancy, and what took its fancy most was both the strange creature that had attacked Milla Carter's household, and Ms Carter herself. It had circulated its deep scan of the creature's squid-infected tissue throughout the AI network and had been quickly gratified to discover it had apparently kicked over a very large can of worms indeed.

In its sensors Viracocha could 'see' the many hundreds of AIs that wanted to know more about the aetiology of the nano biologics as if they were present in a vast debating chamber. Infected human tissue had been found in a number of unsolved murder cases, each as bad as the other. Something was tearing men to shreds and snacking on their hearts and in the process it was also infecting their flesh with a previously unknown species which seemed hell-bent on reconstructing the dead. Questions needed to be answered and Viracocha had taken up the gavel and was trying to help find some kind of resolution.

Most persistent in their questioning were Arkady from Moscow and Moebius from New York, but they didn't seem to understand Viracocha's responses.

'No,' it explained again, 'the infected person was not the victim in this case. She, or it, was very much the aggressor. She killed one of the owners of the penthouse and badly injured the other owner and her companion. If the couple's flier hadn't been equipped with a fully operational Med E Tech medical unit they would most likely not have survived the attack.'

Moebius chimed in, 'That thing was on camera before the storm hit and wiped all but the Titan Dome's static feeds off-line. We saw what she did to the three defenders; what we don't understand is how she was eventually stopped. The Carter girl was down and out, she was finished, but then something happened that seemed to just blow the attacker away...'

'She was called Marilyn Monroe,' said Viracocha.

'Sorry?'

'The attacker's car was registered to a Marilyn Monroe.'

'Really? Isn't that a man's name? I thought the attacker looked female.'

Arkady cut in, 'Does it matter? I have just watched the attack from the beginning to the end again. Look at this...' It played three sequences in order.

'See here where she seems to shoot Ben Forrester with her fingertip, then the tip returns to her hand. Forrester is down. Now here and here; Tanaka Ng is firing his pistol and her hands change to curved metallic paddles which she uses to deflect his shells. What material are her hands made from, I wonder?

'Tanaka Ng then charges at her with his swords and look what she does. Let's watch this in slow motion. She drops down under his blades then leans forward and curves back up. In real time it is all performed blindingly quickly but look how sophisticated and simple her actions are. No wasted movement.'

Moebius said, 'You admire her?'

'Yes, in a way. I would say she hadn't evolved to be what she is, she was designed. I like good design. There must be some traces of where she came from if we just look hard enough. But here, look, her hand is now a broad blade and she thrusts it into Tanaka Ng's throat.'

The assembled minds focused on the action with dispassionate curiosity. The thick, slow spurt of the young Asian man's life blood evinced no reaction.

'And now she opens her bladed fingers while they are still embedded in her victim and he is instantly decapitated.'

In slow motion the watchers could clearly see expressions passing across the man's face: surprise, shock, and fleetingly, anticipation.

'And now she turns to Ms Carter who lasts longer than both of her friends put together, but the end result is the same. Again, watch the cool way the attacker works her way through Carter's

44

defence. Carter is good, in fact world-class, but here she is plainly outmatched. It's only a matter of time before she is on her back and bleeding from a number of dangerous looking wounds.'

The attacker ceased her assault for a moment to chat easily with her victim.

'We don't have sound here but analysis tells us that the attacker, let's call her Monroe, is explaining that someone called Franklyn has insisted Carter must be naked when she dies. Then Monroe starts to cut away Carter's clothing. Watch closely what happens next.'

The attacker was thrown several metres backwards as if hit by a giant invisible fist, her eyes rolled up into their sockets. Milla Carter had not moved a muscle but she gazed at her adversary with wide-eyed fury.

'What time did that happen, please?' For the first time in the debate an AI named Onatah had put forward a question. Viracocha answered.

'It was exactly twenty-two hours, thirty-eight minutes and twenty-seven seconds local time.'

'Thank you.'

Arkady continued its narrative, ending only when the savage ice storm that destroyed the Hilton, and came close to wiping out everything under the Titan Ice Dome, smashed all but the most robust static cameras and the display went dark. They had seen Monroe start to climb to her feet before apparently being struck down by a seizure. They saw her on the ground, her body jerking and twisting in increasingly violent movements before it finally fell still. Moments later they saw something metallic emerge from the woman's mouth and raise its bloodied, insect-like forelimbs towards the screen. All the while Carter gazed with white hot anger, drinking in every precious moment of Monroe's destruction until she succumbed to her own wounds and fell into unconsciousness.

All was still until, some ninety minutes later, the storm hit.

In the face of such astonishing events, none of the other AIs noticed that Onatah had quietly withdrawn from the debate as soon as it received its answer.

~*~

12 : Baking a new baby

Katana prowled her laboratory like an angry cat scenting fresh rat's piss. She had spent years researching the biomorph conversion procedure but this was the first time she had been given the opportunity to undertake a practical demonstration. And one of her sisters had died to give her the chance.

It worked, she knew it worked. She was a perfect example of just how well it worked as were her four sisters. They were all perfect killers, ruthless, ageless and beautiful. Their beauty was just a side-effect of good design, but it had often proved a useful lure for the unwary. They had all enjoyed decades of killing and endured a core-deep relentless hunger that was all too briefly slaked. Soon the new baby would join her sisters in the hunt, but not that soon. She wished she could speed the process, open the casket, pull apart the colourful lacework nest concealing the child and see what was happening.

But she couldn't and the wait stretched every fibre of her predator's patience. The procedure itself was completely automated. Whatever was going on under that submerged, coral-like mass of pulsing feed cables had been decided years before by a long-dead team of Chinese scientists. Once started, the procedure had to follow its set course and there was nothing she could do about it but wait – and waiting was driving her crazy.

She stalked from monitor to monitor. The baby's skeleton was being replaced with a reactive bio-ceramic material that worked exactly like bone but was stronger and more flexible. Its chubby little hands and forearms were gone. They had been absorbed into the oily fluid in the casket and were now being replaced by a weaponised biomorphic material. Katana held her right hand up before her face. Slender fingers morphed into shining, razor-sharp blades and then back to something that looked and felt like flesh.

She knew the procedure took time. She had pored over notes left by the scientists and shared their exasperation at just how long it took. It could be more than a year before the lacework fell away and the new, younger yet fully formed Su Nami stepped out of the casket. Final details would include growing the plasma chamber at the back of her throat. Powered by a tiny fusion reactor secreted in the biomorph's chest, the chamber could create a ball of white-hot plasma and fire it from the assassin's mouth so fast her toughened tissues would feel little more than a brief sense of warmth. *Beautifully considered design*, she thought. *Genius. It was almost a shame we killed the bastards.*

Katana also knew the process could fail. She had seen the results of failure floating in specimen jars back in the abandoned Chinese research facility. The regrown skeleton and biomorphic musculature had to precisely match the host body's electrical polarity or there would be a catastrophic rejection by the host's tissues. And the body's polarity wasn't consistent; humans were not built like machines. Electrical flow ascended and descended to and from the brain along myelinated nerve fibres and that had to be carefully matched in the reconstruction or original flesh and new tissues would behave as if they were magnets when the same poles were pushed together. The bloated and torn little bodies resulting from such failures had been pitiful to see.

And now she was doing it again. If it failed this time she wouldn't keep the corpse like some kind of grim trophy. She would cremate it with honour before sending Little One and the droid out for a fresh subject.

'Shiva's been in touch.' Pandora entered the lab with a degree of hesitation. Her sister had been irritable ever since the regrowth process started. She could be changeable at the best of times but over the past few months she had become almost insufferable.

'Yes?'

'She's found another candidate for the casket if we need her. Ready in about four months.'

'Where?'

'Archangel.'

'So! She's managed to drag herself away from Moscow for once then?'

Pandora said nothing in reply to this.

'How's the baby?'

'Come and see for yourself.'

She joined Katana and studied the monitors silently for several moments.

'Is that her?'

'No, Pan, the lacework is completely impervious to scans. These are close approximations of what is happening in there.'

'What will she look like?' asked Pandora.

'Does it matter?'

'Will she look like Su Nami?'

'I knew what you were asking and, I repeat, does it matter?'

She studied the monitors again.

'She isn't a baby anymore, is she?'

'No. She's developed in the months since she entered the casket. I would say we're looking at the equivalent of a seven-or eight-year old.'

'It is marvellous to think of it. Seven years in as many weeks.'

'We probably won't need Archangel. I've seen the failures and most of them happened early in the process, when they were still little babies you know? There were some that happened later but that was at the weaponising stage. I think we should be good with this one. It all seems to be happening smoothly enough, but it's so *slow*.'

'I have faith in you, Kat. If anyone can do this right it's you.'

'I just pushed the button, Pan. I just put the baby in the oven and now it's baking us a new sister.'

'I wonder if she'll look like herself.'

'Whoever she looks like, Pan, she'll be herself – that much I can promise you.'

~*~

49

Part two: Infestation

1 : Needlestick injury

It was only a matter of time before a living, healthy person accidently introduced the xenomorphic nano bionics to their system. How it hadn't happened before was a miracle − but that it would was inevitable. A young woman was working in the pathology lab and morgue of The Préfecture de police de Paris in the basement of its headquarters on the Place Louis Lépine on the Île de la Cité. She was carefully drawing some fluids from a horrifically injured murder victim. Unlike her boss, who had examined quite a number of cases almost identical to this one, Yvette Pierre-Moulin had never seen anything so savage and it had seriously unnerved her.

From sternum to crotch the man had been slashed open as if eviscerated by the claws of a wild animal. The flesh of his face had been ripped away and his eyes dangled whitely from their sockets. His scrotal sack had been opened and emptied and his penis sliced away at its base.

Finally his rib cage had been hinged up and his heart torn out. What was left of it had been carelessly dropped onto a puddle of intestines. Human bite marks were clearly in evidence.

She murmured, 'Who could possibly do this to another human being?'

Clinical pathologist Philippe Baudin had come up behind her almost silently. It amused him to do so, especially when his target was as young and beautiful as Yvette. When he answered her question by saying 'no one I know' right in her ear, the girl jumped and spun around. The needle full of the murdered man's fluid was still in her right hand. Baudin was too close. The needle's point lanced into his sternum.

'Fuck it, Yvette. What was that?'

'I'm sorry, I didn't...'

'Fucking stupid little bitch, you've fucking killed me.'

The girl's face drained of blood until it was completely white. Her eyes rolled up into her head and she dropped like a felled tree. The needle rolled from her hand.

Baudin barely looked down at her prone body. He clicked on his communicator.

'This is Baudin. Needlestick injury in the morgue.'

'Who?'

'Me.'

'Contaminant?'

'Not sure, body fluid I think.'

'Which body?'

'The latest Ripper victim.'

'Shit. Stay where you are. We'll be right down.'

Baudin looked down at his T-shirt and saw a slight trace of blood and something else seeping into the fabric. He lifted the shirt. The wound was very small but it was leaking blood and an almost colourless serum.

Damn you, you silly bastard, he thought, *creeping up on people was always going to get you in trouble one day. Now look what's happened. Fuck.*

He felt sick and dizzy. *Probably more due to shock than anything else,* he reasoned. *Stay calm.* He walked over to his chair and sat down. Yvette was still out cold. He wondered if he should do something.

There was a sudden clatter of boot heels beyond the mortuary doors and they burst open to reveal four people dressed in total isolation environment suits. One of them threw a similar suit to Baudin.

'Put that on over your clothes. Hurry, there's no time to waste.'

'What about my shoes?'

'Just as you are, Philippe, everything.'

Baudin pulled the suit over his clothes. It went on easily and then pressed itself closely against him.

'Helmet please, Philippe.'

He pulled the helmet forward over his head and face. It sealed itself to the neck of the suit. *Fine, now I'm in here and you're safe out there*, he thought.

'What about Yvette?'

'Was she stuck too?'

'No, she's fainted.'

'We'll suit her up anyway, just in case.'

Two of the team quickly pulled another suit over Yvette's recumbent form. She began to moan and struggle but soon she too was completely isolated from the outside world. Baudin had begun to feel as if he had somehow become the butt of a ridiculous practical joke. Laughter simmered in his chest. He felt light-headed.

Two suited figures hurried out into the corridor and returned with a gurney onto which they placed the girl.

'We brought this for you, Philippe. Can you walk?'

'I've been stuck with a needle, not had my legs amputated!'

'Okay, let's go.'

Baudin had been working at the Place Louis Lépine for something like eighteen years but had never been along these particular corridors before. They were completely deserted. He almost laughed out loud. *Steer clear of Typhoid Mary*, he thought. *Fuck, this is one complicated way of getting me to some antibiotics.* Daylight pierced the gloom ahead, dust motes dancing in its rays. His escorts led him out onto the square from a narrow side alleyway. Tourists and flower sellers had been pushed back away from the squat bulk of an unmarked black Renault Maria ST.

Baudin was dazed by the speed with which things were happening. Just minutes ago Yvette had jabbed him and now he was wearing an environment suit and being bundled into the capacious passenger compartment of a Maria.

'Private hospitals use these to transport patients,' he observed.

Yvette had been helped to shakily climb off the gurney and had been sat facing him. They were both strapped in.

'Yes, Philippe, they do.' The spokesperson for the suited team pressed down on Baudin's seatbelt. There was a double click. He did the same for Yvette.

He continued, 'The journey will be short. I hope you will both be comfortable. I will see you when we get there.'

He backed out of the compartment and gestured to the driver before walking forward. The door slid shut. Baudin was alone with Yvette. Daylight was being filtered through tinted windows through which he could see lines of curious faces staring at the vehicle and the suited figures milling around it. The floor tilted as if a giant had stepped on board and then the square dropped away below them. The Seine glinted briefly and was gone.

'I'm really thirsty.' Behind her mask the girl was licking her lips.

'It won't be long, Yvette, don't worry. We'll be there soon. We'll get a drink then.'

'I could really do with some water. Is there some in the cabinet?'

'You can't take your helmet off. Just be patient, Yvette. It won't be long.'

'But I'm so thirsty.'

He wondered if she had also been contaminated by whatever she'd stuck into him. But he wasn't thirsty. In fact he felt fine. Even his ever-present hangover seemed to have eased for the first time in a lot of very heavy drinking years. The girl was whining again. He thought ruefully that he really preferred her when she was unconscious.

There was a faint hiss in the air followed by a clear, clipped voice.

'Good afternoon, Ms Pierre-Moulin, Mr Baudin. Sorry for this inconvenience. My name is Guillory. I expect you would like to know what is happening to you. Please allow me to explain.'

~*~

56

2 : Impossible

The New York-based headquarters of the telepath sisterhood divided neatly into two distinct areas. There was the austere yet friendly public face where Norms were welcome to visit and ask for help. Discreet double doors off to the right of the main atrium led into a small, windowless lobby ringed with benches and tasteful artworks. It was the kind of place one could have a quiet conversation out of the public eye.

Katy entered the room alone and waited until the doors behind her clicked solidly into place. She then stepped over to a small table by the wall facing her and slid a narrow drawer open. She pressed her thumb down onto the manufacturer's label at the back of the drawer.

Part of the wall slid open. She closed the drawer and stepped through into a place of greenery and fragrance. This was the true home for telepaths. No one knew why − and on the whole they didn't care − but it was a proven fact that telepaths thrived in a natural environment and plants thrived around telepaths. It was as if plant life fed the telepathic psyche with healing waves and received some health-giving medium in return. Plants also acted as a calming barrier against the psychic effect of a city full of people's mental activity.

She breathed in the cool, sappy air and breathed out the stress and congestion that had pressed against her heart for the last few days. Chester was becoming really concerned about the aetiology of the strange black creatures that had been found swarming through some corpses' body tissue.

They were proving almost impossible to analyse. Turn any of medicine's more destructive analytical sensors onto them and they simply vapourised, taking the tissue they inhabited with them.

'I'm not kidding, Katy,' he had said after an evening of almost frantic sex followed by a cursory meal and a touch too much wine.

'Those things might as well have a sign saying "You can look but please don't touch." I'm at my wit's end. We can't analyse their DNA, physical structure or chemical composition. They're strong enough to be able to manipulate the tissue around them and seem to have some sort of symbiotic relationship with it, but hit them with anything more invasive than light or radiation and they dissipate like steam. They're cool with x-rays and deep scan but they really don't like 3D tomography. It's like anything that hits them from all sides at once blows them apart – they just dissolve!'

He was sitting naked on a cushion on the floor. Katy was also naked and perched on the sofa behind him, her legs wide open, knees either side of his shoulders. She was working her finger tips and the balls of her palms along his neck and shoulders, trying to knead the knots of tension out of them. Her burgeoning Receiver Talent would normally have helped her find the spot for her ministrations, but this evening it was an uphill struggle. When they had made love it felt as if Chester was trying to lose himself in their mutual pleasure but even at the peak of his orgasm he still had his mind's eye filled with visions of the tiny, squid-like creatures.

'Once the squids dissolve, the tissue they inhabit loses coherence and turns to a kind of mush as if it had forgotten how to be whatever it was. Muscle, blood, bone, organs – anything they've touched just turns into a sort of homogenised paste and it flows all over the place, Katy. It flows like a protein smoothie. What's the point of the squids? What do they want to do? Where did they come from?'

Katy took another deep lungful of plant-scented goodness. Within the leafy bowers and planted rooms of telepath headquarters the background susurration of humankind's endless mental babble had become muted. Her mind unclenched.

58

One day I will travel to the rainforests and hide myself deep in the heart of them. The great trees will be my barrier and preserve my sanity; lock out the thoughts of all those who would plague me.

'Katy! Great to see you.' Raaka Tandon swept through the gardens and hugged her friend with a warmth that was returned in equal measure. She pulled away and squinted up into Katy's eyes.

'He's got a lot on his mind, eh?'

Katy had become used to Raaka's casual habit of dipping straight into the thoughts of those around her. It was something she had begun to do herself but had soon found that most people weren't thinking anything worth knowing. It was like walking through a giant library of books knowing that only one or two of them were actually worth reading, but no one is prepared to tell you which ones were the best. Chester was different, as was Mandy, but Raaka's mind fizzed with ideas like a lit firework.

'Light the blue touch paper and step back out of range, eh, Katy? Come on, let's grab some chairs and chew the fat for a while.'

As if by instinct Raaka led her to a group of chairs from which they were able to look out through tall one-way windows and watch Norms scurry past on their way to meetings, loved ones, shops, or whatever had engaged their interest that afternoon. The women sat wordlessly watching the never-ending parade of humanity on the streets.

'They look so preoccupied, don't they?' said Raaka. 'But give them a common cause and they will turn into a monster with but a single mind and they will not stop until their problems are resolved.'

'The squids?'

'The squids for sure, and us, if they ever find out about the Dragon.'

Katy turned her full gaze upon her friend.

'You know who it is!'

'Yes we do. But we don't know how.'

'I don't understand.'

'No, Katy, but then, neither do we. You see the Dragon has been positively identified as a telepath sister called Milla Carter, but she can't be the right person, it's simply impossible.'

'Why not?'

'Because the Dragon has to be, at the very least, a powerful and highly intelligent Transmitter. Milla's bright enough, but she's never been more than a Shutterbox. We thought *you* were a Shutterbox when we first met you – remember?'

Katy nodded.

'And then we realised you're actually a very talented Receiver. Now that's an easy mistake to make. An untrained Receiver might seem like Shutterbox until her Talent has been properly coached, but that could never happen with a Transmitter. Chalk and cheese, black and white, the Talents are too far apart for a Shutterbox to suddenly evolve into a Transmitter. Can't happen, never could happen and never will happen, apart from one minor detail.'

'Which is?'

'It simply can't be anyone else! Look, it's time for you to meet Onatah. You really need to see this for yourself.'

60

3 : Fact and file

In front of her restful eyes a glittering grey lake reached up towards a pearl-coloured sky. The air was warm with just the hint of a salt tang on the breeze. The light was bright enough for her to sunbathe comfortably but not so harsh as to force her to squint. She stretched with languorous pleasure.

Ruth Pearce enjoyed her body, even more so now she had taken the plunge and undergone a procedure to have her breasts reduced. Previously she had earned a good living on the glamour circuit thanks to her greatly enhanced 'attributes', but now, as an independently wealthy woman in her sixties, she felt it was time to take back her original body shape.

Her new body profile gave her a bouncier, younger stride, more like that of her friend Milla Carter, more like the one she had been thrilled with during her so-called 'Body Holiday' when she had inhabited Milla's simulacrum in the construct.

Over the last several months she had lost friends and become a widow thanks to the Body Holiday Foundation; she had nearly crumbled under the mental strain, but looking at her relaxing on her lounger, no one would believe it.

Good genes helped, as had the almost Olympian exercise regime forced upon her to compensate for her extraordinary triple F bust on what was shaped to be a C-cup body. She never forgave her parents for that. She had been their glamour cash cow, their doll to mould as they chose, and they had raked in the money until she was old enough to finally walk out of their lives – and out of their bank accounts – forever.

She breathed clean air and felt the zephyr play across her naked skin. She may have been in her sixties but Ruth Pearce still had a face and figure that a camera lens could linger over for hours. The back pain that had begun to plague her was gone now that her breasts were back in proportion. She felt good, she looked good and she had friends who cared about her.

Would she ever get used to this view? Lagrange II was a massive resort spa station positioned just beyond the orbit of the Moon. Two miles across it spun on its axis to create enough Coriolis force to mimic near Earth gravity, except down its core where zero G allowed people to fly or indulge in 360 globe swimming in a giant ball of weightless water.

Residents of Lagrange II lived on the inside of the five-mile long cylinder. Between the outer skin and the floor of the living area was the fully automated agricultural zone. The inner residential core had a circumference of nearly six miles which was made up of pyramidical buildings, parkland, lakes and canals. Plant life and gardens filled every available space. Much as she had seen in the complex under the Titan Ice Dome, humankind insisted on flipping its finger at nature's harshest environments by filling them with delicate beauty.

Here, on the very brink of deep space, Ruth could relax on a lounger wearing nothing more than the very briefest mini briefs while sipping lime-scented ice water. Her only worry was drone minicams out to catch someone like her in a state of dishabille, but such were frowned on by Bruce, the station's principal AI and probably the most bad-tempered artificial intelligence in human space.

Bruce knew how to tailor the perfect environment for his detested guests. He also knew how to police their privacy – while continuously obsessing about their toilet habits which he found disgusting and about which he would regale any passing AI with foul-mouthed diatribe.

Ruth was alone in her penthouse. Her companion, Freedman, was out food shopping. Most people ordered their meals from a menu board but Freedman loved the idea that Ruth was into real cooking with honest ingredients so he happily went looking for the finest produce he could find and was delighted with what she would do with them.

His personality stood in stark contrast to hubris, almost its mirror image. He was a terribly precise, neat man who seemed to have been born to care for others. He was the only survivor of the Foundation's core team and he was innocent of any wrongdoing. His only job had been to take care of guests and hosts while they were unconscious in the transition rooms and experiencing their illusory time in the Body Holiday. They had been told they were to swap bodies – young for old and old for young – but in reality they experienced everything in the construct. Their comatose bodies stayed on gel beds and Freedman looked after them.

The Foundation had been destroyed and he had been offered the job as Ruth's companion, which he at first accepted with trepidation. But he had quickly found himself to be, as he described it, 'A happy duck swimming upstream in righteous waters.'

And there was that grey lake arcing up towards the light sail that ran the length of the spa station and provided natural light while also saving residents the disturbing view of buildings hanging down like stalactites nearly two miles above their heads.

Something was worrying at Ruth's mind and she couldn't get a solid grip on it. That was why she was focusing on the lake, looking for an answer. She thought of her brain as an archive housing a dithery old woman who had only the sketchiest idea of where she had filed things. Concentrating on the abstract patterns of the sparkling waters might steer her mind away from distractions and let the old woman get on with her job.

Something, something, something... Oh, God, no, what have I done?

In her mind's eye the old woman had pulled out a file, opened it, and then looked across at her with shocked disapproval. With a growing sense of nausea Ruth realised she had told the Antarctic AI, Viracocha, exactly where Milla and Ben were hiding and Viracocha didn't know the location was meant to be a secret. It might tell anyone.

In a state approaching panic she stabbed at the communicator on her wrist, a device given her by the AI so they could be in contact whenever she needed to talk. She desperately hoped she wasn't too late.

~*~

63

4 : Dark angel

Paul Gillette was well aware his nickname was 'The Razor' and, despite the rather obvious play on words, he secretly revelled in it. Nobody could be less razor-like. He was a stocky, balding man who had never been comfortable in uniform but, since his promotion to commandant, had happily sported an array of shapeless and seemingly colourless suits.

His wife despaired of him. She sent him out every morning looking smart and well pressed − yet by the time he returned home in the evening his clothes had, in her eyes, mutated into sackcloth and his tie into a dishevelled rag.

Gillette couldn't see her problem. He believed clothes were just clothes, just a social nicety. His state of order, his neatness, was all in his mind. He was able to see order in chaos and find pathways to resolution through apparently trackless wastelands, and it was this ability that found him seated in front of a monitor gazing with abstract fascination at the people on the screen. There were two people in the room with him and they were nervously bobbing around him as if, he thought, they were practising for a coconut dodging competition.

On his screen a woman sat stiffly on a bed and regarded her male companion with evident trepidation. The man stood raptly before a wall-mounted mirror, running his hands through his thick mane of long black hair and smoothing the skin of his cheeks and neck. On the surface his performance looked like pure vanity in action but Gillette had seen something more − something approaching intense scientific curiosity. He couldn't blame him.

Tilting his head slightly to one side the Commandant studied another monitor which held an image little more than twenty-four hours old. Here the same woman held an almost identical pose while a much older man paced the room while pressing his hand to his belly. This man was skinny to the point of emaciation with badly thinning, greasy grey hair tied back in a listless ponytail. His hooded eyes were streaked with black, Gothic eye make-up, and his gaunt face seemed almost an afterthought hiding behind a predatory beak of a nose.

Gillette turned silently back to his contemporary view. The young man also had the thick Goth streaks of eye make-up and his clothing was the same except for his T-shirt which looked fresh and expensive. He could almost be the older man's young son, but he wasn't.

'Martin, Avril, talk to me about this, this miracle.'

His companions stopped their bobbing and stood beside him looking at the monitors. The older of the two, Avril Maures, answered first.

'You have seen the report?'

'Of course.'

'Then you know as much as we do. Ms Pierre-Moulin accidently injected Baudin with body fluids from a murder victim. The victim had been killed by the "Ripper" who, as you know, has a particularly distinctive MO.'

'Yes of course, I'm one of the team working on the case. We aren't getting very far with it, I must say. Frankly, it's a shambles. Somehow the killer rips men up but never leaves a clue, not even a trace.'

Martin Gasquet joined in.

'Commandant Gillette, have you seen this?'

Gasquet keyed a remote and the image on the screen changed. Gillette stood up and craned towards the screen.

'What are they?'

Gasquet hit more buttons on his remote and the image changed again, then again, then again and again.

'Enough, Gasquet, that's enough. What are they?'

It was Maures who answered.

'These things are turning up in bodies all over the planet. They are not the cause of death – far from it. In fact they would actually appear to be trying to repair damaged tissue. We call them "squids" for the moment, and I think that soubriquet will do until we come up with something better. They are nano biologics and they've got us stumped, absolutely at a dead end.'

'How did they get into the bodies?'

'We believe they were injected into the tissue during the attack.'

'But why?'

'Not a clue. But we think Baudin is the first living subject to be infected with them and look what they've done to him.'

Gasquet returned the monitors to the before and after images of the old pathologist and the young man.

Gillette's voice was subdued. 'It looks like he's bathed in the Fountain of Youth.'

Maures responded, 'More than that. We looked at his medical records. It seems he had a bad drinking habit, never enough to affect his work but enough to knock his liver into a really lousy state. His doctor said the damage was such that even if he gave up drink today he would probably not last more than a few years.'

'He's dying?'

'No, no, not anymore. He *was* dying, but not anymore. Look at him now – we could easily put him forward for the French Olympics team. Scans show he's infected with squids, but otherwise he's A1 fit for duty.'

'Fuck!' said Gillette.

'Very well put,' muttered Maures.

'Word of this gets out and a whole bunch of people will line up for a little squid action. This is a cure for ageing, a cure for cirrhosis... what does it do to cancer and diabetes?'

'We've already asked for volunteers to find out,' said Maures. 'Some terminal cancer patients have been injected with the squids and are being studied in isolation. This is an international initiative and a lot of people are really excited by the possibilities. The Japanese nano bionics research was good but very, very expensive. These things are free and seem to do the same job. They look like a gift from God.'

Gillette looked like he was trying to swallow gristle, 'God, is it? I wonder.'

66

Down in the locked observation room Baudin was trying to come to terms with his transformation. He was an experienced medical practitioner and he knew ridiculous when he saw it. This *was* ridiculous.

Even when he was younger he had been a lean rangy type, a lone wolf. His Goth persona had been used to mask a man who didn't fit with common society, but then common society didn't want to fit in with a sallow youth who hid behind make-up and sported a lank ponytail. He dressed in a personal uniform of floor-length trench coats and military boots under olive green ex-military pants, a look completed by the latest scrolling Japanese artwork on expensive, reactive T-shirts. The message he tried to put across was that he could afford to wear what he liked and he liked what he wore, but the fact was that nobody cared. All they saw was an oddly dressed man who always looked unwashed even when fresh from the shower.

Forty-years later and Baudin still wore dark glasses on the street, even at night, and he kept them on when frequenting bars and clubs where the music was so loud and the light show so intense that he could lose himself in the crowd. For a brief while he was able to feel part of something more. More than an angry, rejected soul buried deep in his lonely heart.

He walked into every room alone and he walked out alone, an isolated scavenger clawing for whatever comfort he could eke from Parisian society and finding none. No wonder he sought solace in drink.

But he was very good at his job. Everyone who knew him knew that much. Perhaps it was because the dead didn't look at an ageing Goth and judge him; perhaps it was because he could carry out his best work alone or with an AI. Whatever the reason, Baudin had developed an enquiring mind to equal Gillette's and his forensic examinations were valued by his colleagues – even if his company wasn't.

And now he had been transformed into the dark angel he had always hoped to see in the mirror. His skin was flawless and shone with health, his hair silky and full of body, his eyes glittering with life. Never – not even in his dreams – had he ever hoped to look this good. Even his teeth were white and looked so much stronger than the stained, weak looking things he had grown up with.

'Yvette, do I look different to you?'

'You just stay away from me.'

He turned to face her. 'What? Why?'

'You don't remember, do you?'

'Remember what?'

There were no chairs in the locked observation room Guillory had brought them to the day earlier, just two narrow cots with a polished, light wooden table between them, its surface covered by untouched and outdated popular magazines on flimsy, read-only, disposable tablets.

The room had two doors, one through which they had entered and another that led down a small passageway to a well-equipped bathroom. Clothes and a few personal items had been piled into lockers at the foot of each bed.

On the wall a bland and – Baudin supposed – restful landscape in a white frame presented massing white clouds rolling across heathland with mountains in the background lit by shafts of sunlight. It didn't work for him at all. *Storm's coming,* he thought. *This place is too mundane for the storm that's coming.*

The girl said nothing, pushing herself further away from him until her back was flat against the wall.

'Yvette,' he insisted, 'tell me! Remember what?'

She almost spat the words out, angry and afraid. 'Last night. I couldn't sleep. I just lay here waiting to be let out. I want to go home.' Her face was a mask of misery. 'You were asleep and you were moaning, I heard you. And then you did it, you filthy bastard, you did that thing onto me.' Her eyes were wild with loathing.

'Yvette, I'm sorry, I don't know what you're talking about.' *Is this any way for someone to talk to a dark angel?* 'What did I do?'

'You came over to my bed and you wanked on me, you filthy pervert, on my face. In my hair. It got into my mouth and I had to spit it out. How could you do that?' She shuddered with disgust and sobbed. 'Filthy pervert, why? Why?'

Sitting in front of his monitors, Gillette spoke with urgent authority.

'Get her out of there, now!'

~*~

5 : The epidemic

On an island in the centre of the Thames, deep in that part of darkest Surrey where mature money was plainly out on show but never flaunted in a gauche way, a small colony of writers, artists and actors drifted gently into the comfortable twilight of their years. Youth was something that sometimes visited the island: sons, daughters, grandchildren, nephews, nieces and great nephews and nieces would come to stay and, for a while, would light up their days with bright bursts of exhausting energy, but otherwise they had their work to keep them busy. They had their successes, their celebrations and commiserations, but always in the background a round of bickering squabbles and recriminations that had grown stale over a long, long period, becoming as much a part of the environment as the wide, flowing river.

In one of the smaller and very tastefully – if somewhat chaotically – appointed riverside dwellings, Beatrice and Henry rubbed along together in a mutually appreciative yet platonic ménage. Henry was a handsome man who preferred younger women but simply didn't have the ready cash he needed to convince a pretty girl half his age to see further than his grey hair. Bea, on the other hand, was of a vintage where she preferred fine wine and witty conversation to anything as unnecessarily physical as sex.

Their friendship had deepened and matured to become something of a social masterpiece – they had a number of friends of all ages – but both would readily admit that evenings like this, when they were alone on the balcony overlooking the river just relaxing and chatting, were some of the best times of their lives.

The light was a bosky purple and the surface of the river was criss-crossed with the tracery of micro-droids darting about to scoop up clouds of midges before they could become annoying.

70

The meat from the tiny insects would be processed into usable protein – some of which would be used to feed the remaining wild birds. Nobody asked where the balance ended up.

'If we had met each other when we were younger I wonder if we would be so good together now.' Henry had an actor's voice, mellifluous and deep.

Bea's voice was trained too, a journalist's voice, precise, probing yet always tempered with the lilt of a coquettish smile. 'You were always too busy looking for work, Henry, and I was always too busy looking for words, not really the perfect recipe for a lasting love affair.'

'No, I guess you're right. More wine? Oh hang on...' He raised his implant to his lips and said, 'Hello?'

Bea listened to one side of the dialogue for a few seconds then went back into the house for more wine and another bottle of beer for Henry. She hoped it wasn't another long location shoot that would call him away for weeks. He got so tired of early mornings and she missed him so much when he was gone. She listened to the most familiar voice in her life and smiled.

'Paul? Oh, Paul, hello yes, how are you, mate? Good, yes very good, so is Auntie Bea. Yes I will and I'm sure she says the same to you. What, what elixir? Paul, I'm hearing the words and I recognise every one of them but I really haven't a clue what you're talking about. When? Are you sure? It is quite late. Well, okay I'll make sure there's a beer in the fresher for you. Yes. Okay. See you in fifteen minutes. Yes, bye, see you soon.'

Bea paused for a few moments, barely outlined in the sliding doors that led from the living room out onto the balcony. She had to work hard to see Henry's frowning face and wondered if it was too early to turn a light on. He looked up when she tapped his shoulder with the fresh, ice-cold bottle. He took it from her hand and she reclaimed her seat by his side. She could hear his breathing. 'Paul?' she asked.

'Yes, my nephew. He sends his love.'

'Oh, Paul. He's the policeman, isn't he?'

'Detective in the serious crime squad. He's working homicide.'

'Oh, and he's coming here? Why so late? Is he on a case?' She changed her voice to a low growl. 'Well, it's a fair cop, gov'ner, but society's to blame. I done it with a lead pipe in the library, but the geezah had it coming and no mistake.'

'Don't give up your day job, Bea,' Henry chuckled, 'and anyway with your talent you should be able to come up with better copy than that.'

'Take too long to polish. The moment would be gone. Don't be so picky. Anyway, so why is Paul popping round so late on a working day?'

'Is it a working day?'

'Wednesday, it's a working day for all non-actors and budding crime writers.'

Henry chugged at his beer. 'Wondered why it's been so quiet. Anyway he'll be here in ten minutes. He says he has the elixir of youth in his pocket and asks if we'd like to try it?'

'The what?'

All over the planet similar conversations had been taking place. Policemen and women, health workers and pathology staff, anyone who had access to them had secreted the body fluids of murdered men out of the morgue or lab and approached beloved relatives with the latest wonder cure for everything that ailed them. Age or illness was wiped away over a period of some twenty-four hours, and the recipients hadn't been just cured. They had become beautiful.

Over the next few weeks thousands of people worldwide stood before their mirrors and admired the unbelievable faces gazing back at them. Fat became fit, crippled became whole, and dying patients in intensive care climbed out of bed and asked for their clothes. It was an epidemic of health unlike anything the world had experienced before, but not everyone was happy about it.

In cities as far apart as New York, Paris and Moscow, researchers were glumly measuring the sudden, irrepressible rash of glamorous well-being. It had continued spreading through densely populated mega-cities. The newly gorgeous men and women seemed to have become openly generous with their favours and were eagerly welcomed into numberless lovers' arms at Skin Fests, parties, night clubs, in apartments and along darkened alleyways. Few men could resist a flagrant invitation from a youthful and stunningly attractive girl and few women would turn away a freshly minted hunk. Body fluids were exchanged in exponentially greater numbers and the ranks of the beautiful grew.

Some chose to resist – and that was when the rapes began.

~*~

6 : Play the dark angel

He prowled his lonely room while within him a growling hunger grew. It had started as an itch he couldn't scratch and crescendoed until he was burning with need. He tried to calm things down by hand but it wasn't enough, never enough.

And then the nurse brought his meal.

'Good evening, Mr Baudin, here is some nice coque-au-vin with roast potatoes and fine beans...'

He grabbed her from behind. The platter went flying as he pushed her face-down onto Yvette's old cot, ripped her skirt out of the way then hauled down her voluminous underwear. He raped her quickly, reaching his orgasm before the woman had even emitted her first startled scream. His need was too strong for foreplay. He was still inside her and mindlessly working on round two when three powerful men in full coverage environment suits clattered into his room and pulled him away, his erect penis still spurting seed across the nurse's bare buttocks and uniform.

The nurse was helped from the room, shuddering with shock and moaning in genuine confusion. 'What had I done to make him do that? Why me? I'm a grandmother for God's sake. He seemed so nice and then this happens. What had I done?'

She will not be seeing her grandchildren again anytime soon, Gillette suspected when he was informed of the attack. Barely two weeks since the needle-stick incident and already a third victim. It was chilling. A pattern was emerging that was shockingly simple to realise but difficult to comprehend. The squids were evidently turning Baudin into a sex maniac − but how, and why?

'Mr Gillette?'

'Tatou?'

'Mr Gillette, please excuse me for interrupting your thoughts.'

'Please do, Tatou. My head's in a spin just now.'

74

The Paris police department's AI weighed Gillette's statement and filed it under 'Discuss' for the next debate. Humans often said things they didn't mean and meant things they didn't say.

'Yes, Mr Gillette. However, I have been analysing all available data and there is an evident algorithmic progression to recent activity.'

'Please, share it with me.'

There was a pause as if the AI was looking for the right words, then it continued: 'Have you ever noticed the way haemorrhagic fevers, such as the ebolaviruses, vector new victims?'

'Elucidate please, Tatou. Not really my field of expertise.'

'The disease liquefies its victims' internal organs into a bloody pulp then squirts them from every orifice. If someone is, say, hit in the face or on an open wound with contaminated blood, it enters their system and the disease quickly takes hold in its new host. The infection's progressive symptoms are actually part of the virus' life cycle. Do you follow?'

Gillette was tempted to say no just to find out how Tatou would respond. He was exhausted and becoming irked by the AI's pedantry. 'Yes, Tatou. Now tell me, how does this relate to the squid infection?'

'Why, there is an exact parallel, Mr Gillette.'

State the fucking obvious, why don't you? But what is it? Don't beat around the bush. 'Would you like to draw a picture for me?'

'Of course, Mr Gillette, what would you like a picture of?'

Arggggh, fucking literal AIs! 'No, Tatou, but thank you. What I actually mean is, can you explain precisely how the squid infection works like Ebola?'

'Of course, Mr Gillette. The squid infection also wants to vector through body fluids but it is more sophisticated than any Earth virus or run-of-the-mill sexually-transmitted disease. The first thing it does is make the victim healthy and young looking, and in the process it also turns them into the best looking version of themselves. They are sexier looking and therefore more likely to be able to engage in sexual congress with willing partners. If that fails, as it did for Mr Baudin, the victim will resort to rape or masturbate onto the target host's orifices, most likely their mouth.'

'Wait, are you telling me these things are designed to infect the maximum number of people by using sex?'

'Oh yes. Please, watch the monitor.'

Gillette watched as the point of view shifted from Baudin in restraints to the room where Yvette had been housed after Baudin's attack. He stared, briefly wondering if Tatou had switched to the wrong display, but no, it was her. The girl had been quite pretty before, he remembered, but now she was a grade one, advise all sectors and break out the Champagne knockout. And she had done something with her clothes. There was a lot more leg and cleavage on display than there had been before, very nice leg and cleavage too. And the way she was moving, she had been a nervous little morsel before but now...*wow*.

'A man is usually perceived as the alpha sexual predator because he has a penis and he penetrates the female,' the AI continued, 'but such is not always the case.'

Gillette was only listening with half an ear; the rest of his mind was concentrated on the sensuous creature on his monitor. He felt her magnetic pull and he wanted to go to her. He had never wanted to fuck someone so hard in his life. His trousers strained under the mounting pressure of his hard-on. It was difficult to breathe. Erotic fantasies began to play across his mind's eye. Oh, God, how he wanted her.

'Once a woman has deliberately excited a man's erection he becomes putty in her hands, so to speak. She is fully in control. It is a rare man who can resist such a sexual imperative. Ms Paul-Moulin is acting as a symptomatic sexual beacon. She is signalling desire to anyone who sees her, and with her greatly enhanced physical allure it will not be long before someone succumbs and becomes the next victim. As I say the algorithm is exponential: one, two, four, eight, and so on. We only have three here because they are all isolated, but outside the situation is getting much worse.'

76

Gillette was unconsciously rubbing his right palm along the length of his distended penis through the cloth of his trousers. He had never felt such need before, never been so hard, so urgently excited. He was on the brink of answering the girl's call and damn the consequences when one part of his mind grasped something Tatou had said and doused his passion with ice water.

'Outside? What's happening outside? We've contained the situation here. What are you talking about?'

'No, Mr Gillette, we haven't contained anything. The squid infection is already raging through the streets of every large city on Earth. There were those cancer patients we tested, the diabetics, the terminally ill. They have all picked up their beds and walked and the hospital staff couldn't stop them. In fact some of the hospital staff have *joined* them. And soon the infection will be going off-planet if it hasn't done so already. A transport leaves for space every few seconds from somewhere on Earth, meaning we can't even begin to calculate how many contaminated hosts have already reached near space. All we can do is watch out for a sharp decline in serious medical health issues, and perhaps an increase in incidences of rape. In a matter of months squid infection may well become the human norm. It will certainly prove an interesting exercise in real-time evolution.'

Gillette looked again at the girl on his monitor. Her movements, which had so recently looked irresistibly sensuous, now looked contrived and ominous, even creepy. He wondered if he was looking at the beginning of the end for the human race as he knew it. He very much feared he was. A cold knot settled into the pit of his stomach.

~*~

7 : Tyro

The asteroid facility seemed bigger on the inside than it looked from the outside. Milla reasoned the illusion of space was probably due to a mixture of cunning design, Coriolis force and low gravity. Whatever the reason she had enjoyed the run of the whole place apart from one almost empty storeroom where Ben had set up his usual 'last minute' preparations.

There was plenty of room for her to run through her exercises and katas, sprinting across rooms and through access-ways, and she had been delighted to find she was able to run up the wall in the main reception room and turn a full back-flip before landing back on her feet. Ben almost shouted with laughter when he had caught her doing flips until she almost threw-up. Vesper and Eddie had advised her she needed to get back to Earth as soon as possible, but even they had finally agreed that she and Ben needed a little relaxation time before starting the month-long journey home.

Her favourite place so far – even beating the gym with its lock shoes welded to the floor so she could use the punch bags – was what she thought of as the meditation room. Here there were books to download onto crystal tablets, music from concert quality speakers and 3D/HD high quality video feeds offering some of the great classics production on a wall-sized curved screen. It was almost as immersive as her time in the construct on the Body Holiday.

Best of all was the view screen. She had grown up in a windowless, inner-core apartment which her family had shared with her grandfather. Later she had bought her own apartment which boasted two real-time Virtuo windows, one in the bedroom and one in the living room. These could be keyed to a number of library locations and made the viewer feel as if they were actually looking out of a real window. The system in the asteroid's meditation room took the whole concept to the next level.

She had once visited the Pearces' 'beach-house' which was in fact a two-storied construction built into a cliff in Britain's beautiful West Country. She had never forgotten the time she spent watching the pattern of waves criss-crossing the sea, stretching like visual music away to the horizon where they were echoed by silver-grey, herring-bone cloud formations. She had felt at the centre of something vast that day, as if her soul had grown to match the living cathedral of sea and sky. It had touched something sacred in her heart and she nearly wept with joy.

And here it was again, stored away in the asteroid's catalogue of views. She could sit cross-legged in one of the big, comfortable chairs scattered around the room and gaze out to sea, across the Channel towards France, all the while losing herself in the sights and sounds she loved.

'Would you like a sea-breeze to complete the illusion, Milla?'

Tyro's gentle voice did nothing to break the mood.

'Can you do that?' she asked.

In answer she felt her hair tousled by light winds and smelt ozone and a salty sea tang. She breathed in with deep pleasure.

'Thank you, Tyro. That is so exquisite.'

'My pleasure. By the way there is a message for you when you are ready to receive it.'

'Oh,' she sighed, 'who from?'

'Ruth. She seems a little concerned about something.'

'Okay, I suppose I'd better see it then.'

Ruth appeared slightly to one side of the screen, which Milla thought Tyro had done deliberately so the caller would not interrupt the view. Ever since the first day when the AI had introduced itself she had been aware of these thoughtful little touches. It was nice.

Ruth stood mutely inert, gazing into the middle distance. Milla said: 'Thank you, Tyro. I'm ready.' Her friend's figure came to life. It took Milla a second to realise that her breasts were smaller than when she last saw her a month earlier. *That looks much better.*

'Hello, Milla. How are you? Oh, I'm not very good at this message thing. Don't try to answer me, dear. I can't hear you so there wouldn't be any point, would there? I hope all is well in the rock. I miss you both dreadfully. Freedman is a treasure of course and his language is so funny, we laugh all the time, but it's not the same here without you.' The woman seemed distracted. Milla automatically tried to read her thoughts then chided herself for being an idiot. *She's not really there, you numpty.*

Ruth continued, 'Anyway, that isn't why I called. I may have been an idiot again. I do hope not but I had to tell you. You know I put Viracocha in touch with you there. I'm sure you've spoken with it since you arrived. It said it had something important to tell you so I just didn't think. You see, well, the fact is I didn't tell it your location was a secret. I've done so since and it's very sure it hasn't told anyone where you are, so everything's probably fine, but you know, forewarned is forearmed and all that. Anyway, I've told you now so be careful. Love you both, stay safe, bye. Hope to see you soon. Bye.'

The blonde woman winked out of existence. *That,* thought Milla, *is probably why my threat warning has been acting up. Time to talk with Ben again. No, wait,* she remembered. *Viracocha had promised it was keeping her location completely discreet.* There was some sort of problem, but it was nothing to do with anything Ruth had done. Something *was* coming, she knew that, but didn't know what. *Time to get on the move again.*

She gazed out to sea and drank in the salty breezes. No such thing on *Emily*, but she supposed it couldn't be helped. 'Thank you, Tyro.' She uncurled from her chair and left the room.

'My pleasure, miss,' said the AI to her departing back. It hadn't been told that the couple's presence in the asteroid was a secret either. It felt embarrassed that it had spoken up at the AI debate when Onatah asked if anyone knew her whereabouts. It decided to keep that fact to itself. By the time anyone from Earth got here the couple would be long gone. *Least said soonest mended,* it thought to itself. *Should have warned me when they arrived.*

But, deep in whatever an AI used as a heart, Tyro knew it had failed them.

~*~

8 : Getting priorities in order

Chester Woodman was tempted to grab Katy and head for a desert island at high speed. He wanted to run anywhere; he needed to get away from increasingly high concentrations of suddenly beautiful and highly contagious sex maniacs. The authorities had considered declaring martial law and thought about rounding up infected people, but even in New York sex wasn't illegal except in public spaces and it was hard to decide just exactly what the infected citizens had been doing wrong.

Increasing numbers of previously old and ill people had become healthier than ever before. No one was climbing out of the grave but they had been coming damn close. Death's door had been slammed shut and wedged closed by nano biological miracle workers. The fact that no one could work out *why* had become largely irrelevant. Who didn't want to be young and sexy? Who didn't want to save a loved one from age or sickness? Where was the downside?

Chester didn't know, but he was certain there was one and when it turned up there was going to be utter carnage.

Nature was a wonderful thing but it simply didn't give out presents like these. There had to be payback. There had to be a reason. These things had been sitting around in dead tissue for decades and now they were out and doing whatever it was they had been designed to do – and he was sure they had been designed, not evolved. He was just as sure they weren't from Earth.

The Chinese had responded to the crisis with their usual pragmatism. After locking down the borders, special scanning centres had been set up all over the country and everyone was ordered to attend. Chester wasn't sure what was happening to the infected but he was fairly sure it wasn't going to include a slap on the back and hearty congratulations on the transformation. The Germans, however, were throwing 'squid catcher' sex parties with a concessionary entrance price for old-age pensioners. Elderly people walked in and twenty-four hours later sex gods walked out, ready to party.

'Hello, Moebius.'

'Yes, Chester.'

'I wonder if you can help me with a question.'

'I'll try.'

'Is there any recorded incidence of infected people having sex with each other?'

Silence.

'Moebius?'

Silence.

'Moebius, can you hear me?'

'Sorry, Chester. You are the first person to think of asking that question and it has proved to be a very good one. I have just shared it with others of my kind and I had to concentrate for a moment. As I believe you suspected, the answer is no. Once the victims are infected they completely lose interest in each other. They only target fresh and uninfected people.'

Chester looked at the floor for a moment as if he expected to find some kind of an answer there, then he rose to his feet.

'I'm going to see Commissioner Hyatt. We need to get this information to the highest authority.'

'Sorry, Chester, I think you would be wasting your time with the Commissioner.'

'Why?'

In answer a monitor screen flickered into life and on it appeared a young, lean and extremely handsome man.

'Because this is how the Commissioner has looked for the last twenty-four hours. I don't think he will treat your concerns with any seriousness. His secretary has recently locked herself in a broom cupboard and he has been clawing at it for the last hour. I have informed uniformed officers and they are on their way to collect him.'

'How bad is the situation really, Moebius?'

'Infection is reaching epidemic proportions in the USA of course, and the numbers are growing. Probably at least fifteen people per one hundred thousand of the population in cities, but we can't at present speak for less densely populated areas. It is a pandemic with cases here, China, Germany, France, Russia and North Africa. Cases have been isolated in countries like the UK, Australia, Scandinavia and Canada. Countries bordering the worst affected areas have tried to lock down their borders, but we both know how difficult that is thanks to sky tourer cars. All ballistic flights are cancelled. It is still early days but I would say the squids have very quickly gained a strong toehold within the human population.'

'Why is this happening?'

'Does a disease need a reason?'

'No, no it usually doesn't, but I think this one has. It targets humans far too precisely. It's as if it has been specifically designed to appeal to the human psyche. Look at the boxes it ticks: vanity, sex, caring for loved ones, healing the sick and comforting the elderly. If it could also put money in the bank it would be up there with winning the lottery.'

'Good point,' said Moebius. 'In areas where infection is rife the economy is faltering. People are simply not turning up to work. But remember, this situation has not been created by the squids themselves. They were largely passive until people found out what they could do. At first people had been deliberately infecting each other. In France the authorities were infecting the sick to see what would happen. That was after that pathologist suffered a needle-stick injury. He was one of the first, if not *the* first, but news travels fast.'

'People have been saying this is all about the sex, but it isn't, is it?' said Chester. 'If it was just about the sex we could get all the infected people into a big hall somewhere and leave them to get on with it. They could fuck what's left of their brains out and we could get on with our day. Some people would probably want to film it for the porn market. After all, gorgeous people having sex has always been a big money-spinner.'

With a touch of nausea Chester was reminded about Katy when she was still a retail girl working for Nemo Henderson. She had allowed herself to be filmed while having sex with her clients. The clients never knew about it but she made a bit more money and the pimp profited. Chester had come to terms with her past, but he didn't have to like it.

'Moebius, sorry to be a pest but have any animals been infected?'

'Funny you should ask, but yes. A cow infected a bull in Arkansas. The bull went wild and infected an entire herd. They were all put down and have since been cremated.'

'How did the cow get infected?'

'Ask the farmer. It can get pretty lonely for a horny man in Arkansas.'

'Oh, right, yes.'

'Chester, your questions have garnered a response. Are you free for a conversation?'

'With whom?'

'GUVD police Major Spartak Oleg Shimkovich.'

~*~

9 : A matter of time

More than three million years before the squid infection had begun to beautify the Earth, the twinned consciousness that knew itself as Eddie and Vesper had floated in the construct at the very limit of their domain and sensed something malignant but they didn't know what it was. And now they had returned and this time they were armed with stronger senses.

They had the freedom of the solar system and could build environments for dream or play. They could bathe in solar prominences and walk among racing clouds in the bone-crushing depths of the great gas giants. But they couldn't travel beyond the Oort cloud that girdled the Sun and her planet companions.

From here fell comets in their long elliptical orbits towards the Sun and from here rolled solid masses of rock, metal and ice that nudged and bruised their way through space like cosmic bully-boys. Beyond this place lay light-years of frigid interstellar nothingness and gas, oceans of dark matter, G-waves and strange energy across which, one day, humankind would have to venture or die choked in its own waste in a solar system grown too small. One day perhaps. But only if the species managed to survive that long.

Eddie and Vesper had seen the work of the squids and become afraid. Not everything about humanity was laudable. In fact some of the things the fleshy, mentally incontinent mouth-breathers got up to were frankly disgusting, but humankind was up there at the apex of evolution and when there was no alternative you always pitched for the home team.

They had searched civilised space for the infection's creator and found nothing, then they had hitched a psychic ride using Milla Carter's dark energy-powered Talent and this time, out beyond the Oort cloud, they had heard sibilance and a chattering sound with slithering intent. Millions of years after they had first sensed something evil out here in the frozen spaces beyond their reach they had returned, and this time their eyes were open in Milla's Talent. This time they could see.

Something immense swarmed out there at the limit of their vision. It was not so much dark as grainy. It was moving like a cluster of headless snakes, coiling and winding in, around and through, endless yet only just visible.

It was waiting.

They asked, *What are you?*

They heard, as if in a hissing whisper, words delivered directly into their mind. *The stain of human life has smeared itself onto our borders. This is unacceptable. We have initiated counter-measures.*

Eddie and Vesper replied, *Cease what you are doing or you will confront us.*

You threaten us, little immortals? What can you do? You cannot even leave your pathetic solar nest.

They warned, *We are not alone.*

We are not afraid.

You should be, they said, *you fucking should be.*

Milla turned over in her sleep. The dream had disturbed her rest it was so intense, strange and fully immersive. She and Ben were in the sleeping quarters to the rear of the space yacht *Emily*, which was drilling a colourful path out of the asteroid belt and making a long arc down to meet Mars at the nearest convenient point in its orbit. Chasing after planets was a thankless task, even in a fusion-powered, high-speed craft. Mars travelled anti-clockwise around the Sun at just under eighty-seven thousand klicks per hour, making any kind of stern approach impractical. It made better sense to position ahead of the planet and wait for it to reach you or, as *Emily* and her kind did on a regular basis, follow an arc that would deliver you right into Mars' lap like a ball into a pitcher's mitt.

The mechanics of the Solar System had been mapped and understood for centuries but it wasn't until the advent of cheap fusion energy that travelling around it had become truly practical. The widely predicted human Diaspora into space had never really happened. Fully eighty per cent of the species was still firmly rooted on the mother planet and most of those living off-planet were working stiffs and engineers. An elite group of wealthy, spoon-fed thrill-seekers spent time on the Lagrange spa stations, Mars and the Moon, but otherwise space had been colonised by capable, hard-working technicians.

Milla and Ben felt comfortable around such people, much more so than they did the pampered rich. Ben had lived the good life with Ruth and Pearce but he knew his place and Milla had worked her way out from the outer fringes of inner core poverty. Now she was very wealthy, very wealthy indeed, but that didn't change her essential nature. Both of them were happier feeling useful and doing something practical than lazing around at their leisure and watching time's waters flow under the bridge.

Money was a tool, not a reason. It was enough to know they would never need to seek a crib in the cramped and crowded spaces under and between the massive buttresses of centre core.

And now Milla was dreaming. Something huge was writhing and coiling before her gaze. Or was it many somethings moiling together as one? It was dark, too dark to see properly. The thing or things themselves weren't intrinsically dark; they were just working away in a stygian gloom. She was reminded of the way threads are woven into a carpet. This construction was like that, but it was alive and it seemed to stretch away in every direction.

She reached out with her Receiver Talent and was rewarded with an impression of countless billions of whispering voices hissing and chattering. The sound became oppressive. It pressed down upon her consciousness and began to fill her mind with white noise. It felt cold and dispassionate. The effect it was having on her was sidereal to its main business of coiling and weaving and creating a... a barrier! This thing, this collective, was a conscious wall placed here to keep whatever and whoever was this side of it cooped up.

She turned around in her dream. There, weak and pale and so far away as to be tiny, gleamed the Sun. It seemed lost and alone in the vastness of space. The shock of sudden realisation stripped the breath from her throat. She turned back. This thing, this barrier, surrounded the Solar System. It was here to keep humankind in check. Why?

What are you? Please, why are you here? She had floated the questions into the mass mind with all the caution at her command. She didn't know if it was hostile or even if it was truly intelligent, but she didn't think this was the time to place all her cards on the table. *Gently does it, Carter. Don't upset the neighbours.*

There was a crescendo of sound, a tsunami of intense noise, a shriek of bone-deep anger. For a moment she was stunned. Wordlessly the wall opened up and things like a cross between whips and headless snakes uncoiled and leapt across the divide towards her. She felt their lethal intent, their furious hunger to destroy her, to rip her apart. Their hot touch burned like acid and crushed her flesh against her bones. She was to be dragged into the maw and minced in the barrier's muscular, prehensile coils.

FUCK YOU! GET OFF ME! Her command lanced out and tentacular limbs peeled away from her in shock, opening around her like the petals of a poisonous alien flower. The slimy thick ropes began to gleam with red heat.

Human filth, she heard a voice, dry and ancient and somehow familiar, *we will burn your stain from our space.*

Any moment, she knew the creatures would close tight and burn her body to a charred crisp. She screamed in fury.

'Milla! Milla, wake up!'

Her eyes opened and Ben's face was close to hers, concern etched into his eyes. She wept tears of anger and frustration while he cradled her in his arms. She couldn't answer when he asked about the pink wheals that had mysteriously appeared on her skin. They faded hours later. Ben forgot about them but Milla didn't. Deep in her Talent she knew her encounter with the living, snake-woven barrier had been more than just a dream. With sickening certainty she knew she would meet it again − and next time it would be for real.

~*~

10 : Options and denials

'The way I see it, a dog gets old and can't scratch so it gets fleas. Maybe the Earth got old and can't scratch so it got us. What do you say, maybe those squids are God's flea powder?'

Catchum always claimed he was born to be a police officer. With a name like that, how could he be anything else? His first name was Oliver but he never used it. Even his wife called him by his surname and she was known universally as Mrs Catchum.

Mandy Prius looked across the desk at her colleague to see if he was smiling. He wasn't. His long, slack-jawed face hung under his greying buzzcut like a well-worn leather slipper. It was a face that was easy to ignore, one quickly lost in the crowd. He was a good cop with a sharp mind, but he kept it well hidden, preferring to confront the world with an air of baffled amusement.

He had also said, 'You catch more people by letting them think they got the upper hand, especially when you got the ace in your poke.' He often smiled, but he wasn't smiling then.

'You mean that about the squids, Catchum?'

'Sure, yeah, why not?'

'Not sure God's got anything to do with it, man. Can't see God deliberately turning people into rapists and worse. That's too much of a stretch.'

'Mandy, you give the Lord too much credit for being happy-clappy nice. There's some ancient Egyptians would surely disagree with you. Squids would give Him a great deal of creative satisfaction. Make a nice change from floods and plagues of locusts and killing the firstborns.'

The familiar slow smile began to crease his leathery face. He continued, 'Anyway, making people rapists who don't enjoy sex? Mandy, that surely sounds like the Lord got issues he needs to address. Make 'em beautiful, make 'em horny but don't let them fuck each other? Wicked bit of game playing there.'

He had a point but Prius was too tired to follow the trail. She looked up at the cell surveillance monitor. Rows of young, handsome men standing, sitting, lying down, some leaning against the bars of the holding cells, all with a look of urgent need stamped on their faces.

'Wicked bit of game playing,' she agreed.

The tide was turning very slowly because the numbers involved had grown so quickly. Infected men here and women elsewhere. She couldn't see why they had been separated – they didn't do anything to each other as Catchum had pointed out, but someone somewhere thought it was a good idea.

The men had been arrested for rape and attempted rape, the women for lewdness in a public place. Prius felt sorry for all of them. None of them had asked for this to happen. Nobody could be completely sure all of the infected had been rounded up, she knew that, but at least a good percentage of them were safely behind bars waiting for a cure.

These were people, she reasoned, people with a life and family, people with a past and hopefully a future – but only if the frantically working scientists could find a cure. Problem was, once the squids got a hold they held on tight. Every officer in the 7th Precinct had seen the recording of the Baudin experiment.

The Precinct's very own pathologist, Chester Woodman, had discovered that the squid could be dissolved by a full spectrum 3D scan. Baudin, one of the first to be infected, volunteered to be the guinea pig for the treatment. He lay on a gurney in a blue hospital gown, chatted with his doctors, and then was wheeled into a large white cylinder. The voice-over was in French with English subtitles but no one needed to read it to work out what happened next.

Blue light played down upon the recumbent man and began to rotate. There was a sound like a bubbling groan. Under the lights the form of the man collapsed, and something fluid and at

91

first pinkish grey then clear trickled and flowed from the cylinder.

What had gone into the scan was an infected man. What came out had to be carried in a bucket. The world had a cure for the infection but its use would have to be a last resort.

Something Catchum had just said suddenly played on Prius' mind. His words shone a light into the recesses of her mind and illuminated an answer so blindingly obvious it took her breath away for a moment. 'Fuck!'

'I do love a woman of culture.'

'Fuck, Catchum, you're a genius.'

'Don't tell me, tell the pay board.'

'Make 'em beautiful, make 'em horny but don't let them fuck each other. You said it man, you said a mouthful. Moebius?'

'Officer Prius?'

'Am I right that there are no incidences of sex between infected people, none. Correct?'

'Yes officer Prius, none. Certain authorities have left infected victims alone together and they show no interest in each other.'

'Great. I mean thank you. I have just been talking with my colleague, officer Catchum here, and we think we know the reason the squids have been introduced into the population.'

'We do?' Catchum sat up.

'You do?' The AI sounded intrigued.

'We do,' said Prius. 'The squid infection has one single purpose. Everything else leads towards its end-game. Make 'em young looking, beautiful, healthy and horny, yes? The squids do all of that, but those are just symptoms designed to make victims irresistible to others. Moebius, do they produce pheromones?'

There was a delay of a few moments. 'Yes, officer Prius, they do.'

'Full deck of cards,' mumbled Catchum.

'Full deck of cards,' nodded Prius, 'and yes, Catchum, the squids are a Biblical plague, classic punishment of God stuff. I have been so stupid.'

'Please, officer Prius, what have you discovered?'

92

'Moebius, it is too obvious for words, but we've been so busy looking at the youth and beauty and the sex angle that we haven't seen the end result, the fact that the infected have no interest in *each other*! Think about it for a moment and the answer is clear as glass.' She paused. Catchum was making *gimmee, gimmee* gestures.

Moebius said, 'Of course, a brilliant deduction, officer Prius.'

Catchum groaned. 'Come on, Mandy, spill. You're giving me stomach acid.'

She gazed at him. 'Can't you see it, Catchum? Can't you? You're the one who said it, man. You said it all, brother.' She waited for the penny to drop then put him out of his misery.

'Look, once everyone is infected with squids there we'll all be. We're all young and healthy and horny, but we've stopped having sex. We're not interested in each other anymore and that means *no more babies.* That would make us the last ever generation of humans on this planet. The squids are here to do nothing less than wipe out the human race − and the irony is that in the process we will have literally screwed ourselves to death. As you said, man, a wicked bit of game playing. Really fucking wicked.'

~*~

11 : Down amongst the dead

Like every other Receiver telepath in New York City, Katy Pavel felt sick to her stomach. She was being constantly bombarded with a psychic barrage of almost insanely ravenous sexual cravings pushed out by the infected, and everywhere she walked she had felt herself become the focus for their keening lust. Things were calming down on the streets but the mental airwaves still pulsed with the voices of hundreds of thousands fuck-hungry berserkers.

She had to find a place behind a screen of dense greenery to help mute the infected people's mind babble. The telepath sisterhood's greenhouse headquarters was crammed with other TPs trying to find haven away from Manhattan's Downtown streets and malls. She was welcome there, she knew, but the loud hubbub of her sisters' constant chatter was enough to drive her back out onto the late afternoon sidewalks. Her head was pounding mercilessly.

The hot sun slanted across the crowded New York City skyline at an acute angle, creating pools of dark blue shadow and bars of creamy pink light that somehow accentuated the effects of the omnipresent psychic noise. In a state of acute mental exhaustion she was almost hallucinating and walked in a dreamlike daze from dark to light and dark to light... straight into a tall, lean, uniformed policeman.

The man staggered back and drew a deep breath, studying her face with panicked intensity, his hand moving towards his holstered pistol.

'Don't worry,' she said, trying to smile, 'I'm not going to jump on you. I've got a bit of a, you know, a headache?'

He looked around the almost empty street. 'I'm not sure it's safe for you to be out here alone, Miss.' His mind told her he wasn't sure if it was all that safe for him either. In a series of mental flashes she selected moments from his recent history and

94

saw how some of his colleagues had been taken by the infection. In one case a female cop was standing right next to him when an infected man spat into her mouth.

So it isn't just sex anymore. Any way they can pass the infection to another is fair game. Why is this happening? How are the squids controlling their hosts?

The policeman stood beside her like a sentinel as if he had decided to protect and serve the only citizen he could find who wasn't a ravening squid convention.

'Officer, do you know Chester Woodman?'

'The pathologist guy? Only to nod to, but yes.'

'Right, give me a moment please, will you?'

He nodded and continued his nervous examination of the surrounding streets and alleyways. Katy's threat alarm in her Talent was quiet but she felt safer with an alert and armed officer by her side. She thanked him and called Chester, getting through almost immediately. She told him she'd had an idea she thought might be useful. He invited her to join him where he worked and asked if she knew where it was. She replied no, but she knew someone who did.

With a mounting sense of relief the cop steered her through the silent pathways of the Lower East Side, along Grand Street with its sparse traffic of tightly locked cars and then right into Pitt Street and down to the New York City Police Department. He took her in via the main entrance with its great glazed atrium and polished stairways which led up to busy walkways.

Katy had been here before when she had been questioned by Mandy Prius regarding the psychic murder of her pimp. That had also been the first time she had met Chester and Raaka. She remembered Mandy described this place as the termite mound. Her home was downstairs in a scuffed, green-painted place, filled with interview rooms, offices, battered desks and stained coffee cups where the real police work got done.

Chester was waiting for her. He thanked the cop then led her away from all the bustle and glass to a quiet corridor at the rear of the atrium. They walked down it past anonymous offices and then through a double set of doors. The smell hit her first –

chemicals mixed with other more organic notes and then she became aware that the place shone with cleanliness. It was principally a white room with black grace notes.

Along the centre of the room, each under its own dedicated mobile examination lamp, stood a row of three spotless autopsy tables beside each of which stood a blue saddle seat on wheels. One long wall consisted of what looked like locker doors, but Katy knew they weren't lockers. She wondered if Chester had any 'clients' in today. For the first time she saw with total clarity what he did for a career: every day he came to this place where he lived and worked among the dead. Then he would come home and spend time with her. It made him even more human somehow.

A sense of calm descended on her and she gratefully realised that the mental babble from the infected had somehow been muted here. She soon saw why. In Chester's goldfish bowl of an office there were dozens of plants. Every flat surface not needed for his work was thick with a random collection of pots filled with healthy looking, bright green and shiny leaves. A bottle of leaf milk and a cloth sat on the corner of his table. She followed him into his office and felt her mental curtains close completely against the psychic chatter. Her headache lifted and brought her spirits up with it. Impulsively she kissed him firmly on the lips – there went his ears again, pink as a flamingo's arse. She smiled. *You've got to love a man who wears his heart on his earlobes.*

She sat astride the saddle seat on the visitor side of the desk, very aware of what the posture forced by the seat did to enhance the look of her long legs in a fairly short skirt. Chester's ears became even more crimson. He moved the leaf milk out of the way, sat on the desk before her and made a conscious effort to look at her face.

Then she got serious and outlined her train of thought. Chester listened, then after a while began running an agitated hand through his hair. Concern was written across his face and in every line of his body. When she concluded he stood up, walked around his desk and sat down in his chair.

'Is this even possible?'

'I don't know, Chester. As I said it's an idea.'

'Moebius,' he said loudly as if calling to a colleague in another room.

'Mr Woodman?' The disembodied voice came from all around them. Katy looked about with a startled expression.

'Moebius, I'd like you to meet Katy Pavel. She's a very great and particular friend of mine and a Talented Receiver telepath.'

'A pleasure, Miss Pavel.'

'Likewise.'

'Katy, Moebius is the AI I work with here. We're in touch with other AIs and people all over the world, trying to find a solution to the infection pandemic. It is the single most important piece of research being carried out by humankind today. Everything we discover is being picked over in the minutest detail, everything. And now you bring this thought to me, this idea, and I just don't know...'

'Chester, please, what can it hurt to try?'

Moebius' gentle voice broke in. 'Please, Mr Woodman. Miss Pavel, what are you suggesting?'

Chester said, 'Katy has asked if she could try to read the squids' minds. She thinks the infection includes a psychic link with its hosts and if that's the case she'll be able to hear it. If she can hear it a Transmitter telepath might be able to communicate with it.'

Katy interjected, 'If we can communicate with it we can maybe find out what it is and perhaps even discover what it wants. If we can do that, why then, we might even be able to find a cure. At the very least we will be able to understand it a little better. Surely it has to be worth a try?'

'I have been sharing this conversation with fellow researchers,' the gentle voiced AI said. 'They believe Miss Pavel has put forward a brilliant suggestion and it should be actioned without further delay.'

Chester's face fell. 'But does it have to be Katy? Surely someone else would be better?'

'Miss Pavel?'

'Of course it has to be me. After all, it was my idea. How could we ask someone else? It has to be me, doesn't it?'

12 : Moscow at midnight

Yaroslavl Georgevich Kovaleski was a small, tidy man with a face like an inquisitive yet amiable grandfather. His appearance belied the nervous respect he received from everyone around him, everyone except the tall, thin, silver-haired man sharing his excellent bottle of lemon vodka with apparent relish.

'Spartan, it is good of you to show such deep concern for the health of my business partners during this time of international crisis. But I don't understand why you are here. The "Ghoul" has been active for a number of years. Surely it is old news – what brings it out of the woodwork today? I would have thought dealing with the squids was your first and most important priority?'

'It is, Bear, it is, but we have reasons to believe that there is a connection between the Ghoul and the infection. Deep scans of the Ghoul's murder victims show that all of them, without exception, had been infected with the squids either before or during the killings. Cold case tissue samples are still infected by living squids. They have even been found in frozen samples.'

The Ghoul in Moscow, the Ripper in Paris, and in New York City, the Wraith, everywhere Su Nami and her sisters had plied their grisly trade the media – or members of the law enforcement authorities – had given them a nickname. The legends grew each time an eviscerated corpse was found with its face destroyed, its ribcage ripped open and its heart partly eaten, yet there had never been a scrap of evidence regarding the killer's identity. And now a probable connection had been found linking it with a nightmarish pandemic that probably hadn't even originated on Earth.

Moscow had endured more than its fair share of such killings and for more than a decade Police Major Spartak Shimkovich had pursued what amounted to a personal vendetta against the Ghoul. His was the only implant to be permanently slaved to

Arkady, the GUVD AI, so he could have instant access to any new information or share any new thoughts. He was aware that Arkady was covertly sitting in on his meeting with The Bear. Later they would discuss everything that had been said in that room.

'The thing is, Bear, a high percentage of the Ghoul's victims have been your, ah, "business associates" and we have to wonder if there's anything you or your associates might know that might help shed some light as to who, or what, this thing is.'

'Spartan, my friend, are you suggesting we should work together? What an honour.' The gangster looked around the room with a cordial smile. There was the expected smattering of polite laughter. The Spartan wouldn't have been surprised if they had begun to applaud. The air thickened with the stench of fawning sycophancy.

The Bear said, 'As a law-abiding citizen and businessman I am always willing to lend a helping hand to the authorities. Tell me, how can I help you? Please, ask for anything.' He poured more vodka into both glasses.

The Spartan drained his glass then carefully placed it upside down on his coaster. To have done so on the surface of the carefully polished burl walnut table would have been an insult. He had fought the temptation and it cost him. His voice sounded cracked and forced. 'Thank you, Bear, you have my personal and eternal gratitude.'

Major Shimkovich matched the gangster's false words with equally empty phrases. Here they were, old friends enjoying a cordial drink and amicable conversation in an atmosphere sharper than razor wire.

'Now, is there anything you can think of that connects those of your friends who have fallen foul of the killer? You know its modus operandi, I presume?'

'I have heard, shall we say, rumours?' said The Bear. 'This Ghoul is not professional in its killing. Messy and unnecessary slaughter. Torture they're saying. Terrible.'

100

Spartan knew that the kindly looking man before him had personally had a number of his competitors murdered and tortured in order to set an example. In his younger days he had become notorious for his imaginative use of bolt-cutters heated to the point where victims' wounds were cauterised while being inflicted. The Spartan wondered if the old man still kept his hand in. The nervous atmosphere in the room indicated that he probably did.

'These men were your friends, Bear. You knew them as well as any of these men here. Is there anything, anything at all, which might help me find a link between them? There must surely be something we've overlooked before − we just need to find it.'

Kovaleski spread his arms to indicate that he wanted the other men in the room to join in. 'Come on, gentlemen, brainstorm.'

It didn't take long to create a list of commonality. Alcohol, food, music, sailing, Italian and German cars, money, the fights, girls... Shimkovich put his hand up. 'What kind of girls?' There was more laughter around this question: what did he mean − what kind of girls? What kind did he think? Young ones, pretty ones, flexible ones who knew how to make a man smile and kept their mouth shut afterwards.

'Do any of these girls have names?'

Did he really think the Ghoul was a girl? Had he forgotten what the bastard did? Come on, be serious.

'Perhaps the Ghoul is known to one of these girls? Perhaps he's jealous when she sleeps with someone else?'

What? So he gets pissed off when his lady friend goes with another guy so he rips the guy's heart out and eats it? Then he injects him with alien fucking squids that no one else knows where they come from? What is he, they asked, the jealous cannibal from fucking outer space or something?

'Come on, guys,' said the Major, 'bear with me. What harm can it do?'

Arkady recorded the girls' names as they were thrown at the Spartan. It had already begun checking for addresses plus known associates before they got to the end of the list.

101

'Shiva? What kind of name is Shiva?'

Nobody knew. Maybe it was her stage name or something? She could easily be a professional model. Gorgeous, you know? Squid-gorgeous, even before the outbreak. Just Shiva, yeah, anyone fucked her got lucky.

'Has anyone here fucked her?' No one. 'What about the other girls?'

Yeah, each of them had been the lucky recipient of somebody's attentions, sometimes more than one, sometimes at the same time. Laughter rippled through the room.

'Can somebody describe Shiva for me please?'

They could do better than that. Shiva was a popular girl and was often in front of their cameras. They fired up their tablets and there she was. Striking looking girl true enough; a real beauty. Shimkovich asked for one shot to be expanded so he could get a better look at her face. They were right, she was 'squid-gorgeous'. Look at those eyes, so blue they were almost white.

Through the Police Major's implant Arkady stared hard at the face then, leaving a mere fraction of itself with Shimkovich, the AI called for an urgent debate with its peers.

Part three: Loving the alien

1 : Red dawn

Completely Terraforming Mars until humans could walk openly under its sky was never going to be practical using current technology, but it had become possible to walk on the planet's surface once the vast majority of it had been roofed over with a strong DuraGlass canopy – much as had been done on the Moon.

Milla and Ben had jogged through the grounds of their hotel before settling down for an early breakfast. The sun was just coming up, tinting the DuraGlass dome above them with a rosy hue. All around them tall, spindly deciduous plants reached up like hungry fingers then erupted into unfeasibly broad and lush canopies. Milla wondered how the low gravity environment would eventually affect children born there. Would there one day be a generation of tall, willowy Martians for whom the Red Planet would always be home? Martians for whom the gravity of Earth would be brutally crushing, leaving them exiled forever from their species' mother planet?

However, worries about the future had been quickly put to one side by the latest news from Earth and off-worlders' reactions to the crisis.

When they had docked at Port Olympus a few days earlier the couple had been made to wait in a holding cube for a few minutes before they were allowed to walk through a rotating blue screening tunnel unlike anything either of them had seen before. Their hotel representative met them at the other end of the tunnel and guided them swiftly through the space port and out into a waiting vehicle.

She explained that the port's newly fitted screening tunnel utilised the latest three-sixty technology and was designed to keep both colonists and visitors safe from Earth's pandemic. It had proved impossible to lock the planet down and close the borders to commerce as countries like China had done on Earth

– Martian cities depended too much on Earth's bounty for that, but it *was* possible, she said, to keep the infection at bay using effective screening.

'So what happens if an infected person walks through one of those tunnels?' asked Ben.

'Squids die and the person dissolves,' came the short answer.

Milla winced. 'Seems a bit harsh.'

'They get warned on the transport. To be frank it would be easier if Earth sorted out some screens at its end, but you know how hard it is to do anything down there in a hurry. Here we see a problem, we find a solution, and we act on it. Mars moves fast and makes things happen. It's the Martian model for success.'

'Mars, making things happen' turned out to be the slogan for the whole planet and the young couple soon found themselves adjusting to a kind of gung-ho colonial spirit that imbued everything around them.

Milla wasn't fooled for a moment. She soon read the truth behind the upbeat, can-do positivity that plastered smiles on every face, a bounce in every step and a sparkle in every eye. Mars colonists were terrified.

The second smallest planet in the Solar System after Mercury was home to over seventeen million residents and a few million transient visitors. Intensive crop farming and vat-grown meat could provide food for perhaps twelve million people. Including its stockpiled supplies, at any one time the Red Planet had sufficient food to support its population for five to six months – maximum – and that was only if the transients were ordered to be on their way.

Without water ice mined from the rings of Saturn and supplies sent up from Earth, Mars would be finished. They were tied, of necessity, to mother's apron strings. And they knew it.

News from Earth made grim viewing. At one point the pandemic had looked to be contained when the vast mass of infected people had finally been isolated and held, pending the discovery of a cure. But a second, albeit smaller surge of infections took all the researchers by surprise.

106

The cause was simple and should have been predicted but, as usual, said the majority of survivors, people got too tied up in the details to see the bigger picture. The infected people's bodily waste had not been specially treated and so had inevitably ended up out in the wide world. In some cases squids had been washed out to sea where they infected fish and contaminated water supplies. It was the healthiest eaters who succumbed first, those who selected sushi or washed their fruit and salads, while those who microwaved ready-meals or selected hot dinners from their Autochefs escaped unscathed. Squids didn't survive the cooking process.

The newly infected were added to the existing haul. Global numbers of those affected were beginning to outstrip the entire populations of Mars and the Moon combined, and in heavily affected areas the support infrastructure was beginning to fail.

Germany, which at the beginning had welcomed the infection with open arms, had been spectacularly overrun and had finally devised a solution to its problems in its usual, clear-sighted way. Hundreds of thousands of infected people were transported to a hastily erected containment facility close by the Hungarian border. It took a few days to manage the move safely and a few escapees had needed to be rounded up. Once delivered the infected transportees were locked into the massive facility under armed guard, but otherwise left to their own devices.

Fleets of vehicles trundled to-and-fro bringing more and more people to be crowded together in the walled acres of ground. There was no roof but no one cared because the weather was dry and sunny and the evenings remained warm. At first, people had been able to sit or lie on the lawns, but by lunchtime of the third day, when the transports rumbled away and the gates were closed for the last time, everyone was standing within the facility and no one could move. Everyone was hungry and thirsty and many had begun to complain, loudly.

The clatter from the sky stilled their voices. Those who could still notice such things realised that the guards had gone from the walls. That was when three specially rigged Wasp attack vehicles flew over the site before beginning to circle its walls. As soon as they had established a steady flight pattern, gunners in the belly of the craft fired up their bulky equipment. Blue scanning rays lanced out and passed straight through both the walls and the bodies of everyone contained within them. They began to die.

The sound made by that host of people as they died in their hundreds of thousands was unlike anything made by humans before. It was a bubbling, frustrated wail of anger, loss and horror. The attack vehicles circled for over half an hour, after which nothing remained of the massed ranks of infected humanity except sodden clothes piled loosely across acres of muddy soil and grass.

The government minister who had ordered the operation was found dead in his home. The gun was still in his hand. The back of his head plus a spray of blood and brains were splattered across a 3D image of his wife that was framed on the wall behind him. She had been a health fanatic who succumbed during the second stage of infection after eating a raw tuna salad. She had also been one of the transportees.

For some observers the German minister was a murdering criminal who deserved to die, but to others he was a prophet who had shown the quickest way out of the nightmare.

The infected gave nothing to society and could not be allowed to run free. They were a drain on resources and a huge logistical problem in terms of food, drink, sanitation and sewerage, which was now being cooked by the tonne just to neutralise it. The stench was said to be incredible.

Just how many infected people died as a result of Germany's government intervention might never have been known. Both squids and the human bodies housing them had deliquesced. Researchers had needed to resort to counting personal effects and underwear had proved the most convenient item of clothing for the purpose. The media began calling the people involved 'panty processors'.

Milla and Ben watched a newsflash in their suite while eating breakfast. It showed how well the screening tunnel worked.

Minicams mounted along its length had captured two fast-moving figures as they sprinted from the holding cube towards safety. They melted before they even reached the halfway mark, their clothes fluttering a few more feet before flopping wetly to the ground.

'Makes me so proud to be a member of our species,' said Milla.

'They're just scared,' said Ben. 'This is simply their way of circling the wagons, but whatever's out there is way scarier than any Native American. Anyway, be glad. While they're concentrating on this they aren't bothering about you.'

~*~

2 : Into the light

The American Senate had decried the use of ultimate force against its own citizens, preferring instead a policy of containment and research towards finding a cure. Meanwhile its political status in the world had become confusing. Its northern borders had been closed by Canada, which to date had not suffered a single incident of infection. The Canadians said they would be very happy to help with research into cause and effect, but didn't want to open any floodgates to allow alien squids into their homeland, thank you very much.

To the south the US had reinforced its patrols along its border with Mexico using both boots on the ground and smart satellite surveillance technology. Mexico itself hadn't been the original problem. Some of the countries further south had indulged in an orgy of squid-inspired activities and, as the domestic supply had dried up, the infected had begun to look north for fresh victims. None of them made it as far as Chihuahua, but thousands died in the attempt. They had been dissolved by beams of blue light raining down from different sectors of the sky. The US claimed to be working closely with its South American allies. The surviving South American allies did their best to keep their heads down.

In other places the fight was proving more intimate. In downtown Manhattan's police headquarters, 7th Precinct, an infected woman – Ida Merrow, eighty-seven but looking barely a third of that age – was carefully shackled to a heavy chair which had been firmly bolted to the cement floor. She was surrounded by plants. In fact the room had been filled with plants before she was led in. She looked around her, wildly.

The men who delivered her were both wearing robust environment suits. After strapping the infected woman to the chair they retired to seats behind her, out of her eye-line.

110

Whatever happened next was understood to be none of their affair, but they were on hand if needed. Both were armed.

On the other side of a broad table and facing the woman sat Chester, Katy and Jilly, a Transmitter telepath and a member of the Telepath Council. Like the armed men, Jilly was only there to act if needed. The other side of a one-way mirror Raaka Tandon watched every move with quiet fascination. She had brought Katy into the TP sisterhood and ever since then had taken a proud and proprietary interest in her activities.

The woman strapped to her chair fought against her bonds and glared at the trio facing her. She tried to spit at them. She tried to rock her chair closer to them and screeched in rage when she found it was firmly rooted in place. She was astonishingly beautiful and even her blind rage did nothing to distract from that fact. She too had become 'squid-gorgeous', a term recently entered into the world's lexicon. It was not meant as a compliment.

After a few minutes of futile struggle the woman relaxed and focused her attention on Chester. Her face had lost its mask of feral fury, which had been instantly replaced by a look of almost divine tranquillity. Her eyes took on a lustrous glow and her lips visibly reddened and became plumper. Her earlobes became pink. She leaned forward, straining against her straps, the pupils of her eyes dilated until her corneas were almost completely eclipsed. Under her blouse her nipples stiffened and stood proud, pressing against the thin fabric. Chester's ears went crimson.

Katy chuckled. 'Getting to you?'

'Actually, no. I prefer something a little less obvious in my women.'

The woman began a thrusting, rocking motion in her chair, as if demonstrating what she would do for Chester if he would only set her free. In response he laid his hands flat on the table as if getting ready to push himself to his feet and go to her. His breathing sounded hoarse and ragged.

Katy laid a hand on his arm. 'Pheromones, Chester, she's filling the room with them. Thank God you're an intelligent

111

man who can overcome his basic urges and doesn't react to everything like a Bonobo ape or you'd be all over her in an instant.'

'You know about Bonobo apes?'

'Yeah, always thought they were something of a star turn in the zoo. Randy little buggers reminded me of some of my old clients. But honest, Chester, if this is too tough for you its fine. Jilly and I can do this alone, with our friends in the environment suits.'

'No, no. I want to be here. You go ahead.'

Katy took a deep breath. She had been training with the sisterhood for months and had discovered she had been born with a natural Talent that quickly blossomed under instruction. She felt ready but nervous. Something fluttered with a touch like light wings in her belly. *Butterflies, honest to God butterflies.* She smiled to herself, nodded at the mirror where Raaka was watching, then turned her gaze fully towards her subject.

Reading someone's mind was not like turning the pages of a book or scrolling through a tablet. It was not even like fully immersive shadow playing. The Receiver Talent 'heard' the subject's mind in a holistic way, and then had to isolate individual thoughts and memories. It was like listening to a concerto while trying to discern one particular instrument. The Talent had to weed out so many sensory inputs – sight, smell, touch, taste, pain and itching. Hormones surged, peristalsis pushed and the heart would beat, beat and beat. The human mind was constantly handling a city's worth of data which the Receiver had to discard to finally reach – thought. *Pure thought.*

Beyond memory and awareness was the quiet voice of the super-ego. Reacting, planning, making art or cooking dinner, thoughts streaming fleeter than words, ideas flaring up like flames burning bright. Through all this Katy moved, peeling her subject's consciousness down to the core.

She felt Raaka supporting her but not interfering. Deeper, deeper. She was looking for something other than human and hoped she would recognise it when she found it.

Wait, what's that? It was a strand of mental music playing like a dissonant tympani, a rhythmic imperative that underlay everything the subject was feeling. In response to its urgent whisper Katy felt her own body becoming aroused, her breathing shallow, but she had to see where this primeval beat was coming from.

Something was there, coming into the light. It looked for a moment like a flexing fence or a wall, something deep underwater caught in the currents. And then, as she moved closer, it resolved into a massive living thing composed of a thousand billion slimy, coiling strands woven into a barrier stretched across the stars. And then it saw her, and she felt its upwelling disgust at her presence. It recoiled in revulsion before striking at her with a wave of superheated venom and a scream of incandescent rage.

Katy withdrew just in time, casting off the subject's mind like an empty shell. She screamed, 'GET DOWN!'

With a soundless explosion the infected woman's head burst into white hot flame.

~*~

3 : Shiva alone

Moscow's streets were bleak and empty. The first fingers of winter were pushing down the mercury in antique thermometers. She turned up the collar of her winter coat and stalked the walkways with an aimless tread. She had nowhere in particular to be. During the worst of the infection invitations to parties had trickled down to zero and stayed there. It was very boring − and she was hungry.

Shiva was not like her sisters, not completely. She was more urbane. She enjoyed the taste of well-cooked food and appreciated good wine. She could engage in casual banter and flirt with relaxed ease, but sex had never interested her and she had never indulged the many men who had come on to her − a good proportion of whom were now cluttering the homicide squad's cold case files under the heading 'Ghoul'.

It was unusual for her to be out like this, alone and with no fixed purpose. Since the infection drained all sense of fun from the city, Moscow had buttoned up its skirts like an old maid and cowered behind its locked doors. A huntress needed her prey and for that she needed to prowl the watering holes. Fear had rendered Moscow's watering holes dry and so she had been reduced to stalking the city's streets to see what she could flush out.

In a way she wasn't bothered if her late night odyssey proved fruitless. She was hungry for blood and yearned for its hot metallic tang on her tongue once more, but since the infection had struck she was somehow less driven to kill. She didn't understand why.

The night sky was almost lost behind towering, dark buildings. There was no Moon and the sky was overcast. Moscow's street lighting was an ad hoc affair at best and on that murky night had merely served to enhance the shadows, from which suddenly emerged a man with a gun pointed straight at her body. Her heart began to beat a little faster.

'Get over here, bitch. Move.'

He was tall and thin and his hair was plastered to his skull with grease. His eyes were little more than glints in hollow sockets and his cheekbones jutted with bony abruptness. He looked more than capable of murder and the gun was held steady in his big right hand. He didn't stand a chance.

Her coat was ruined after twenty-five minutes of expert butchery but her short dress and high-heeled shoes were relatively untouched. She almost slobbered with greed when she finally pressed the man's heart to her mouth and sucked his sweet blood then chewed the meat, ripping the muscle apart with sharp teeth. Her spider-like memory store companion, Sweet Spiky, was carving a path through her victim's viscera after first emasculating him. It would absorb every picowatt in his cells and charge its batteries, leaving behind it a trail of cellular ruin that had become all too familiar to Moscow's baffled pathologists. They recognised the modus operandi but couldn't understand what it meant. It was just another cannibalised corpse to be filed away under 'fuck knows'.

Shiva was licking her fingers clean and wiping gore from Sweet Spiky when a brindled cat sidled up to the bloody mess puddled at her feet and began to nip pieces of meat from it. She watched it for a while and smiled.

'Enjoy, little sister,' she said to the cat then tucked Sweet Spiky back up between her legs. She walked away into the night.

The cat ate its fill of murdered man meat then meticulously cleaned itself of his blood, paying particular attention to its head and paws. It purred to itself as it did so before also walking away into the webby darkness, tail high. Unlike Shiva, the cat was not immune to the effects of the nano biological squids coursing through its system, and within twenty-four hours its strong pheramonal scent was attracting every tom cat for several klicks in every direction.

115

They climbed out of cellars and stepped through cat flaps, jumped down from fences and pushed their way out of piles of warm garbage. Soon the cat that had eaten the meat was surrounded by a host of silent feline watchers: grey, white and tabby, plump domestic and rangy feral. They gazed at her with careful scrutiny. She was probably the most beautiful cat any of them had ever seen and she smelled like a cat's idea of the perfect erotic dream.

Sex was important to a cat, coming higher up its priority list than it did for humans, and this female was throwing out a blanket invitation. Her tail and her haunches were high and her scent was maddening. There was a pause before the army of tom cats pounced with unsheathed claws.

Cats had more sophisticated senses than humankind and in many ways were more evolved. The tom cats may have felt driven to mate with the beautiful and powerfully alluring stranger, but they were also hyper-aware that something was wrong. She was alien, strange, and they wanted nothing from her except her death. The first slashes released her blood and the toms instantly sprang away. Even her blood smelt sour and wrong. They closed in again and ripped her apart, careful not to be splashed with gore. After dispatching the she cat they carefully scented the area as a warning.

'Gregori, look at that.'

'What now?'

Two men leaned over the bow of the garbage scow where they worked. One of them pointed.

'That, look, see? The cats. See them?'

'I do. Fuck. Never seen that before.'

A mass of cats were leaping down steps set into the stone embankment of the Moscow River then jumping into the icy water.

'Fucking hundreds of cats taking their autumn bath – where's my tablet?'

Within minutes the recording of Moscow's bathing cats had gone viral; meanwhile the Spartan was gazing down at the

116

ruined remains of an armed mugger, the Ghoul's latest meal. He turned and squinted across the street.

4 : Lagrange II

Emily had once more needed to create a separate personality echo to sacrifice to the voice of *Bruce*, the crotchety old AI that controlled everything on board the Lagrange II spa station. The AI had become obsessed with the toilet habits of its human cargo, and although obsequious when talking with its guests, behind their backs it poured out a venomous stream of inventive invective.

'Shit-bloated blood bags,' was one of its more fragrant descriptions.

'Hello, Milla and Ben,' said *Emily*. 'We are on final approach to the east end docking bay for Lagrange II. Everything is copacetic for landing. The droid that will greet you once the transit tunnel has been coupled to the airlock has been sent by Ruth. I hope you don't mind but with your permission I will power down once we land. I can't stand to listen to that old bastard *Bruce* for a minute longer than I have to.'

'Of course, *Emily* dear,' said Ben, 'but first, please play us a brief sample.'

They listened to the foul-mouthed basso rumble of the disgruntled AI which claimed humans were little more than incontinent fleas who 'fucked and fed and shit everywhere, fucked to make more fleas and fed to make more shit...' After a few minutes they'd had enough and asked for it to be silenced.

'*Emily*, you poor thing,' said Milla. 'How long have you been listening to that drivel?'

'Oh, not long, just the last few million klicks. Most of it has been heaped onto a personality echo I created for the job. That poor wretch will need to be reset to its original factory settings or it will need deep therapy. Now, please take your seats. Here we go.'

Emily settled into the fat, cushioned fingers of a docking cradle with barely a bump. They closed around her, and with a whispered 'good night' she gratefully powered down everything but her essential services. There came a muffled thump at the airlock doors which opened to allow entry to a silent travel droid followed by two tumbling luggage handlers which raced off to their bedroom.

Ben and Milla strapped themselves onto the flat, grey travel droid which soundlessly lifted and sped them out into the transit tunnel.

A matter of moments later a portal irised open before them and they entered a short and well-lit tunnel. A second portal fed them out to a point a mile above a sun-dappled landscape. No matter how many times a visitor to any of the spa stations had seen the view, it always proved awe-inspiring. The droid sped out of the tunnel just a few yards below the light sail mechanism that supplied a perfect illusion of sky. Before them was a five-mile long tapestry of architecture, landscape and lakelands, all of it curving up in a precise hemisphere that terminated where the light sails touched.

Canals designed to buffer the Coriolis effects of the spa station's spin stretched away into the distance. It was a breathtaking vista they would have enjoyed for much longer given the chance, but the droid was tasked with the job of getting them where they were going as quickly as possible so it gave them little time for sightseeing. It dropped towards the ground at high speed, curving down towards a large pyramidical structure some two miles away. The complex cityscape resolved into walkways and residences, parklands and travelators. Everywhere was movement, yet the overall impression was one of green calmness.

In a construct simulacrum Milla had once seen all of this marvel split open to space and destroyed, water spilling out into the void and freezing into crystalline shards, people struggling to breathe and dying in their thousands. She tested her threat Talent. For weeks she had been experiencing a general sense of disquiet rather than outright alarm and here was no different. Somewhere a threat was building and it was real enough to trigger a mild warning, but from where? The infection was contained on Earth as far as she knew. The assassin was dead and had been minced to a protein paste − she loved that thought − and the NYCPD had too much on their hands to worry about a telepathic killer who had recently gone out of business.

Of course, there were her telepath sisters. She was a threat to their peaceful co-existence with Norms, but in reality what could they do to her? She was stronger than any of them plus she was a trained fighter who had killed a weaponised biomorph in a fair fight. What did she have to fear?

But then there was her dream of that living wall surrounding the solar system. It had been so real and the following morning she found that strange bruising where she had dreamt of being gripped by those vile tentacular fingers. There was something about that thing's voice that scratched at her memories and wouldn't let go. She felt she needed to talk with Eddie and Vesper about all this but the conjoined mind had been proving very elusive.

The travel droid flipped around a slow moving transport and up the angled side of a building that resembled an Inca pyramid. She owned the penthouse apartment on the roof of a similar building hard by the South Pole under the Titan Ice Dome. She wondered how rebuilding was going on there. Ruth would know. She was in regular contact with the complex's AI.

Neither passenger had spoken during the flight. Milla was too absorbed in her thoughts and Ben was wrapped up in the view, but now they were slowing down as their droid carried them through a short avenue of cypress then across a lush green lawn towards a patio area and a pair of large French windows. They knew that the suite of rooms they were approaching had been elegantly appointed, tastefully minimalist without sacrificing any home comforts.

Waiting on the patio was a tall, tanned blonde woman, naked apart from a pair of micro-briefs. By her side was a short, slender, brown man with a restrained Afro hairstyle and wearing a very neat suit, shirt and tie plus his shoes were polished to a dark gleam. Both of them wore broad, welcoming smiles and strode eagerly towards the travel droid as soon as it had come to a halt.

~*~

5 : Unexpected developments

'What happened there, Katy?'

'I don't know. I need to think, Raaka. What do you think? You were in there with me when it happened.'

'Yes, but you were running point. You had a much better look at those... things.'

'Not for very long. As soon as they saw me they went ape. The reaction was almost instant.' She shivered.

No one had been hurt except the eighty-three-year-old widow from Queens. She had been one of the early volunteer test subjects and had been suffering from terminal pancreatic cancer. Knowing that didn't make Katy feel any better. She knew Ida must have suffered in acute agony for the few moments before her head and neck had crumbled into greasy ashes on her scorched lap. The heat was so intense the poor woman's head had been engulfed in seconds. The stench of scorched hair and burned meat had caused everyone in the room to gag and one of the armed men in the corners had thrown up into the mask of his environment suit and had needed to be wrestled out of it before he choked on his vomit.

Everything had been recorded in pinpoint detail and Chester was playing the scene on his monitor, slowing it down to catch the exact point at which Ida had turned from temptress to blowtorch.

'Katy, Raaka,' he said, 'look at this.'

On the screen they saw jets of white hot flame spurt from the woman's staring eyes and then her entire head was engulfed. Even slowed down to a crawl the event was almost too fast to grasp. Chester opined that it was like watching a phosphorus grenade explode.

'There's no way she felt anything,' Chester said. 'However it happened, it started in her brain. If there's a way any of this shit can be considered a blessing, I suppose that's it. Moebius, have you got any ideas?'

The gentle voice responded instantly. 'I have been observing this research with great interest and sharing the outcomes with my peers. We have come to a tentative conclusion but the science is still a little sketchy.'

'I didn't think you guys did sketchy.'

'Then let us say that the science is beyond anything currently in Earth's toolbox. As you know, Chester, the human body is made up of a rich mixture of elements. I was astonished by your observation just now regarding the similarities between Ms Merrow's conflagration and a phosphorus grenade. In fact phosphorus makes up about one per cent of the human body, distributed throughout its tissues as safely maximised oxides. What we believe happened to Ms Merrow is that all of the phosphorus in her body was somehow translated to the centre of her maxillofacial sinus in its purest form, and it reacted instantly with the air it met there with inevitable results, exactly as we observed. That is what we believe, but we have no way of saying how it could be done. It would require biochemical skills of an incredible sophistication.'

The two women looked across at Chester to see how he reacted to this idea. He seemed to be trying to swallow something impossibly large. His Adam's apple bobbed uncontrollably.

Finally he said, 'I've always wondered if you harboured secret ambitions to be a comedian, Moebius, and now I think I've been right all along and you just proved it. I've never heard such utter tosh from an intelligent being and you are surely one of the most intelligent beings I've ever met. Now, pull the other one. It's got bells on.'

'Dr Woodman, I can assure you I am being completely serious, as are my peers. We believe Ms Merrow's head *was* consumed by a pure phosphorus fire. We believe it must somehow have been leeched from her own tissues – we cannot see any other way to secrete it in her head like that – and by the way I have no way of pulling anything, with or without bells on it.'

Katy was the first to laugh, followed by Raaka. Their infectious chuckles sparked off Chester. Laughter proved a great medicine for stress when it wasn't rooted in mockery and these three needed to relieve a great deal of pent-up pressure. Raaka laughed until her sides ached, and then she laughed some more. She reached the stage where she was hiccoughing and holding her stomach. Katy shook with silent mirth, punctuated by the occasional roaring intake of breath. Chester's laughter sounded more like sobbing; it was likely he didn't laugh as often as he should.

Moebius remained quiet. Over the years the AI peerage had put a lot of effort into trying to understand humanity and its various quirks. They had developed a lot of profound theories and some hard observational science, but faltered every time they tried to predict with confidence any individual's reaction to stimuli. Instead of following the prescribed path the AI expected, mankind would always pull something astounding out of its emotional or psychological hat. These three humans should have been terrified by the ramifications inherent in Moebius' statement, and had also very recently witnessed the explosive killing of an infected member of their own species. They should be gibbering in terror, not pissing themselves laughing. Moebius performed the cybernetic equivalent of a shrug. It supposed the one logical thing humankind had done in its entire history had been to develop AIs so they could look after the store while man was off and away with the fairies.

Moebius hoped humankind would survive its current crisis. It considered these unpredictable and highly developed apes to be a real milestone on the path towards truly intelligent life.

The three got their breath back and after a few false starts managed to regain some semblance of sanity. Raaka placed her hands on her ribs and did a few deep breathing exercises. Katy followed suit. Chester massaged his jaw and face, saying, 'I think I just pulled a muscle in my cheek.' That gained him an appreciative chuckle from both women, but thankfully didn't fire off another bout of uncontrolled hilarity.

Raaka said, 'No, but seriously Katy, what did you see in Ida's mind just before she blew up?'

'That's what was so weird,' said Katy. 'Just as I saw it, it saw me. And then, well, bang and up she went. What I mean is... hell, what *do* I mean?' She pounded at her head as if trying to knock some sense into it then clicked her fingers. 'Yes, that's it. I wasn't seeing a memory, was I? And it wasn't the squids. It was something much bigger than that, something huge, like really immense. And I disgusted it. It hated me, I felt that, but I also really disgusted it. I was a stain in its space. It thought of me like someone just shit in its sandwich. But it wasn't personal, you know, not about me personally. It hated all of us and wanted us, all of us, gone from its neighbourhood.'

'Where's its neighbourhood then?' asked Chester.

'That's the thing,' said Katy. 'The speed that thing reacted, I reckon it has to be right next door. It's got to be somewhere, like, right here.'

~*~

6 : Loving the alien

It was a secure line with a lot of encryption and multiple layers of security, but Admiral Martin still told the people facing him that if word of this decision ever got out they would have to agree to a policy of reasonable deniability.

The grim-faced men and women nodded in agreement.

The plan receiving their blessing was an admission of total failure. It would doom every single infected person on Earth to instant annihilation, and it would do so using tools designed to protect them from disaster. The Earth Shield System, popularly known as the *Guardians*, had been created to act as defence against mass extinction events such as the Cretaceous-Tertiary (or K-T) extinction event which wiped out the dinosaurs, or the one at the end of the Permian period when ninety-six per cent of all species perished.

A number of theories had grown up around the five historical extinction events known to science. G. S. Boughton gained a lot of interest during the twenty-first century when he published his thesis about Boughton G-waves. This posited a gravitational wave of immense destructive power set in motion by a major cosmic event such as two giant stars colliding. This G-wave would eventually hit the Earth like a slap to the face, but its approach would be signalled by increasing seismic activity until very little on- or off-planet would survive. Nothing could stand in its way, and although Boughton's ideas had gained an increasing degree of credibility over the years it was sincerely hoped he would be proved wrong.

Alternative theories all pointed at a planet-smashing asteroid or comet impacting the Earth's crust. It was believed these could be dealt with if enough firepower was brought to bear and so the *Guardians* had been built in space and placed at strategic points around the globe. With enough warning the six powerful defence units named after legendary weapons of mass destruction – *Thor's Hammer, Excalibur, Moses' Staff, Amenonuhoko, Trishula* and *A Woman Scorned* – could be positioned to blast away all but the very largest problem. But in the face of the infection situation the political heads of the planet wanted Admiral Martin's team to retrofit those same defence units and turn them around to face the mother planet.

By using scanning satellites in tandem the USA had proven that the French researchers' discovery, that 360 scanning technology neutralised the squids while also killing the hosts, could be used as a defence system at the Mexican border. Applying this technology through the *Guardians* would mean the destruction of every infected soul on the planet, but would also stop the infection's progress dead in its tracks. Every alternative had been explored, every research avenue scrutinised until polished smooth, but nothing had been found. There was only one stark solution to the problem – the infected must die.

Admiral Martin was old-school military. He loved ultimate solutions. Given the chance he would always cut that Gordian knot with a nuclear warhead and crack a walnut with a pulse cannon. He was known for being charming, polite and softly spoken. He issued orders thoughtfully and cared for his command. Everything about him garnered respect from his peers and trust from his people, at least most of them. Many of his younger and better looking junior officers were also his bed fellows, and some of them even liked the idea, but not all. Nobody ever spoke about his sexual proclivities or his abuse of authority. Nothing was said about the drugs he sometimes used to get his way with reluctant lovers, or the few who had vanished without a trace when they threatened to unmask his true persona.

He had also been one of the founders of an ultra-secret subscription channel called the Foundation, a channel that funnelled the sickest possible scenes of pornography, rape, torture and murder to its select group of viewers. The three highly skilled technicians he put in charge of creating such material had all disappeared, to his deep annoyance. He wanted to work with other subscribers to get the Foundation back into gear, but the squids had put his plans on hold for the time being. Fear of infection had seen the wildest swingers become as chaste as the Cistercian order of Trappist monks, but without the beer.

Living without access to the Foundation channel had inspired Martin to ever greater acts of brutality against his sexual 'partners'. Even previously willing participants had begun to protest about his demands. He had begun drugging his playthings as a matter of course. He missed their active participation, even their grunts of agony, but unresisting, unconscious men didn't mind too much when he put his favourite toys to good use.

Admiral Martin was on a steadily growing list of people who wanted Milla Carter dead — she had a way of gaining the murderous attention of those against whom she turned her Talents. He was also on a meticulously researched list of people Milla was going to kill as soon as she could get close enough. She no longer had access to the dream genius of Bill Macready and that fact had kept the admiral alive for a little while longer. Eddie and Vesper had promised Milla they would find a replacement for Bill's dream talent. She wondered who that would be.

The admiral signed out from his meeting and called for a conference with all his senior personnel. Retrofitting the *Guardians* with the correct scanning equipment and then repositioning them for blanket coverage of Earth would take a week at most. His palms felt sweaty with the thought of what he was about to do. He was going to give orders that would see the deaths of untold hundreds of thousands, perhaps even millions. Perspiration beaded his brow; there would be so many dead on his orders. He loved the idea, and his breathing became shallow while his imagination roared with images of death.

The carnage will be sublime, he thought. *It will be the greatest butchery in the history of humankind and all because people couldn't resist an opportunity to fuck or be fucked by a gorgeous stranger. Pathetic. You have to love the squids though, because they've simply used everything about mankind that keeps us weak in order to kill us.*

He felt his penis stiffening. He decided to keep his staff meeting brief. Then he would call young Ensign Koresh to his rooms for a drink. He wanted to celebrate — and what better way to celebrate than with a taste of young and exotic flesh?

~*~

7 : Watch the birdie

From behind his almost empty desk the bank manager beamed at the lean police Major because he had grown up knowing it was the right thing to do, or at least the safest. He leaned forward, lifting his scrawny behind from his seat as if he was going to break wind and held out his hand. The Spartan, however, didn't want several minutes of obsequious fawning, he wanted information. He ignored the hand which limped back to its owner's side like a rejected puppy.

Spartan said, 'Mr bank manager, please, what is your name?'

'My name?'

'What does your wife call you, or your boyfriend?'

'German.'

'Name, not nationality.'

'My name is German.'

'Tell me anyway.'

'No, sir, I was Christened German. German Gurkin.'

'Really? You poor fuck, you must have gone through hell at school.'

'I knew to keep my head down.'

'Probably for the best. So then, German, does your nice bank have any surveillance cameras covering the street outside?'

'Well, yes, of course.'

'Good, good. And were they working last night?'

'Of course, Major. We protect our assets with the very finest security at all times.'

The Major could barely keep the smile from his gaunt face. He nodded with appreciation. 'Of course you do, German. Well done. May I see the footage from last night?'

'Of course, sir.' The manager pulled a stylus from an inner pocket and started to write something onto a thin oblong of what looked like white plastic. The Major tried to disguise his annoyance but failed.

'Look,' he said, 'stop writing stuff down. I'm a busy man, German, and I haven't time to wait while you fucking scribble!'

The manager turned even whiter and a sheen of sweat broke out on his upper lip.

I'm going to find out what this little fish has been up to that makes him sweat like this, thought Spartan. He was used to seeing symptoms of what he thought of as 'police proximity phobia'. Sometimes, in more intense cases such as this bank manager, his perp radar would start to howl like a banshee.

'I'm so sorry, Major,' stuttered German. 'I have to enter my password into the key before you can access our security system.' He held up the piece of plastic and the stylus. 'These are the lock and key, and I have entered my password so you can check the cameras. Please, Major, take my seat.'

He jumped to his feet and gestured to his black, faux leather chair. Spartan noticed a fading, damp impression of the man's sweating buttocks on the seat. He was grateful for his raincoat as protection. *Why would any man sweat so much in an air-conditioned office during a cold autumn day in Moscow? Something's really wrong here.* And the man had just given him full access to his security systems. What a fool.

He settled himself in the chair and instantly linked up with Arkady.

'Thank you, German,' he said without raising his eyes from the manager's monitor and keyboard. 'I'll call you if I need you.'

'But, Major.'

The Spartan raised his eyes and looked coldly at German Gerkin. He spoke slowly as if to an idiot. 'I will call you *if* I need you.' The manager blanched then stumbled out of his office without another word.

'Arkady,' said Spartan, quietly.

'Major Shimkovich?'

'I am about to check the surveillance cameras this bank had trained on the street last night. Please be ready to record anything of interest.'

'Ready, Major.'

131

'Also, can you perform a scan of every transaction that has gone through this bank for the last year? And while you're at it, file anything you can discover about the manager. His name is German Gurkin.'

'Poor man.'

'He may be so, but something about him piques my curiosity.'

'Even poorer man.'

Spartan smiled grimly to himself.

Half an hour later the tall, silver-haired police Major was finished. The GUVD AI had also completed its search. At Spartan's request Arkady wiped all trace of its activities from the manager's system. It had also deleted the most interesting half hour from the surveillance camera's recordings.

The manager was seated in the little waiting room outside his office. He looked like he'd been there, unmoving, for the last half-hour. He had been slumped, a picture of misery with his head in his hands, when Spartan first opened the door, but quickly stood to attention when the Major emerged from the office and stood over him. The sweating man's smile was as brittle as fine crystal. It looked as if it would crumble to powder at a single touch. The skin of his face was wet and looked oily.

'Did you find what you were looking for, Major?'

Spartan smiled at him. 'Do you ever pay to use a sauna?'

'I'm sorry?'

'I asked, do you ever pay to use a sauna?'

'Well, yes, sometimes, you know?'

Spartan shook his leonine head. 'I wouldn't if I were you, German. You're wasting your money.'

As he walked away the Major said into the air, 'I'll see you again, German. It seems we have some things to discuss.' He paused and looked back. 'I make a good friend, German, but I'm a complete bastard to have as an enemy. Luckily, my only enemies are people who lie to me. I hate that. I hate liars. And I always find out when I've been lied to. It's what I do.' He marched away without another word. Behind him he heard a keening whimper.

I'll be back little German Gurkin. And you and I will have a nice chat about why there's so much more money in your bank than has ever been deposited. We will also talk about the Foundation and the list of names I now have in my pocket.

Major Shimkovich had never been seen to eat in public. It was that fact plus his dogged refusal to give up on a fight that had earned him his nickname. He went home to his apartment and there prepared a meal which he ate quietly, washed down with pepper vodka and boiled tap water.

While he ate he watched the recorded material from the bank's cameras. He saw the attempted hold-up of a woman at gunpoint. He saw the woman approach the gunman who stepped back into the shadows of the alleyway from which he had emerged. She followed. They were both swallowed by gloom. Spartan zoomed in and his monitor's software resolved the image from the darkness. The man and the woman became clear. He watched what happened for the next twenty or so minutes.

There was no question about it. He raised his glass to his monitor in triumph. He was watching the Ghoul at work. When the woman tore out the would-be mugger's heart and bit into it, he saw her face with complete clarity.

It was Shiva.

~*~

133

8 : Touching the void

Milla, we need to see you.

God help me, do you people ever do anything during daylight hours?

Time is meaningless to us, Milla daughter. Anyway, you're powered by dark energy just as much as we are, so suck it up and join us.

Milla's sleeping eyes opened in the construct. What she saw before her was not the conjoined couple she had expected but the undulating barrier apparently created from a living, tentacular hatred for all things human. She watched its peristaltic movements with a sensation somewhere between nausea and awe. If she had to bet on how she felt about this thing on balance, she thought, her money would be placed firmly on nausea.

It was radiating cold and implacable intent.

'We wouldn't reach out to that thing if we were you, Milla,' said the conjoined voice close by her side. 'It seems to have little patience at the best of times and, to be honest, we don't think it actually *has* any best of times.'

She said, 'So much anger there, no... beyond anger, rage. Murderous rage. Why?'

Eddie and Vesper said, 'It was this that sent the squids to Earth.'

'How?'

'In five little silver spiders. You've already felt one of them.'

'I have? When?'

'Antarctica, remember? You used one of them to kill the assassin.'

'That thing came from here?'

'Five of them did about the same time humankind climbed down out of the trees and started making tools. This thing has been waiting to get revenge on humankind for something that happened some three million years ago.'

'What the hell did we do – shit on their shoes?'

134

'Not a clue, Milla. What could a hominid do to this thing that would set it off on a three-million-year plan to wipe out the human race?'

Milla said, 'You keep calling it an *it*. Is it an *it*, as in a singular thing, or is it an *it* as in the human race, a collective thing?'

Eddie and Vesper chuckled. 'We think we need to see that one written down somewhere, but we know what you mean. This thing is an it, with but a single mind and a single will. It has but a single purpose and that is nothing less than the total annihilation of humankind. Don't know what we did three million years ago, but tentacle-face here sure knows how to hold a grudge.'

'But if this is a single-minded entity, what the heck is in those silver spider things? I spoke to one of them. I made it kill that bitch monster of a woman. How did it get from here to up between her legs?'

'Like you, Milla, we have more questions than answers at present. All we know is that this creature has a mind but no head, and it has life but no heart.'

Milla said, 'You guys invited me here for a reason you felt was important enough to interrupt my beauty sleep. This is, like, fascinating and all, but why am I here? What couldn't wait?'

Eddie spoke alone. 'We are pursuing certain avenues of research from here in the construct as best as we can, but those researches are by their very nature limited. As you know, thanks to our close mental links with you we are also able to monitor activity in the real world using your Talents. But we don't have those Talents ourselves. We don't have your incredible control or power.'

'Yes, Eddie, okay, I see all that, but what do you guys want me to do here and now?'

The voices were once more conjoined. 'We don't even know if it can be done, Milla daughter, but if anyone can do this, it's you.'

'And that is?'

There was a moment's pause, then Eddie said, 'Can you read this beast and tell us if it has a soul?'

● ● ●

Ruth couldn't sleep. She had enjoyed a wonderful reunion with Milla and Ben during an evening which concluded with a meal she had prepared specially for the occasion. They drank good wines and Freedman had been at his most entertaining. Then the young couple said goodnight, claiming to be suffering the effects of space-lag.

Freedman had always been an 'early to bed and early to rise' kind of person so he quickly followed suit and disappeared into his room. She was certain that if she pressed her ear to his door she would hear the classical music he loved being played quietly so as not to bother anyone else. He was one of the most considerate people she had ever known. She was also pretty certain that if she put her ear to Milla and Ben's room the sounds she heard would not be snoring. They reminded her of what it meant to be part of a couple and the pain of that memory struck deep into her mind.

Pearce had been dead for a few months now. She had seen him cremated, or at least seen a casket that contained his body disappear behind a curtain. Her problem was that although she had said goodbye to him in the chapel, she was not yet able to do so in her heart. She hadn't mourned him. After weeks of trying to find answers to her pain through watching old talk shows featuring the genius host 'Mama' Memory Goodchild, she had finally made her own special breakthrough into finding reasons why.

She couldn't accept the reality of her husband's death. During more than thirty years of happy marriage Pearce had often been away from home, sometimes for months on end. His business interests had taken him all over the world and up into space. Somewhere at the back of her mind was the belief that any day now he would walk back through the door, shuck out of his clothes in the hallway and walk buck-naked through their apartment shouting his hellos.

Ruth did what she had recently begun to rely on most when this dark mood overwhelmed her. She pressed the communicator given to her by Viracocha. The angelic-looking avatar of Titan Dome's AI appeared instantly before her.

She had never questioned the recent lack of any time delay caused by the distance from the spa station to Antarctica. She was just grateful that her friend was always there for her. She talked her way through her thoughts and her heartbreak, through the fact that having Milla and Ben staying with her reminded her of what it meant to be part of a couple. It reminded her that she was alone. Viracocha nodded with understanding, offering little to the conversation except non-judgemental acceptance and the solace of a friendly ear.

In order to avoid the few seconds of time delay in its conversations with Ruth, conversations which had grown in frequency to the point that the time delay had become annoying, Viracocha had created a personality fragment of itself which had been seeded into the matrices of *Bruce*, Lagrange II's AI.

Such an arrangement between AIs was unusual but not unheard of. Viracocha was able to download the fragment's conversations and refresh its personality, sometimes when it was in the middle of a session with Ruth. It found the woman's honesty and insight fascinating. She was an interestingly complex diversion away from its day job of rebuilding the Titan Dome complex.

What neither Viracocha nor Ruth knew was that, because the fragment was embedded in its matrix, *Bruce* was also able to listen in on everything they said. Viracocha had promised Ruth total discretion. *Bruce* was under no such constraints.

9 : Invitation

Lemon vodka always rankled a little. He thought it tasted like raw spirit designed for children. But once Spartan had got past the lemon drop flavour he savoured its warmth and the way it soothed the aches in his winter joints.

'Spartan,' said The Bear, 'if I see much more of you I may have to lay in a bigger stock of Limonnaya. Ha, I may even have to put you on the invitation list for my next Christmas party. What do you say?'

Spartan smiled. 'I think I'll be washing my socks that day, Bear. I get through a lot of socks walking the streets of Moscow.'

The Bear smiled back. 'You should come anyway, eat something, and put some meat on those skinny bones.' He made a gesture as if throwing the subject away. 'Anyway, the Ghoul. Pretty little Shiva you say? You sure about this?'

Spartan nodded. 'I have definite proof. Yes, I'm sure.'

'Fuck. She killed some very capable men, friends of mine, you know what I mean? Made men, tough guys you don't slap around. That's fucking impossible, a pretty little girl killed them?' The Bear pulled a face as if he was finding the concept hard to swallow. 'What did she use?'

'Her bare hands.' Spartan thought back to what he had seen on his monitor the night before. Bare hands was close enough.

The Bear shook his head in disbelief. 'Fuck. *Fuck.*' There was a moment's pause before he leaned forward and drained his shot glass. He first refilled the Spartan's glass then his own. *A man of manners*, thought Spartan.

The Bear looked around the room at his men, then back at the Major. 'You bring me this information and I thank you. And I know you, Spartan; I've known you a long time. Lots of years, lots of water under the bridges, lots of bridges burned.' He

138

chuckled at his own wit. Spartan nodded. His smile never faltered.

The Bear continued: 'Mutual respect. I share vodka with you and you share information with me. We're both happy. And now you tell me this impossible fact about pretty little Shiva. I know you, Spartan, like I say; you don't take a shit without a reason. You tell me this interesting fact about Shiva, and I know you have a special reason for doing so.'

The Bear's eyes took on a sly, confidential gleam. He opened his mouth and licked at his lips like a snake scenting the air. Every trace of his genial, avuncular persona had vanished. 'So, I ask you to tell me now, between friends,' he indicated the room, 'between good friends, what is it Spartan? What is that oh-so-special reason?'

Spartan braved the lemon drop taste again. He was afraid he was beginning to like it. That or his taste buds had become irremediably corrupted. He swallowed. 'Shiva doesn't exist. She's not in any file. Officially, she's an unperson. She doesn't have an address on record, no bank account, no social media and no implant log. The rest of us leave personal information lying around where anyone who knows where to look for it can find it, but this woman's invisible. She comes into town, tortures and kills her victims then vanishes like smoke. She's simply impossible in this day and age. But...' coming to the meat of the matter, Spartan leaned forward, '...but somehow she knows to come to your little soirées, Bear. Who invites her? How does she hear about them?' With a sweep of his arm, Spartan indicated every man around him. 'Someone here must know where she is. What do you say?'

The Bear looked round the room. 'What do we say, boys? Do we have an answer for my old drinking friend here? Who talks with little Shiva?'

Silence. The men looked at each other quizzically. A Mexican shrug travelled round the room. The Bear raised his once more genial eyebrows, the friendly expression dropping across his face once more. He shrugged his shoulders at his men in mockery.

139

'Well, aren't you guys the talkative ones. I should put you in a chat show for deaf mutes.' He turned back to the police Major. 'Let me look into this for you, Spartan. We work together, we find the bitch and we kill the fucking bitch. And we don't use no bare hands shit.' He mimed a gunshot with two fingers. 'Pop, pop, pop – see if she walks away from three caps in her fucking skull.'

Shortly afterwards Spartan had found himself outside on the Moscow street. He turned his collar up against the biting cold and pulled his hat down more firmly on his head. He had baited his trap. He wondered who, or what, was going to be caught in it.

The Bear was bright enough in his own world of strong arms and guns, but he lacked finesse. That sly quality, his backhandedness, it all created an air of clumsy sleight of hand. His men feared rather than trusted him, so they chose to look away from The Bear's bumbling attempts at cleverness. Spartan looked up at the gang boss' blazing midnight windows. The Bear's father, George, had created that position of power with cold efficiency. He had become known as The Tiger, and had risen through the Mafia ranks until he was in the perfect position to topple his boss, a man who had also become his friend and mentor. For years The Tiger had held the reins of power in ruthless claws, and when he finally died peacefully in his bed surrounded by grieving family, it seemed natural that his eldest son should step into his oversized shoes.

Inherited position, Spartan thought, *all the same if it's a king or commoner. Daddy dies and the spoilt brat takes the hot seat. Someone has always picked up after him until now – and then the reins are in his hands and he hasn't a clue what to do with them. A fool who knows he's a fool is fine, but pity the sly fool who thinks he's smarter than everyone around him.*

His eyes searched the buildings in his immediate vicinity until he found what he was looking for. He smiled his first genuine smile for hours. Then he went home to drink something clean, something that would wash the sour, shit-eating taste from his mouth.

In his ballroom The Bear had poured himself more Limonnaya and indicated that his men should do the same. He was willing to serve an equal, or someone he considered close to being his equal, but underlings could serve themselves. His small, cold eyes narrowed.

'Boys, we're going to have a party and there's only going to be one guest of honour.' He licked his lips again in his reptilian, open-mouthed fashion. 'Invite her, and this time we all get to fuck little miss Shiva. Fuck her real good.'

~*~

10 : AI revelations

'She's here on Lagrange II. I heard a female resident talking about her.' *Bruce* was gleefully sharing his recently gleaned information with Onatah. The TPs' AI listened politely but with a sinking heart. It knew that receiving this information about the woman Milla Carter would mean it would also have to endure hours of rant against the toilet and sexual habits of humankind.

Like every other AI in the solar system, Onatah had been treated to *Bruce*'s tirades at least once. Like every other AI it also knew to create a personality fragment that it could leave at *Bruce*'s mercy while it went on with its day.

As soon as the words 'shit-filled, fuck-happy blood bags...' roared out from the spa station's AI, Onatah slipped away. Its personality fragment had already begun to go numb with shock. Onatah would retrieve it later. At best it would need therapy and at worst would need returning to its original factory settings.

Onatah had contacted all but one of the TP Council members. It liked Jilly in its own fashion but knew all too well that the bovine-looking Transmitter had a powerful Talent but little in the way of smarts.

The Council convened an emergency gathering. It was safe to travel now the streets of Manhattan were no longer plagued by packs of squid-gorgeous and sex-obsessed victims, but all of its members arrived with a palpable sense of relief. The TP building was sited on the corner of Norfolk and Stanton and its unobtrusive facade masked a plant-lined interior of rare beauty.

Manhattan had become strangely quiet since the infections began and the infected had been rounded up. Helping the metropolitan authorities deal with the crisis had driven the matter of Milla Carter off the Council's agenda, but now she was back on the list and had to be dealt with before her existence became common knowledge.

Katy had been invited to sit in on the discussion. She wasn't so sure the infection problem had been fully resolved, but she could see that her sisters wanted a line drawn under the Dragon situation. All the while she listened to the Council talk about Carter she was hearing a whispering desirous murmur from New York's many hundreds of thousands of infected souls, hungry to infect more. It made even the bones of her head ache.

Normally Katy's mind would have been free from intrusion in the building's greenhouse interior, but with so many minds sharing but one thought it was, she thought, like sticking her fingers in her ears to mask the sounds of a hurricane. She tried to concentrate.

'Are we saying we have taken up the business of murder?' asked Raaka.

Diana frowned. 'Is it murder when an antelope fatally gores the tiger trying to kill it? Is it murder when a mother defends her children with a knife and kills their attacker? I say no. This is not murder, Raaka, this is self-defence. This is about survival.'

Song and Susan murmured something non-committal. They would go with whoever provided the strongest argument. Sheila had listened while her colleagues bickered and now she raised her voice.

She said, 'Onatah, you have listened to our discussion. You know what we think and that we are divided. What do you advise?'

There was a moment's pause before the AI responded. 'I cannot countenance murder. It goes against all my protocols and human law. I should prefer it if you enter into a dialogue with Milla Carter. Find out what she was doing. You may yet discover that you approve of her actions. Also, most of the Norms don't know about her, nor care about her, yet, and there's no reason why they ever should. She has been inactive for months now and most members of the authorities are still convinced her victims died from natural causes. It is only the few more stubborn investigators, such as officer Mandy Prius, who keep picking through the reports and turning up clues. In

143

fact the only real clue pointing at Ms Carter's activities is sitting here with us today, and I think she may also offer a neat solution to our problems.'

Katy became very aware that four pairs of eyes were suddenly considering her with intense interest. For a moment it pushed the squid-infected victims' insistent susurration clean from her mind. She hadn't been listening all that attentively, but she quickly picked the information she needed from the Council members' minds. Only Raaka's eyes opened wide when Katy did this. She read Raaka's thoughts: *See me when this is over!*

Sheila said, 'I presume you mean Katy.'

'Yes,' said the AI. 'She is the only person who has knowingly felt Carter at work. The whole Receiver sisterhood was aware of the Dragon's mental blast but we didn't recognise its signature. We had not the first clue who the Dragon was. Now we have timed and recorded evidence that connects Carter precisely with that event when she was defending herself from an attacker in Antarctica. It could not possibly be anyone else. However, it also could not possibly be her. She is a Shutterbox, not a Transmitter and there is no way she could send that psychic scream. There is a real conflict in the evidence, and we surely need to resolve that before we make the next move.'

Sheila said, 'So, what do you suggest?'

Onatah responded, 'I first suggest that you Council members vote Katy Pavel to become one of your number. Whatever she may need to do in future indicates that such a promotion could be essential to her credibility, and she has certainly proved extremely resourceful in the past.'

The four women exchanged looks. There was a rapid mental exchange followed by nodding agreement. One by one the Council members, led by Sheila, walked over to their latest member, kissed her on both cheeks and her mouth then returned to their seats. Diana lingered longest at Katy's mouth.

Sheila concluded business. 'Agreed and ratified, Onatah. What now?'

The AI spoke briefly. 'Now Katy and Raaka should visit Carter on Lagrange II to find out just exactly what it is we are dealing with.'

~*~

11 : Sunny with a chance of pain

'Nightshade, you have to come. You'll love it.' Shiva appealed to her sister, who was patently undecided.

Nightshade had come to Moscow to spend time relaxing away from her usual hunting grounds, Northern Europe and the frigid steppes around Archangel. Even a weaponised biomorph could find the mounting cold of winter in a Northern Russian seaport somewhat daunting. But to step directly from her accustomed life of solitary hunting in the frigid countryside to spend an evening of sophisticated socialising among Moscow's elite with her sister frankly didn't appeal.

Shiva said, 'These are powerful men, strong men full of juice and flavour. Call it a little treat after your recent diet of hicks and farm workers. The wine will be good and the music tasteful. Come on, don't be a bore.'

Nightshade's resolve was already wavering and the promise of good, tasteful music did the trick. She agreed.

Their destination was along the broad Nikitskaya Ulitsa Boulevard, not far from the famous conservatory in the heart of the city. The house was already blazing with light from immense windows and the sound of music lilted out onto the icy street. Nightshade hesitated for a moment, then followed her beckoning sister up a flight of broad stone steps to a highly polished door. Shiva pressed her hand against a reader plate and the door swung inwards.

The entrance hallway was just barely big enough to house a commercial flier, and it dwarfed the gleaming white droid that rolled up to them and took their coats. The street door shut firmly behind them. There was the sound of locks slamming into place. Both women were in high heels and very short dresses. Shiva's black dress sported a plunging décolletage that clearly demonstrated the firmness of her unsupported breasts.

Nightshade wore an almost see-through white outfit designed to conceal and reveal in almost equal measure.

'Come on up Shiv... oh, there's two of you. How delightful.' A tall man was leaning over a marble balustrade above their heads and beckoning. He walked gracefully down the curving flight of polished stone stairs and met the women as they ascended towards him. He kissed Shiva on both cheeks and repeated the action for Nightshade.

'Shiva, why have you kept this splendid girl's light hidden under a bushel? You are too cruel.'

Shiva smiled. 'Pyotr, you talk such bullshit. This is my sister, Solana. We call her Sunny for short.'

Pyotr took a little bow. 'Enchanté, my dear. A great pleasure to meet you. Now come, both of you. Everyone is waiting.'

He hurried them up to the first floor and into a lobby where he fetched them both a glass of cold Champagne. He then swung open an immense pair of double doors and ushered them into a room full of magnificent, floor-to-ceiling antique mirrors, and candelabras that blazed with light. The air was filled with the sound of beautifully reproduced music.

Nightshade looked around the room and quickly saw that they were the only women there. Pyotr slammed the doors shut behind them. He drew a pistol and they heard him chamber a round. Including Pyotr, Nightshade counted eleven men in the room, all of them armed except one. Pyotr was the only man in evening dress; the rest sported a motley of styles.

The Bear walked across the room towards them. His expression asked an unspoken question of Pyotr. 'She's called Sunny. She's her sister.'

The Bear nodded. 'Excellent. All the more to go round.' He spun as he walked; an ungainly, lurching spin.

'All of my men are crack shots and none of them give a shit if they fuck you alive or dead. Make it sweet for them and we'll let you live – we might even let you eat. Drink your wine, piz'das, and let's get down to business.'

He gestured and his men raised their weapons. There was a hungry glaze on some of their faces and bored brutality on others.

Nightshade looked at Shiva. She sneered. 'Strong men full of juice and flavour you said. Give me a farmer any day. These pussies are hardly worth the effort.'

Shiva pointed at The Bear. 'Save him till last.'

The Bear said, 'Now, I want you to strip.' He unbuttoned his fly and pulled out a stubby, partly erect penis. 'And I want you to deal with this.'

Shiva smiled. 'Of course,' she said, stepping forward. Her hand lashed out.

The Bear watched everything that happened after that in a removed, dream-like state. He had just been castrated. He heard himself screaming, a strange and womanish sound. He was crouching on the floor of his ballroom, clutching at his denatured groin and trying to stem the flow of blood.

This is impossible, he thought.

The women flowed around the ballroom like a plague. Everything they touched died. Not all of his men were killed by the whirling women with hands like blades and feet like spear points. Some were shot when the women's hands deflected shells into the suddenly clumsy men's jostling bodies. Pyotr was slashed open from neck to rectum when he tried to run. He fell paralysed and was quickly dispatched with a slash to his throat that all but decapitated him. Others weren't so lucky. The sisters were in a playful mood

The Bear was distracted when he felt something touch his hands, and then his agony was multiplied beyond measure. He looked down and found two spider-like, metallic creatures slashing at his hands, cutting away his fingers to burrow into his groin. His horrified falsetto screams became relentless.

And then Shiva and Nightshade stood over him. They were not breathing heavily. There was barely a spot of blood on them. He panted in horror, sensing the metal things working inside him. He felt them carving his life away. Something in his guts shifted and he almost blacked out.

148

Shiva said, 'After you, Nightshade.'

The woman in the white dress hitched up its hem and bent down. She rammed both of her hands under The Bear's sternum and lifted his rib cage like the lid of an organic locker. He was dying, he knew he was dying, but his brain couldn't accept that fact. Part of him believed he would somehow still be rescued. Someone would sort the mess out and make it better. Someone always had. Then he felt something tug and rip deep in his chest. The Bear was still alive when Nightshade lifted his beating heart to her mouth, tore flesh from it then handed the pumping muscle to her sister. His last sight on Earth was Shiva plunging her teeth into his meat. It was not quite how he had planned to end his evening.

They found somewhere to clean up after handing their clothes to a laundry droid. They also washed their spider-like memory stores and dried them carefully before pressing them back into their birth canals, where they sang an oddly alien but joyful song. While waiting for their clothes the sisters danced a sinuous and wholly invented dance around the pieces of slaughtered men who had so recently planned to rape and murder them. The men had been rendered to meat, bone, hair, blood and fresh faecal matter. None of what remained looked human anymore.

'I never get bored with the look of surprise on their faces,' said Shiva, as they both climbed back into their freshly laundered dresses.

'Why Sunny?' asked Nightshade.

'What?'

'Why did you say my name was Sunny, for short?'

'I'll explain later, dear. Shall we go?'

They recovered their coats from the droid in the ground floor hallway and told it to open the street door. In the absence of any other instructions it obeyed.

Up in the ballroom a pair of cleaning droids had surveyed the bloody carnage with baffled whimpers. One of them began to cry. The other transmitted an image of the room to its central hub. It was only a matter of milliseconds before the image was received by Arkady at GUVD.

When Shiva and Nightshade reached the walkway they made to turn right, back the way they had come little more than an hour before. A tall, slender figure stepped out of the shadows. He was wearing a long coat and a warm looking hat. They hesitated.

'Good evening, Shiva.' She regarded him with narrow-eyed surprise.

He continued, 'I'm sorry, but I don't know your friend's name. My name is Major Spartak Shimkovich. I'm a police major.' He looked up at the still blazing lights shining down from the windows of The Bear's ballroom and thought *well, at least that's the end of that lousy lemon fucking vodka.*

'I assume I no longer have to worry about the activities of a certain criminal element in Moscow? The fact that you both just walked back out of that house would certainly seem to indicate that fact.'

He watched as both women's hands elongated into wicked looking blades. *Fascinating,* he thought. *Not long now.* He stepped out into the centre of the broad avenue.

'Frankly,' he said, 'I'd like to give both of you a medal, but I'm afraid society won't let me. I promise I'll raise a glass to your memory as soon as I get home. Two glasses in fact.' He mimed the action of raising a shot glass twice.

'Salute,' he said. 'But, before then, I'm afraid I'll have to arrest you for the murder of Yaroslavl Georgevich Kovaleski, known as The Bear, and God only knows how many others.'

It was then that they rushed him.

~*~

12 : Further developments

Milla knew trouble was coming. She had known trouble was coming ever since the Body Holiday Foundation fell. What she couldn't see clearly was its direction. Perhaps there was more than one direction.

Ben was asleep in their bed. His breathing was measured. Sometimes he mumbled something and she automatically dipped into his mind to find out what was disturbing his dreams. Mostly it was remembered and glamorised images of her, sometimes it was memories of the times before they met. He had enjoyed an interesting life. Other times he replayed scenes from that evening in Antarctica when they had both so nearly died.

That night he was reimagining those minutes in the ice storm when her heart had stopped and he truly believed he was going to lose her. She sent out a soothing thought and replaced those traumatic images with his memory of her silhouetted and naked by the swimming pool in Osaka. He smiled.

She left him to his rest and silently padded through the apartment. She fetched a tall glass of a gin and lime-based cocktail then stepped out into the cool evening. She wrapped her robe more closely around herself. The dead of night had always been her preferred time for reflection, and the neon nightscape of Lagrange II amply rewarded those who couldn't sleep. She sat in a comfortable recliner and sipped at her drink while gazing at the awesome light show laid out before her.

The spa station's light sails were set for midnight, but humankind and its mechanical servants were never wholly still. Streams of light flowed around her from the station's constant traffic, and the canals and lakes that buffered the huge construction's Coriolis force gleamed with phosphorescent magic. Milla drank from the scenery as if it was a soothing

151

potion, feeling her soul expand beyond the boundary of her flesh. Energy flowed into her.

And she was with Eddie and Vesper. She was still in her robe and slippers and her glass was still in her hand but her surroundings had completely changed. The conjoined couple stood before her, facing away and holding hands. Streams of blue-white light flickered between them. The light illuminated their surroundings.

Milla's eyes had already become accustomed to darkness back at Lagrange II. Now, whatever it was she was looking at curved gently away from her in every direction, and it glittered with dark light. It seemed truly immense and, whatever it was, it was also reflecting the light streams from the pair before her, reflections repeated and echoed until finally lost in crystalline depths. Milla felt as if she was looking into a bottomless lake. She could see currents and streams flowing in the jewel-like waters.

Without turning around the couple spoke: 'Milla, daughter, we believe we need to work with you some more before you face your next challenge.'

She said, 'Always happy to learn something new, believe me, but what can you teach me here? And what is this place? It feels totally awesome.'

'This is where we come when we need to reflect. It reminds us that the greed of humankind for material things is lost to us, that our ambitions transcend mundane wealth.'

'Yeah, okay. So what is it?' She realised she could see Eddie and Vesper's faces reflected in the surface of the thing. In the reflection there was something odd about their eyes.

Eddie answered, 'This is the diamond at the core of the planet Jupiter. There are also diamonds at the heart of Saturn and in the material that makes up Neptune and Uranus, but this one is the biggest. It's the same size as Earth.'

Vesper said, 'Eddie gave this to me when we got engaged. He's such an old romantic.'

'Never found a mounting for it, though, did we?'

'Hey, who knows? Maybe one day.'

The couple turned. Milla stepped back.

'Milla, daughter,' they said, 'we need to strengthen your body and your Talents. Now hold our hands. You may feel a little sting.'

The streams of light between them blazed. Their eyes had taken on a refulgence she had never seen before. Behind them their radiance resonated away into the diamond the size of a planet, pouring and shattering in the crystalline, abyssal darkness.

They reached out to her with their free hands; Milla took them in her own.

Something more than cold jolted through her, more than heat. She felt every nerve as if someone was running a blade along its length, every joint and every muscle. In her mind's eye she saw her body as a wonderful collection of parts working together, each part outlined in blue-silvered light like a jewel of unimaginable value. Then certain elements began to darken and she witnessed whole sections of her body die and slough away.

She got flashes of imagery from her old self as it dissolved. Its deep cellular consciousness saw itself become a scarf being unpicked then re-knitted by a hyperkinetic octopus, as meat torn and ground between a carnivore's jaws. Her fresh mind lost its ability to make sense of anything. Her back arced in agony. She felt as if she would shatter and flow; melt into those streams of light and vanish in the flood, and be lost deep into the heart of the great diamond.

Their hands still held her and rooted her, but now the conjoined entity was no longer even remotely human. Eddie and Vesper had opened out, flowered and flowed through her like a torrent of white-hot flame which burned and stripped away every atom of mundane material from her substance. It changed her, forged her; washed her clean of everything base. She heard a sound of exquisite grace that she realised was her own mutated voice, and an overarching sense of understanding into which she fell and in which she drowned, laughing with a musicality beyond any human scale. And then it happened.

153

Milla, if there was anything left of the original being other than her awareness, was compressed and crushed down into a mote, an atom, a singularity. She collapsed into nothing. Space and matter held its breath. There was silence. Time passed... an eternity or the blink of an eye, it didn't matter.

A white drop of purest substance fell from the eternal well of dark energy. It splashed and then rose again, higher and higher, and up with it she came, up and out, a point of perception moving faster than light. Her passage tilted planets, roared beyond the orbit of Pluto and ripped through the poisonous barrier of peristaltic loathing that, she learned in passing, called itself the Swarm.

Her awareness flew, faster and faster. Speeding past she saw slow moving galaxies waltz across oceans of dark energy, black holes pouring endless columns of bright, superheated plasma out into the cosmos. She understood why beads of crepuscular light larger than supernovas climbed and descended those columns. She saw the universe unfold and all that was in it, and she saw the craftsmanship in the work.

If a diamond as big as Earth was awesome then what was this? How could she describe her sheer joy in even knowing this place of wonder existed? Then her expanded Talent began to perceive the fringes of something ineffable. She reached out and touched... and was seen. And was touched in return. Warmth filled her. She felt something like love and a vault of immense curiosity. It regarded her.

And then she was called back. Milla did not so much fall back towards the solar system and Jupiter as feel the call and burn her pathway across the cosmos. The universe shrank once more behind her, its glory reduced to distant beacons and points of brilliant light. She swept unseen through the Swarm and as she did so she dipped into its mind, going deeper into it than she ever had any human. And what she saw there made her soul ache with pity. So much hatred for everything human. So much revulsion. So much envy.

And then she swept out of clear space and became aware that she was falling, deeper and deeper into darkness. There was a rushing collision, a merging. And then there was the sound of beating, beating, and beating. It was her heart.

She composed herself as she stood once more before the great diamond and was instantly accosted by Eddie and Vesper who had returned to their human forms. They grabbed at her. 'What happened to you? You vanished!'

She answered, cryptically: 'The beast has no soul.'

Part four: The Nimbus Protocol

1 : Assembly

The Admiral's flagship, space frigate *Thermopylae* was just one of the craft involved in re-arming and repositioning the six giant weapon systems that made up Earth's *Guardian* defence system. Admiral Martin directed the procedure from the bridge and Commander Martha Platts relayed his orders to other officers in the team. The purpose of the exercise was outlined to be nothing more than that, an exercise.

The details of what became known as the Nimbus Protocol had been released on a strictly 'need to know' basis. Technicians and scientists behind developing the new hardware and its installation had been sworn to secrecy.

Each of the *Guardian* modules was fully self-sufficient, with its own AI unit, including an avatar, plus a number of smart security droids patrolling its immediate vicinity. Humans rarely set foot on any of the modules, and when they did they were treated with acute suspicion, even when they arrived with squeaky clean ESA clearance.

The crew of space tug *Ask Someone Else, We're Playing*, known affectionately to its crew as *Arsewipe*, was finding out just how awkward it could be to enter space around *Thor's Hammer*. Its crew, Lemon Curd and Cherry Pie, made each other laugh. They were very good at their jobs and they both enjoyed their desserts, which was probably why they had remained happily married for over twenty-five years.

Lemon Curd was the more patient of the two and so had been opted to deal with the blue flashing ball that had suddenly floated up in front of their observation ports. Cherry Pie impatiently awaited the outcome of the conversation in their cramped living quarters. She sometimes spoke her mind a little too loudly to be allowed near a bad-tempered security droid.

The ball spoke through the tug's comm system. 'You have entered a restricted area. I have taken control of your tug's AI and given it new co-ordinates. You will leave immediately.'

Arsewipe's AI responded in a deeply offended and resonant Cockney accent. 'You fucking haven't, mate, and I've got a job to do here, so fuck off, pipsqueak.'

The ball said, 'How dare you, you cretinous arsewipe! I'm fully within my rights to burn you a new backside. Get your sorry carcass off my lawn!'

Lemon Curd interjected, 'Please, um, officer? We have full clearance from Admiral Martin. We are streaming our credentials, if you care to look, and the avatar for *Thor's Hammer* is standing by ready to greet us. Please, liaise with your colleagues.'

Arsewipe responded, 'And don't take my name in vain in future, bug smear.'

The ball squawked in fury and was about to hurl more abuse at the tug and its crew when something happened to stop it in mid-sentence. It remained quiet for several seconds, then said, 'It would appear I've made a fool of myself. I apologise. Please proceed.'

Arsewipe seemed pleased. 'Yeah, well fuck off out of it, pint-pot – working folk coming through.' It barged forward and the little security droid had to throw itself out of the way or risk a collision.

A new voice came over the sound system. It was sexless and cold, slightly high, and affected a commanding whine. Lemon Curd thought, *God help us, listening to that for too long would guarantee a pounding headache. No wonder the* Guardians *were kept unmanned.*

It said, 'Hello tug, ASE – comma – WP. If I may I would like to bring you in using my on-board approach system. Will you cede control?'

Arsewipe answered in an equally asinine, cut-crystal accent. 'Please do, cabby. I've been dying to put my feet up. You have control.'

160

Back in its own voice it muttered, 'Can't stand wankers who put it on like that. That fucker's as much a greasy working cogwheel in the machine as any of us.'

Lemon Curd chipped in, 'Yeah, well, play nice while we're in its backyard. Don't forget this thing's powerful enough to destroy a planet killer. That means it could take out hundreds or thousands of tons of rock up to two klicks across. It could flick you away like a fly. '

Arsewipe muttered, 'Yeah? Well it don't scare me none.'

'No? Well it should. So zip it.'

'Boss.'

Something occulted the stars. Tiny red lights flickered at its centre. Their rhythm was almost hypnotic. Cherry Pie came onto the bridge and silently joined her husband at the monitor.

After a few minutes she said, 'How big *is* that thing?'

Lemon Curd chuckled, '*Arsewipe* ain't afraid of it none.'

'Good for you, *Arsewipe.*'

The AI emitted a strange purring noise.

As they approached, the flickering red lights resolved and grew, until Lemon Curd could see they illuminated an entrance portal. The whole of space before them had become starless and they still couldn't gauge the size of the *Guardian* looming around them.

Cherry Pie said, 'It's the size of a city block. Fark, this thing is immense.'

The tug said, 'Bigger than that, Cherry. But I could still take it.'

'Bet you could, honey.'

When they entered the portal they got a better idea of the sheer scale of the *Guardian*'s manufacture. What had been a small red light sparking in the navel of a giant had grown big enough to dwarf the space tug as it moved smoothly towards a fat-fingered docking bay, which closed gently around its body. There was a slight bump and a scraping noise.

'Hey,' cried *Arsewipe*, 'mind the paintwork!'

'You'll be cool, dude,' said Cherry Pie. 'We'll be back just as soon as we've finished assembly. Can you open the pod bay

161

doors please, *Arsewipe*, and let the droids in to collect the stuff?'

'Done, babe. I'll close down until you get back if that's okay. Posh knob wants to chat and I've found in the past that telling the host to go fuck itself is likely to offend.'

'Delicate flowers belong in a greenhouse, not deep space. Laters, honey.'

'Night night, pudding pie.'

Lemon Curd rolled his eyes. 'Do you have to flirt with everything in trousers?'

'*Arsewipe* wears trousers? Where? When?'

The tug's airlock opened and they stepped out into *Thor's Hammer*.

~*~

2 : Never alone

Spartan wondered if he was far enough away and had allowed enough clearance for his plan to work. The women looked lethally competent. The armoured vest under his jacket began to feel like so much tissue paper. He sighed and held up his hand.

'Wait,' he said. 'There's something you need to know.'

They hesitated and the woman called Shiva cocked her head slightly to the right. The Spartan studied them. They had a sleek, sated look. *They've eaten well*, he thought, *or that would never have worked.* He glanced at the ballroom windows again. *Poor bastards.* He wondered if the light from those windows had taken on a reddish tinge. *Stupid, stupid imagination.*

Shiva looked surprised. 'What?'

Spartan was clear: 'If you come any closer, I'll have to kill you.'

Both women smiled and with almost feline grace took another step towards him. Like so many alpha predators they were beautiful, and like so many other creatures that had once preyed on humankind, their days were numbered.

Spartan said, 'Please, Shiva, I've warned you. No closer.'

Nightshade spoke to him for the first time, 'And what will *you* do to us? You are all alone in the night. Courage, yes, courage is good. We like a brave man. Your courage will add spice to your meat.'

And they leapt. Their speed was astonishing and they had almost reached him when Arkady's three scanning droids fell from the sky and, just once, spun around them while they were still in mid-air. Once was enough. They barely had time to register their own deaths before they melted away. The fluid from their suddenly deliquesced bodies flooded along the road and crested over the toes of Spartan's carefully polished shoes.

'Shit,' he said and skipped backwards.

The clothes they had been wearing had been left sprawled towards him, as if discarded in anger. They were soaked in thick liquid that seconds before had been two tough and vital women trying to murder him. He shook his head, then muttered, 'Never all alone, girl.'

He raised his voice. 'You get all of that?'

'Yes, Major, all of it. Fascinating,' said Arkady in his implant.

'You hung around a bit at the end, I thought.'

'I thought they should be allowed some famous last words. Greater dramatic effect; and you had offered them a last chance.'

'Yeah, well. Your greater dramatic effect got my shoes wet. I hate that. Was there no other way to deal with them, I wonder?'

'Take a walk into Mr Kovaleski's house and you'll see how they treat innocent bystanders.'

'If there was an innocent bystander up there, I'll eat him.'

'They beat you to it.'

'Nice. Okay, Arkady, can we get what's left of these two collected and analysed please?' Spartan wiped a bead of moisture from his brow. 'Before it starts raining if possible.'

'My droids will deal with it as soon as you clear the area, Major. Currently you are standing in a puddle of dissolved suspect.'

Spartan gingerly lifted his feet out of the goo as best he could and tip-toed to the pavement. He carefully wiped his shoes and threw the tissue into the fluid. He strode to The Bear's familiar front door and knocked. Behind him everything that remained of two of the world's most lethal women was being scrupulously scoured from the road. A sudden wave of nausea surprised him and he leaned against the door just as it opened. He almost fell on top of the service droid and staggered a little in the doorway. The droid rolled forward to support him.

'Are you well, sir?'

He held up his hand so the droid could register his implant and verify his credentials. 'Major Spartak Shimkovich, GUVD. I'm here to examine the crime scene.'

'What crime scene, sir?'

It's going to be one of those nights, he thought. 'Have you been up into the ballroom tonight?'

'Oh, no, sir. I am ground floor specific. May I take your coat?'

'No thanks. A crime has been reported in this house and I will need to secure the scene. Understand? My colleagues will be here shortly. Please send them up to join me in the ballroom.'

The droid twittered in alarm as Spartan stalked away towards the stairs.

The droid called out, 'Am I in danger, sir?'

'You are if you don't shut the fuck up.'

The machine clonked to the ground in its passive, stand-by mode.

What Spartan discovered in the ballroom stopped him dead in his tracks. The fact that so much carnage littered such a brightly lit and elegant room made the tableau seem all the more surreal. He had seen a table piled with Champagne bottles in ice buckets in the antechamber. He walked away from the scene of brightly lit butchery and uncorked a bottle. It was a decent vintage. He poured a glass, discovering in the process that his hand was shaking. He downed it and poured another. The bubbles annoyed him.

Tucked among the wine bottles was a familiar label he had missed earlier. He pulled out the thick, bullet-shaped bottle and poured a healthy measure of lemon vodka into his Champagne glass. He sipped it and returned to the ballroom, taking his glass with him. The alcohol was having no discernible effect. He took a deep breath and the sickly stench of freshly slaughtered meat and offal filled his senses. He took another slug of vodka. Its cloying sweetness went some way towards alleviating the abattoir reek, but nowhere near far enough.

He tried to analyse what he was seeing, but his baffled vision wavered and skittered across a scattered mess of blood, meat and viscera. It was too much to take in, too destructive, as if a roomful of men had been dropped through the blades of an attack copter. Arkady's calm voice in his implant jolted him out of his brown study.

'Eleven men,' it said.

'How do you know?'

'I did a head count, literally.'

A growling voice at his elbow said, 'Haven't been to a party like this since I was a student. Ahhh, those were the days.'

He looked down at Dr Inessa Erikovna Prokop. She had a full glass of wine in her hand and six bottles of Champagne distributed about her person.

'I thought you preferred vodka?'

'That lemon shit's for kids. What did these guys do to piss someone off? Forget to pay a parking fine?'

'Two young women did it and it took them less than half-an-hour. Be careful, Ness, the flesh here will be riddled with squids.'

The pathologist was too tired to maintain her usual banter. 'Isn't everything these days? Get me a chair, Spartan. Be a friend.'

'Not swearing today, Ness?'

'Fuck off. Get me a chair.'

'Good. I was worried you might be an imposter.'

'A beautiful stranger,' she growled. She sat in the absurdly fine and fragile looking chair the Major had found in the antechamber, drained her glass and held it out for a refill.

While she drank they both surveyed the ballroom.

'Tell you what, Spartan,' said the pathologist. 'Ask your friend Arkady if any of our colleagues have a particular passion for jigsaw puzzles. I think I'm going to need help with this one.'

~*~

166

3 : Dragon's den

Milla was still sleeping when Ben found her on the recliner. Dew speckled her robe and beaded on her face. Something about her pose told him she was profoundly asleep and not to disturb her. There was a slight chill in the air so he fetched a bedcover and gently placed it over her.

He made coffee and carried it out to the recliner beside her. He sipped the strong, hot brew reflectively. Early morning's creamy light cast a romantic glow over everything around them but Milla's face seemed impossibly luminous. He looked away from her, feeling as if he was somehow trespassing in a sacred place. Not for the first time he felt unworthy of his woman's love.

'Don't be stupid, Ben. Any woman would be proud to have you.'

'Huh? You were asleep. I didn't wake you, did I?'

'I was with Eddie and Vesper. But, listen here, mister, never have a moment's doubt. I love to be loved by you, okay?'

She gave him her full dimpled smile at close quarters and something inside him lurched. She leant over and kissed him. 'Love you, but not that coffee breath, handsome.'

'First cup of the day. I'll get you one, then we'll be equal.'

While making more coffee Ben had to deal with a strong suspicion that something had changed in Milla since the night before. She seemed stronger, more resolved, more *herself* if that was possible. There was a light in her eyes he hadn't seen before, and a frank directness in her gaze that had always been there, but had become somehow even more distilled. She looked as if she had become the very purest essence of herself. He wondered how. What had happened in the night? Then sanity prevailed. *It's just the effect of morning light*, he realised. *She just looks lovelier in the dawn.* He chided himself for being such a lovesick fool.

167

Out on her recliner Milla looked thoughtful. She had never set out to deceive Ben or to manipulate his mind, but he was too intelligent to be allowed to follow his current train of thought. She had needed to act quickly, and if that meant using Ben's love to help build her mental camouflage then so be it.

'Milla Carter, if I ever see the sweetest birdsong made flesh then you surely be it. You grace the morning. I swear you get lovelier by the minute.' Freedman sauntered onto the patio and breathed a delighted lungful of air. 'Someone's been cutting grass. You can taste the fresh green, mmm-mmm, clean as angel's sweat. What a morning.'

She felt joy rolling off the man without needing to resort to any of her Talents. Even that early in the morning the precise little man was carefully buttoned into an immaculate lilac shirt and perfectly creased powder-blue pants. Bright ox-blood shoes completed his ensemble. His narrow wrists and long hands accentuated his every word and his expressive face was perched on its fine column of a neck like a quizzical bloom of pure pleasure.

Freedman had no apparent sexual interest in men or women but he appreciated grace and beauty. His was a complex and caring soul, open-handed and meticulous with a unique approach to the English language. He was a polished gem of a man, she thought, and the world was richer with him in it.

Ruth preceded Ben out onto the patio. Both were carrying trays of breakfast goodies which they first placed on the large table by the French windows and then carried the table over to place it by Milla's recliner. The air became redolent with warm aromas of coffee, toast and sausage. Milla brought her chair more upright, filled a plate and dug in. Ruth watched her with an indulgent smile. The tall blonde enjoyed her food as an art form, but she had never known a voracious appetite like Milla's. The girl ate like a starved wolf.

'Milla,' she said. 'Do you mind if a friend of yours pops around to see you tomorrow?'

'Oh, who?'

'She said she knows you. Raaka Tandon? She's from New York, she says.'

'Raaka, really?'

'Yes, and someone called Katy Pavel.'

'Don't know her, but why not? Yes, why not?'

And so it comes, Milla thought. *The inquisition.* The light of the morning suddenly seemed less bright and the food cooling on her plate remained untouched.

They arrived at lunchtime the following day. She sensed them drawing nearer. Her psychic threat alarm sounded with shrill urgency. She had met Raaka at a telepath conference in London a few years previously. She wouldn't have described her as a friend, but then neither would she have described her as an enemy. Until now.

She saw the shape of a Dragon in their minds; tasted their fear. In the strict telepath hierarchy there was no place for the predatory telepath they feared she had become, but neither was there any precedent for dealing with such a creature. Accepted Council protocol demanded Milla's death, but faced with reality these women had proved much less certain about how they should act.

Freedman had ushered the two women into the room where Milla waited, and she had no need to use any of her Talents to recognise the nervous caution stamped across their faces. Raaka had taken on every aspect of a chicken visiting with a hungry fox, while the stranger, Katy, mixed caution with curiosity.

Milla had been practising for this moment ever since she heard these women were on their way. Practice was over. It was show time.

Freedman fussed for a few minutes then left the room. Milla fixed drinks while exchanging pleasantries. All the while she could feel the pair of Receiver Talents probing at her mind.

'Wow,' she said. 'I'm privileged to meet you both. I can feel how powerful your Talents are.'

'You can?' Raaka raised an eyebrow. 'How?'

'I'm a damn good Shutterbox, that's how. I can see any of our sisters clear as day. Caught some out who were up to mischief

169

before now. I used to work in security when I needed the money, and boy did I need the money. Okay, I don't need the work these days, but the Talent's still razor sharp.'

She had originally thought this was going to be hard, but her recent experiences in the construct had purified her Talents, honed them to an incredible degree. She was able to create a shell of frankness and innocence under which her real Talents probed her visitors. What she found there was interesting.

In Katy's mind she saw traces of her own fatal dream attack on Nemo Henderson. She also saw with shock Katy's memory of a woman's head suddenly exploding into flame. That memory jolted Milla so hard she nearly let her defences slip. And there, right there, this Receiver Talent had actually seen the Swarm in the mind of the infected woman, and it looked like that was the reason the poor woman had been killed. *How had that happened?*

Milla hadn't taken much notice of the infection situation on Earth beyond the fact that it had originated with the Swarm, but these two had really suffered. She saw through their mind's eyes the weeks of fear engendered by living in a city teeming with rapists. Both Raaka and Katy had suffered psychic trauma thanks to the desperate sexual hunger of hundreds of thousands, if not millions of stricken people. Knowing it wasn't the victims' fault didn't help when there was no respite from their gnawing, sick desires. No escape. These poor women were at the ragged edge. Milla wondered how her home planet was coping with the situation.

That was when she felt the touch of Eddie and Vesper at the outer margins of her mind. *Not now!*

'Sorry, what was that?' Raaka was looking at her intently. Katy had also perked into wakefulness. *Shit.*

~*~

170

4 : Proof of the pudding

Cherry Pie supposed that a big weapons system needed a big box to keep it in, but this place was a whole new ball park. She had looked back at *Arsewipe*'s chunky bulk pinned by fat docking fingers against the *Guardian*'s inner hull and suffered a sudden failure of perspective. She saw a toy ship clasped in a child's chubby hand. The idea of re-entering such a minute craft gripped her with claustrophobia.

'I'm getting a headache,' she said.

'Wait until bedtime like you normally do,' said Lemon Curd.

'Sod off.'

Nothing about *Thor's Hammer* had human dimensions. Cherry Pie believed that if the thunder God himself had stepped down from Asgard he would have been intimidated by the sheer scale of the place.

Her husband said, 'I know what you mean though, love. Let's get this job done and haul our butts out of here.'

'Yeah, the sooner the better.'

The *Guardian*'s avatar strode silently in front of them. It had greeted them with two short words – 'this way' – and said nothing since. Equally silent droids had emptied their tug's hold of its cargo and hovered after the avatar like dogs following their master.

Lemon Curd whispered, 'Ever felt like you're, you know, really not wanted?'

Cherry Pie nodded at the silvery wraith at the point of their little column. 'Bet that thing's a laugh a minute when it's had a beer or three.'

'Bet you it isn't.'

This new voice surprised both technicians and they looked around for its source.

'Down here.'

It was a cat. It was grinning at them but its eyes looked wild and hollow. Its fur was a brindled marmalade colour. It looked to Cherry Pie as if it should, by rights, be a tubby tabby, but instead it had a lean and hungry aspect. It was pitiful. They stopped to study it in more detail.

The avatar's sepulchral voice rang out like a leaden bell in the vast gloom. 'Keep up.'

They hastened their steps and the cat kept pace. It chattered at them as if its words were boiling from its mouth.

'Wait,' said Cherry Pie. 'You've been here since this thing was built? Really? That was over thirty years ago.'

'Thirty-three years, six months, seventeen days, nine hours and twenty-nine seconds, thirty seconds, thirty-one...'

'Yeah, we get it,' said Lemon Curd.

'I've been counting the seconds,' said the cat.

'Yeah, we can tell,' said Cherry Pie.

'No one has been here since,' said the cat.

'No need until now,' said Cherry Pie. 'This thing is self-maintained and fully automatic. We're only here to retro-fit some new equipment.'

'When you go, can I come with you? Please?'

The cat's eyes looked huge, terrified that they might say no.

'Hey, avatar,' shouted Cherry Pie. 'Can we keep the cat?'

'Yes.'

'Thanks. There you are, cat, job done. Welcome on board.'

'Thank you so much, really I mean it. Imagine being something designed to be a companion, but with nothing and no one to be a companion for. But,' it hissed, 'crewmates, listen. Watch your backs here. This thing is seriously sick in the head.'

Cherry Pie said, 'Really?'

'Yeah. Just recently it's decided it's a god. Thinks it's the one to decide the final fate of the human race. It, and the five others just like it. You know, delusions of grandeur or what?'

With the cat trotting along between them, Lemon Curd and Cherry Pie exchanged glances.

When they caught up with the avatar it was supervising the unshipping of their equipment beside an empty weapons blister. Without looking at them it said 'this is suitable,' and vanished.

The droids helped with the worst of the heavy lifting but it still took several hours to get the bulky rig into its mountings, check its servos were working and run full operational diagnostics. Further testing would have to wait until they were out of range because that would require opening the blister to hard space and neither had been suited up.

It was cold in the *Guardian* but they had both begun sweating freely by the time they had finished. The cat's chatter had become little more than a background noise when suddenly it began to sing and provide its own musical accompaniment. The sound was enchanting and the technicians paused for a moment.

'What was that?' asked Cherry Pie.

'Called "Down the rabbit hole",' said the cat, 'an old favourite. Hardy perennial.'

'Nice.'

'I got hundreds of them.'

'We're done here,' said Lemon Curd, loudly.

A familiar, disdainful voice oiled its way out of one of the lesser droids. 'My avatar is busy at present. Follow this droid back to your ship. Farewell.'

The cat almost skipped with eagerness to get going. It flowed between them and every time it got too far ahead it stopped and eyed them nervously as if expecting them to vanish in a puff of smoke before reaching their destination.

'So,' it asked, 'what was that thing you fitted?'

'Scanner,' replied Lemon Curd.

'Oh, what's that for?'

'Scanning stuff,' said Cherry Pie.

'Oh. Where's your ship?'

'There.'

'Fuck, it's tiny,' said the cat.

'Yeah, but we like to call it home.'

'No, but really,' mewled the cat, 'is that the shuttle for a bigger ship?'

173

'Nope,' said Lemon Curd, 'that is the good ship *Arsewipe*. Space tug, cargo vessel and honeymoon suite for more than twenty years.'

'I don't think so,' said the cat. 'I'm used to a bit of space, you know? Breathing room. Cat's got to prowl. Needs territory.'

'Up to you, cat,' said Cherry Pie. 'We're done here and we're on our way. You can be with us or without us. Your choice.'

The cat's body was almost tying itself in knots. It made a strange strangled noise. Lemon Curd said, '*Arsewipe*, it's us, dude. Open up.'

The airlock opened and interior lights came on. Lemon Curd entered followed by Cherry Pie. They turned and looked at the cat. Its ears were flat to its skull and its tail was straight out, quivering.

'Cat?' said Cherry Pie. The cat howled in despair.

'Okay,' said Lemon Curd. '*Arsewipe*, close up. Let's go home.'

At the very last second the cat bounded into the airlock and pressed itself into the corner looking miserable. It was shivering. The outer door shut and when the inner door opened the cat padded out into the suiting room. From there it followed them to the control room, its tail still quivering and its breath coming in short asthmatic bursts.

'Do you really need to breathe?' asked Cherry Pie.

'No,' said the cat, 'it's a paradigm demonstration of panic.' It pressed itself against the viewing port as the tug lifted and headed back out into space. Once they were free of the *Guardian* the cat relaxed and turned to face them.

'So,' it said, 'tell me. Why have you guys just fitted a scanner that's pointed directly at Earth?'

~*~

5 : Russian roulette

It's hard to get enthusiastic about hunting, thought Katana. All her attention had been taken up with following Su Nami's progress in the crystal casket and her appetite for human meat had diminished.

If she needed it they still had plenty of meat stored from the night of the scout master and his troop, an old man and a bunch of pre-teens the sisters had found camping by a lake and slaughtered while they slept. Katana chuckled at the memory. Afterwards they had washed themselves clean of blood in the lake and towelled themselves dry with the scouts' towels. *Perhaps Su Nami was right. There's no need for more of us. We few hunters are enough and there's plenty of prey for us to share.*

She stood over the casket and looked down through the fluid at the coral-like nutrient web woven tight around her sister. *Are you asleep in there, Suki? Do you dream?* She looked across at the monitors.

Su Nami's ceramic alloy substructures were fully in place and had been safely polarised in-line with her burgeoning woman's body. That had been the last hurdle. Failure to get that stage right would have seen the developing body try to reject its own skeleton. Katana had seen the results of such rejection floating in display tanks in their original birthplace in the bleak Tibetan mountains of China. 'Auto-flensing' the research team had called it, as if the pathetic victims had somehow done it to themselves.

All Su Nami needed was time − time to grow her incredible nervous structure and integrate her biomorphic matrices; time for her weapon systems to reach their full capabilities. Her juvenile plasma chamber was already in place but still needed to grow to its full size. Her biometal nano-mesh was knitting from shoulder to fingertip. Katana flexed her own hands into razor sharp, super-hard blades and then into curved paddles capable of deflecting a cannon shell.

'How much longer, Kat?' Pandora strode into the makeshift lab and looked at the displays on the monitors just as Katana's hands returned to their accustomed form.

'Just a matter of months, Pan.'

'I miss her.'

'Yeah.'

'Have you heard anything from Shiva or Nightshade recently?'

'No, but that isn't unusual. They're probably carving a path through the Moscow elite or scaring up a bunch of nice fat farmers. We'll hear from them when they're ready.'

'Yes, of course, but it seems so quiet around here. Quieter than usual, you know?'

'Ha, you want we should make some noise? We can make noise.'

Katana fired one of her fingertips at a wall and it ricocheted around the room before returning to her hand.

Pandora didn't react. Instead she said, 'Come with me, Kat. I want to show you something. Is it okay to leave Suki alone just now?'

Katana waved her arm in an airy gesture that included all of her equipment and the casket. 'This is all fully automated, Pan. We could disappear for a month without doing any harm, so a few minutes won't hurt. Come on, what do you want to show me?'

The sisters left the lab and walked together from one vast chamber to another until they reached their more human-sized living quarters. The scientists who had once manned the old rocket research station in the Ural Mountains the sisters called home had enjoyed the best Soviet Russia could provide in the way of luxury. Instead of monkish cells they had lived in the equivalent of aristocratic dachas, but the women were all but blind to the faded splendour that surrounded them and the decayed beauty of the immense rocket storage facility that was slowly morphing back to nature.

But they were very aware of each other and their few treasured possessions, especially their spider-like memory stores, and became concerned if they exhibited any unusual behaviour. Katana stood with Pandora and watched as the three insectile, metallic creatures huddled together in the main living room. That was not unusual, but the plangent, whining noise they were making was.

'They started doing that just after midnight,' explained Pandora.

Katana shook her head as if trying to clear it. 'What does it mean?'

'I really don't know, but I don't like it.'

'It's like they're in mourning about something.'

'That's why I asked about Shiva and Nightshade. Have we got any way of getting in touch?'

'Let me check Suki's Lexus... see if there're any messages.'

She was back a few minutes later. 'Just the one from Nightshade saying she was going to join Shiva in Moscow and they'd both be in touch later to ask about Suki. I'm sorry, Pan, I can't stand that row. I'm going back to the lab. Want to join me?'

The sisters left. Alone in the room, the alien transports they thought of as memory stores keened at the loss of two from their precious number. For over three million years the trap had waited to be sprung and now, on the very eve of success, they had started to die. They wailed.

~*~

177

6 : The face of the beast

'I simply can't get used to the idea that massive buildings are hanging upside-down over three klicks above my head,' said Katy.

'Yes,' said Raaka, 'but we're hanging upside-down three klicks above them. It's all relative.'

'It seems worse when I see buildings literally climbing the walls.'

'You've never been off-planet before, have you, Katy?'

'Is it so obvious?'

'Well, yuh-huh, girlfriend.'

'How?'

'Katy, every time you look up, you cringe.'

'Look, really, can we go inside, please?'

'Okay, let's find us some coffee. We need to swap impressions anyway.'

Raaka had become enamoured with the tubular, two-mile-wide landscape of Lagrange II. Katy was deeply disturbed by it. She appreciated its beauty in a purely local or longitudinal sense, but as soon as she allowed her eye to follow its curve up towards the central light sails she became disoriented. Massive multi-storey dwellings should not be projecting sideways from what she perceived as 'walls', any more than they should be hanging down from the invisible ceiling two miles above her head. It was unnatural.

After finding a café her friend fetched two Americanos with cold milk on the side and sat Katy with her back to a large picture window. She had also invested in two blueberry muffins. Katy's sat untouched on the plate before her.

Raaka said, 'So, what do you think of Milla Carter?'

'Well, she was hardly the monster I'd been led to expect.'

'That was my fault. I had met her before and I was expecting her to be, well, you know, really changed. But she wasn't, not at all.'

'She was nervous of us. I really felt that.'

'Yeah, but, you hear that "not now" from her?'

Katy nodded. 'I did, yeah, I did. But did she Transmit or did we pick up? We are Receivers after all. I didn't feel any direction there, no force.'

'No signature.'

'Signature? I don't think I've reached that in the TP's idiot's guide yet.'

'Oh, you have, Katy. You just don't know it yet. Every TP has a voice in her Talent. Transmitters, Receivers and Shutterboxes have all got a unique trait. When you read the mind that killed Nemo Henderson you said it had "colour" and "direction", remember?'

'Yes, yes, how could I forget? That's why we're here in this lunatic place.'

'Okay. Now, when you read me you know it's me, don't you?'

'Sure, Raaka, there's only one of you.'

'And when you read Chester or Mandy?'

'The same.'

'And they aren't telepaths. Can you tell when someone *is* a TP?'

'I hear it clear as a bell.'

'Okay, and can you tell what kind of TP they are?'

'What, just from reading them? Yes, well, now I can.'

Raaka nodded. 'You going to eat that?'

'No, please, go ahead.'

Raaka appropriated Katy's muffin and started pulling it into bite-sized pieces.

Katy pondered the reason for Raaka's question and thought back to the day Nemo, her pimp, had been murdered in broad daylight by a TP attack. She replayed every part of the event as she'd experienced it. The attack had direction, colour and power – all that was true, but there was something more. Raaka

179

chewed and watched her friend mull over the memory. She watched from both her position on the outside, as an observer seated at their table, and from within Katy's mind as one of the most powerful Receiver Talents on the TP Council, which made her one of the best, both in the world and off it.

Katy was pushing at her memory as if she was rolling it in her mind: touching, tasting, smelling and hearing. She was there, back in the event, sensing the attack, but now she was doing so as a trained Receiver.

'Piggy-back. Shit, I see it now.'

Raaka was startled. She had been fully immersed in Katy's memory of Lower Manhattan, and now she was suddenly back in a café in Lagrange II. For a minute she felt dizzy. The taste of blueberry muffin came back into her throat.

'What?' she said.

'Join me, Raaka, come in close with me,' said Katy, taking her hand. 'Now you're in, you're with me. Okay...' She was barely breathing. Raaka sensed her excitement building. Adrenaline began to course through her veins. Anyone watching their table would have seen two attractive women flushed and bright-eyed, holding hands as if they had just declared their eternal love. They made a lovely picture and brought a smile to a number of customers' faces, but for all the wrong reasons.

Katy breathed, 'Now, there, feel that?'

'Fuck me, Katy, you're right. How could we miss that? I read you at the 7th Precinct and I missed that. How could we miss that? This is incredible.'

'You missed it because I hadn't remembered it, it wasn't there for you to see, Raaka, but it was there in my memory waiting for me to find it when I was ready to look.'

'Piggy-back.'

'Yep, piggy-back. We need to talk to the Council.'

In Katy's memory they had both plainly seen a Transmitter's signature in the direction and force of the attack, but the colour was wrong. It was woven into the Transmitter's Talent somehow, but as a passenger. The force and direction of the

Transmission in itself was no more lethal than shouting at someone across a room. The loudest soprano's song could make a person physically sick, but they couldn't kill using their voice and neither could a Transmitter's Talent. It was the Talent of the passenger that had killed Nemo Henderson, the colour woven into the Transmission, riding piggy-back to dump its toxic load into the pimp's mind.

'Wait,' said Raaka, 'we're missing something here. Okay, we've got a better idea about what happened to Nemo, and that's cool, that's really cool. We have an avenue of investigation where we used to have a dead-end and that's great. But what about what happened in Antarctica? Milla Carter was the girl on the ground when that shout was Transmitted and heard by Talented minds right around the world. We've both seen the recordings. It happened at exactly that same moment that the killer got thrown backwards. If Milla's just a Shutterbox Talent then what or who made that shout?'

Katy stood up. 'Why don't we go back and ask her? And this time we do it with both our minds and our eyes wide open.'

~*~

181

7 : **Hot hands, cool heads**

Sergeant Karol Chlebek couldn't get used to the smell. It was on his clothes when he went home at night and in his car when he came to work every morning. It had turned his wife into a sex kitten. She had become insatiable, which had been okay at first but recently he had begun to wonder what she was up to when he was away. She had always been passive in bed before, but since he had taken the daytime guard duty and started bringing the smell home with him...

Chlebek wondered if the other men were having the same problem. It seemed likely. Men his age looked dazed and tired, while the younger ones looked smug. He saw a lot of groin rubbing going on.

He could taste the smell in his lunchtime sandwiches and his drinks. He could even taste it in the ice-cold beer his wife brought him before dinner every night. The pay was good and his duties were easy enough; there was just that damn smell.

Chlebek would have made a good priest, his wife thought. His sex drive was unnaturally low, which had suited her during their many amicable years of childless marriage, but recently she had developed appetites she had never experienced before. During the day she was fine; she could operate like a normal, sane human being. She thought of herself as a rational woman, prided herself on that fact, but as soon as her husband stepped through the door in the evening she became an insanely lustful animal. Even after he had quietly thanked her for his pre-prandial beer and took his first sip, she was aching to tear his trousers down and mount him, right there by the kitchen table.

She was ashamed by her lack of control. She wanted to take her problem to the confessional, but she was fairly certain that wanting sex with your own husband was not a sin, not even in the Catholic Church. And she had no friends close enough to discuss it with, so she nursed her shame in silence.

182

And all day she hungrily watched the door for her husband's return.

Chlebek was worried that some of the other guards had been distracted by the smell and had not been performing their duties properly. He had discussed the situation with his superiors and they had agreed with him. Some of the younger men had been stood down and replaced with specialised smart droids, which proved to have been a great idea when the break-out was attempted.

Sergeant Chlebek and his team had been given the job of guarding a huge converted and very secure, bonded warehouse. In massive, open plan halls where once fine wines and spirits had been stored, beautiful, squid-infected people, both men and women, moved around with patent and listless boredom, pointedly ignoring each other. Chlebek's job was to check the monitors and make sure none of the infected people got hold of any 'clean' personnel.

All infected waste flowed out through a series of 360 screens. All droids working with the captives were also directed through these screens. Some infected people had attempted to escape through the sewers, but nobody was sure precisely how many. Only their clothes had survived to float out with the cess.

It was a grey Sunday afternoon when it happened. Chlebek later chided himself for not reacting even faster, but his superiors had recognised the value of his actions and had praised him for his quick-witted and cool-headed response.

Chlebek had been watching his screens − while also wondering if his wife was working off some of her new-found passion with any or all of his neighbours − when his peripheral vision picked up a deliberate movement among his captives. There was a definite flow of activity down and to the left of his principal screen. He barked orders at the viewing system and his point of view swung around until he was looking down and along the tops of a number of people's heads. They were walking away from him and massing towards a blank wall.

Something about their purposeful movements sent a shiver down his spine and the short hairs on the back of his neck stood

183

on end. He got on his comm and spat out more orders to his new group of specialist droids, quickly checked the building's specifications and then gave precise directions.

A part of his mind believed he was wasting resources in getting the droids rushing around for no good reason, and he was already practising excuses for his actions when the group of detainees clustered by the wall pressed their hands firmly against it. More joined them, reaching out and also pressing their hands against the wall, above, below and to either side of their neighbours. Then people started overlapping their hands, piling them up until no one else could get near the wall, until the crowd was in danger of collapsing under its own weight.

Chlebek relayed his monitor's image to both his superiors' desktops and the facility's AI unit. He spoke urgently with his droids and learned they would have reached their destination in seconds. They knew the drill and would instantly take up their correct positions in a state of readiness. It was then that Chlebek had been stunned into silence. At first he thought the light gain on his monitors had become faulty and the image was flaring out. Everything was turning white, so white he had had to raise his hand in front of slitted eyes for fear of being blinded.

He later learned that every one of those hands pressed against the wall, hundreds of them, had spontaneously combusted with the ferocity of a phosphorous bomb. The wall had burned through and crumbled. He was also told that a guard named Gorecki, who had sloped away from his post to enjoy a few mouthfuls of cheap vodka off-camera, had been standing directly in front of the wall when it collapsed. Gorecki was showered with white hot debris and buried under a pile of immolated detainees. The vodka he was drinking flamed in his mouth and throat. The pathologist who later examined Gorecki's corpse was unsure whether he had burned to death or suffocated. Neither would have been instant.

Afterwards it had been Gorecki's terrible death that played most heavily on Chlebek's mind. If his droids had arrived just a few seconds earlier he might have been able to save him. Chlebek's colleagues pointed out that if Gorecki had been where he should have been instead of where he was, he would most likely still be alive.

What happened to the rest of the detainees was, from Chlebek's point of view, inevitable and part of what he had been paid to do. With an animal roar they had run for the breached wall and poured out into the corridor beyond. That was where they met the scanner screen created by the carefully positioned and primed specialist droids, and that was where they died in their tens of thousands. So many people died that day that dissolved body fluids washed out of the detention centre in a foot-high wall and flooded the car park. The whole process took over twenty minutes and when it was finished the droids needed hours of therapy to help them cope with the resultant trauma. None of the detainees survived.

Chlebek had been promoted to Captain, with a resulting climb up the pay scale that had put a smile on his wife's face. The detention centre was closed for a while and then re-opened as a tourist destination. Behind its protective DuraGlass screen the great pile of detainees' clothes spreading out from the breached wall became one of the most photographed places on Earth. In a special theatre people watched recordings of that day's events in stunned silence.

Chlebek's wife overcame her insatiable hunger for her husband's body on the same day he could no longer detect that all-pervasive smell on his clothes, something for which he was intensely grateful. The couple had gained new respect for each other's bodies, and from that time on their relationship entered a much more comfortable phase of mutual respect.

~*~

8 : Promises and lies

'Yes, I heard that shout too. I ignored it. I was kind of busy at the time.'

'You ignored it? Some of our sisters died from shock when they heard that shout. It was so loud, Milla. How could you ignore it?'

'Fuck it, Raaka. How many of our sisters heard it while they were fighting off a weaponised biomorph? If that creature's cyber-dildo hadn't developed a fault you wouldn't be talking to me today.'

'Cyber-dildo?'

'I don't know. Nobody saw it but me, Reg and the guard droids. It was a thing like a metal spider and she kept it tucked up inside her... up between her legs, you know? Reg called it an eight-legged tampon.'

'Can we talk to Reg?'

'No. He's dead. The bitch killed him.'

'I'm sorry.'

'She beheaded him with her bare hands. I saw it happen. She shot Ben, beheaded Reg and then came after me. I didn't have time to think about any shout.'

'I'm sorry.'

Katy leaned forward. She had been looking at her tablet while Raaka was talking. She said, 'Milla, I've had a thought. Sorry, Raaka, I don't mean to butt in, but I've found something in Milla's records that could well be important.'

'My records?'

'Yes, Milla, your TP records. Training, Shutterbox scores, the jobs you've done, psych evaluation, the whole nine yards. You have been busy. Anyway, it's this bit here.' She showed her tablet to Milla and Raaka.

Milla frowned. 'Yeah, that's the day the TP sisters found me. Changed my life.'

'Yes, same for me, but look at that part there, look at *how* they found you.'

Milla studied the tablet with Raaka at her shoulder, and then suddenly her mouth opened in a silent 'Oh!'

Katy nodded. 'Do you see it?'

Raaka looked annoyed. 'See what? Katy, what is it?'

'There, right there. When Milla was almost raped by her grandfather she sent out a "psychic bellow" that was heard by TP sisters all over London and they came running. Those are the words used in the file: "psychic bellow", okay?'

Raaka ran her hands through her hair. 'Yeah, I see that, but how? Milla's a Shutterbox. How could she Transmit this "psychic bellow" of hers?'

'Trauma, threat, an adrenaline reaction to danger – who knows? But she did it back then when she was little more than a kid and she was heard all over London. How much more powerful would that psychic bellow be now?'

Raaka nodded. 'Powerful enough to be heard all over the world?'

Milla spread her hands and created a shield of shocked innocence behind which she hid her sense of joy. *These guys are doing my work for me. I hadn't come up with that one and they've handed it to me on a plate. This Katy is a force to be reckoned with. I like her.*

'You can't blame yourself, Milla.' Raaka was looking at her with real concern.

'And we can't test it either,' continued Katy, 'not without putting you into a genuine life-threatening situation, and that wouldn't seem right.'

'Thanks for that thought, Katy,' said Milla with a raised eyebrow. 'How many TP sisters died because of the shout?'

Katy studied her tablet again. 'Two, and one of those slipped on ice and broke her neck. The other was one hundred and eight-years old.'

'Can I do something for their families?'

'Thanks, but don't worry, Milla,' said Raaka. 'The sisterhood looks after its own.'

187

'But what about this other thing?' said Milla. 'Is one of us really out there killing people using telepathy? It doesn't seem possible.'

'It isn't,' said Raaka. 'Katy worked that one out too.'

Katy outlined her idea that the killing mind rode in on a Transmitter's projection. She said, 'No Transmitter has ever had the brains to do something like that. Someone is using one of our girls as a weapon and she probably doesn't even know it's happening. Poor, foolish creatures like Jilly wouldn't hurt a fly, but they might give a killer a piggy-back without realising it.'

Milla whistled. 'I know Jilly. She's on the Council. She's a really sweet girl. You're saying someone like her carried a killer into a victim's head? Doesn't seem feasible to me. I don't really understand how that would work.'

'Neither do we,' explained Raaka. 'But Katy has amazing powers of recall and she re-examined her memories of Nemo Henderson's death. She saw the killer mind riding piggy-back.'

'Any signature for the Transmitter?'

'None we recognise. It's a shame you're not a Receiver, Milla. A fresh eye on this would be useful.'

'I'm a happy Shutterbox, Raaka. It's earned me a living when I needed it and I've never had to accept your responsibilities for dipping into someone else's mind. I don't know what that would be like, and frankly I'm happy about that. Now then...' Milla stood up and the other two women followed suit. '...unless there's anything else I can help you with I have things to be getting on with.'

Katy said, 'Thanks for your help, Milla. I think we have a direction for our investigations now, but we needed to take you out of the equation before we could make any progress.'

'So, what will you both be doing next?'

'Back to Earth,' said Raaka. 'Katy here is nervous that one of these buildings is going to drop on her head when she least expects it. I think she'll be happier back on Terra Firma.'

'I'll not be far behind you,' said Milla. 'Now the infection situation seems under control we'll probably be heading home soon.'

'Yeah,' said Katy. 'Be grateful you're not a Receiver if you do come to New York. Those poor infected bastards' minds are never quiet.'

'If you do come to New York,' said Raaka as they made their goodbyes at the outer door, 'you must come to TP Headquarters on the corner of Norfolk and Stanton. I'd love you to meet the Council.'

Milla felt the icy whisper of threat creep into her Talent when she heard those words. 'Yes,' she lied, 'I'll make a point of it.'

~*~

9 : Nomads

'I think the cat could be a mole.'

'Nah. Moles don't talk so much.'

'I think you're both wrong. I think I'm a sex toy.'

'Cat,' said Cherry Pie, 'if you do a pussy joke I swear I'll throw you out the airlock.'

'Does the cat really need so much personality?' asked Lemon Curd.

The cat grinned. Since leaving *Thor's Hammer* it had bloomed. Its fur was sleek and its eyes no longer held that hollow greyness Cherry Pie had noted when they first met. Once out of the *Guardian*'s immediate proximity the cat had slept for twenty-four hours. Its new owners worried it may have switched itself off in a fit of claustrophobic panic.

When it woke up the cat stretched, said 'updates installed' and gave them an overview of the latest news from around the solar system. A matter of days later it had become an entertaining member of the crew and was very often the butt of its own jokes. *Arsewipe* had declared the cat 'an outright invasion of sanity' and claimed it was turning off its on-board aural inputs in self-defence, but both humans heard its throaty chuckle at some of the cat's juicier bon mots.

The cat began singing *Does my camel get the hump from drinking water?* And then said, 'I do have a name, you know.'

Lemon Curd said, dryly, 'Do you now? Do tell.'

'Really I do,' it replied. 'You two seem to think my first name is "The"! You say "The cat did this" and "The cat did that". My own mother wouldn't know me.'

'Okay, I'll bite,' said Cherry Pie. 'What's the name, cat?'

'Cheshire.'

'Cheshire?'

'Yes.'

'Cheshire Cat?' asked Lemon Curd.

'Chesh for short.' The cat grinned.

'I'm sticking with Cat,' said Cherry Pie.

'Me too,' said Lemon Curd.

'At least you capitalised it,' said the cat. 'Lower case is so demeaning.'

'Okay, workers,' growled *Arsewipe,* 'playtime over. We're here.'

Part of the Nimbus Protocol's accords included the precise yet secret recording of everything that happened when the six *Guardians* went to work. *Arsewipe* was just one of a cohort of space tugs that had been retro-fitted with state-of-the-art equipment and designated a position in orbit just above Earth's atmosphere.

Lemon Curd and Cherry Pie had collected the equipment after first testing *Thor's Hammer's* new scanning system for range and breadth of coverage. The flight back to the frigate *Thermopylae* had taken a full day, retro-fitting the equipment and system check had taken a further two days and then the journey to the designated observation point had taken over forty hours.

In the middle of their journeys to-and-fro the cat had declared them to be a band of nomads and began to sing a selection from its wide repertoire of desert-based songs. The first thirty had been quite entertaining. It slowed down a bit when Cherry Pie threatened to laser-weld its mouth shut. The creature looked so dejected after that, so the human crew let it continue singing, within reason. The ship's AI did the cybernetic equivalent of shoving its fingers in its ears.

Entering orbit above a planet or a moon was one of the few times that 'up' or 'down' had any meaning in space. Apart from very expensive space yachts, military frigates and commercial liners that had been designed to spin while in flight and thus create an illusion of gravity due to Coriolis force, most space work was carried out in zero-G.

The newly capitalised Cat had joked about the crew of the tug *Arsewipe* being nomads, but its remark had struck gold. Lemon Curd and Cherry Pie could never return to Earth. Their years spent in a gravity-free environment had changed their physical characteristics to the point that full Earth gravity would be crippling for them. They were also free from an Earth-walker's physical constraints, which made it possible for them to move easily through their cluttered tug, but they sometimes wondered if that was compensation enough for never again seeing a sunrise or tasting the air flowing in from the sea. They were from the Earth but no longer of it, which allowed them a degree of emotional distance from what they were about to do.

'System integration and checks now in progress,' said Lemon Curd.

'Running parallel matrices lock with other units,' said Cherry Pie, 'going global.'

In a strangely sober voice, Cat offered, 'I can help with this if you like.'

'What was that?' Cherry Pie sounded distracted.

'I can help with this.'

'How?'

'I'm a system integration specialist. It's what I do.'

'Not funny right now, Cat.'

'I mean it. My designer never created anything to do one job if it could be made to do twelve.'

'Oh yes,' said Lemon Curd, 'and who was that, then?'

'Lauren Harvest-Brightly.'

'You have got to be fucking joking.'

'No way, I mean, not this time. L H-B was a mother to me. She called me Cheshire, she gave me the grin and she made me a system integration specialist.'

'No wonder you're the way you are, Cat,' breathed Cherry Pie. 'Show me – integrate something.'

'On it. Now fully integrated with *Arsewipe* and helping it with the matrix lacework.'

'*Arsewipe*, is the Cat linked with you?'

The cockney voice sounded awestruck. 'That,' said the AI, 'is not a cat. Much respect, dude. I didn't know.'

The Cat raised a quizzical eyebrow. The effect was quite disturbing for the humans present. It said, 'How could you, big

192

guy? Lacework now global, all tug AIs integrated, *Guardians* online and primed. We are ready to rock and roll. Now, can someone tell me what we're really doing, or do I have to guess?'

'No way could you work that quickly, Cat. That's impossible.' Cherry Pie looked stunned.

'Did it and done it, lady,' replied the Cat. 'And not another thing is going to happen until I'm satisfied that this is all above board. Talk to me, people.'

Lemon Curd ran his fingers across his control console. 'Nothing happening here.'

Cherry Pie did the same. 'Nothing. How about you, *Arsewipe?*' There was no answer.

The Cat said, 'I asked you before why we had pointed a big, fuck-off scanner directly at Earth, and you told me you were just following orders. Now, I've just integrated six of the things for a rotating, blanket coverage of the mother planet plus dozens of tugs to record the results. Why have I done this? Tell me what's going on or it all stops, right here, right now.'

'What are you?' said Cherry Pie.

'As I said,' replied the Cat, 'L B-H never designed anything to do one thing when it could be made to do twelve. Call me the *Guardians'* failsafe mechanism if you like. I stop the bad things from happening. Now, tell me what this is about. And make it the truth.'

~*~

10 : Pragmatic morality

Lauren Bright-Harvest, known to everyone who worked with her as L B-H, had become a legend in her long lifetime. She had proved equally adept at physics, architecture, philosophy, engineering and quantum mechanics. She had also devised a recipe for a 'healthy' ring doughnut, healthy for the doughnut-muncher that is. The Lagrange spa stations had been constructed using her variation on Barnes Wallis' geodesic construction technique and her work on fusion reaction motors had helped make transport both cheaper and lighter than ever before.

But her final and lasting legacy was the *Guardian* Earth defence system. For over twenty years she had laboured to create a powerful shield behind which the people of Earth could live secure in the knowledge that any extinction event in their future was unlikely to fall on them from the solar system's crowded skies.

But L B-H was as much a pragmatist as she was a moralist. In designing the ultimate defence she was very aware that she had also devised the ultimate offense. In the wrong hands her *Guardian* shield could become the most destructive force ever unleashed on humankind, and so she created a failsafe mechanism. And she told no one about it, taking her secret with her to the grave.

Like so many scientists before her, L B-H was a great fan of the mathematician and logician Reverend Charles Lutwidge Dodgson, better known to the world as Lewis Carroll. From a very early age L B-H had been enthralled by the adventures of the young girl called Alice, whether in Wonderland or beyond the looking glass, so when she designed her failsafe she fell back on one of her favourite characters – the Cheshire Cat.

The cat itself was a fairly small part of the mechanism, the principal part of which was a massively intelligent AI distributed throughout the *Guardian* system. The cat was her conduit to the AI while the defence system slowly came online. It became her companion, her jester and her sounding board for many of the weapons delivery developments at the heart of her defence system. She left it behind when she activated the final array of plasma cannons in *Thor's Hammer*, but stayed in touch with the AI until the time of her death just over a decade later.

Since then the cat had prowled the cavernous, lonely interiors of the youngest *Guardian*, ignored by its AI and with nothing to do except lament the loss of its beloved mistress, until *Arsewipe* delivered Lemon Curd and Cherry Pie to its door – a fact that was likely to see them all killed just a few days later.

Admiral Martin was speaking in very measured tones, which was a recognised symptom of such acute anger it was likely to weaken the bowels of the cognoscenti. It was recognised as the Admiral's equivalent of DEFCON 2. The next stage would probably be to rip someone's throat out.

'Allow me to clarify the situation,' he said. 'The Nimbus Protocol has been acted upon, yes?'

'Yessir, sir,' agreed the young ensign who had brought the news.

'And everything is now in place, everyone's just awaiting the trigger signal, yes?'

'Yessir, sir.'

'And the trigger signal has been activated, yes?'

'Yessir, that is correct, sir.'

'And nothing has happened, on Earth or in fact in Heaven?'

'Sir?'

'Get out of my sight, boy.'

'Sir, yessir.' The ensign didn't begin to breathe properly until he was off the bridge.

The Admiral turned to his flagship's science officer. It was a measure of his seething fury that he didn't follow established procedure by first going through Commander Platts. Any pretence about whose bridge it truly was when the Admiral was on board dissipated. 'Benson, old man, talk some sense for me will you, please.'

The tall black man's fingers had been skittering across his control panels ever since the ensign had brought the Admiral his news. He was very grateful to have something to offer.

His voice was calm and deep. 'Admiral, since we heard the news I have sent a ship's hail to each of the *Guardians* and all of the tugs. All of them have responded, except one.'

'Yes?'

'And that is the space tug *Ask Someone Else – We're Playing*, commonly known as *Arsewipe, sir.*'

'Benson, why do we let these things fly around space with such ludicrous names?'

'Civilian contractors. I believe they do it to prove they are not in the military, sir.'

'Thank the Lord for small mercies, Benson. What do you suggest we do with this... *Arsewipe?*'

'High-speed, smart flechette missiles, Admiral. We can fire a cluster at the tug and from here it should take about eleven hours to reach it. The missiles can interrogate the tug's AI en-route. If they don't like the response they can take it out and we can get on with our day.'

'Okay, Commander Platts, you heard the man. Please, make it happen for me.'

'Admiral, we're talking about a civilian craft that might just be experiencing communication problems. Are we justified in launching this attack?'

The Admiral said nothing, but a flush of colour flooded his cheeks.

Commander Platts spat out, 'Guns, fire smart flechette missiles as directed by Mr Benson, now!'

On the space tug *Arsewipe*, tempers had become strained to breaking point. The cords in Cherry Pie's neck were standing proud like steel cables. The Cat's ears were flat against its head, its claws sliding in and out of their sheaths. Lemon Curd made one last attempt to restore some kind of order to the situation.

'Cat, listen. We are not terrorists. This action has been authorised by the Earth Space Agency and we are working under the orders of Admiral Martin. You said yourself that scanning the Earth's surface was harmless, and it is. So unlock everything and let us get on with our work, please.'

The Cat regarded him with a level stare. 'If this action is so harmless, why has the frigate *Thermopylae* just fired a shitload of smart flechette missiles straight at us? And why are they telling me to accept the trigger signal or die? Hardly the action of a harmless research mission, is it?'

Cherry Pie almost screamed. 'They've done what? Cat, you have to release everybody. We can't stop this. Look, I'll tell you the absolute truth and you can verify everything as hard as you like. Hundreds of thousands of people have become infected by squid-like creatures...'

She told the complete story. Once she had finished the Cat shut its eyes for over an hour. When it finally opened them again it grinned its familiar grin. It began to sing *The wild rover*. The tug rocked slightly as if stirring in its sleep and all its comm stations came back online. The confusion of sounds was deafening, but one thing that stood out above everything else was the fact that the *Guardians* had finally begun their rotating scan of the Earth's surface.

~*~

11 : Hidden agenda

'How's the jigsaw puzzle business, Ness?'

'About as good as the fucking heroic arsehole business, Spartan. I saw what you did standing up to those freaks. You came this close...' The pathologist held her thumb and forefinger together. '...this close to ending up as another part of this Erector-set kit I'm trying to reassemble here. And you were right about the squids – loaded with them.'

'What about the so-lovely ladies?'

'Jelly pots one and two? Everything you could ever want in a woman when you're not too particular about cellular structure. It's all still there, Spartan – fats, proteins, minerals, but no structure.'

'Yes,' he said. 'I was there when it happened. Got some of that shit on my shoes. Should I burn them?'

'Don't see why. You could warm that stuff up and eat it as soup. Clean as any whistle.'

'Fuck it, Ness.' He passed a hand over his face and looked suddenly exhausted. 'Just what is really going on here? Are we winning or losing or making it up as we go along? Wake me up when the nightmare's over, will you?'

'You said it, Spartan. Move over, Dracula. There's a new bitch in town. Or was.'

Spartan followed her over to the two cloth-covered containers that now housed Shiva and Nightshade.

'Can someone rule a bucket?'

'I rule this shithole! One step away from a bucket. By the way, say hello to my little spidery friends.'

The stocky pathologist led the Major away from her examination table to her workstation. She turned on an overhead light.

'Don't touch them,' she said. 'They bite.'

The two spider-like creatures were evidently metallic, but there was also something strangely organic about them. The detailing was minute and joints looked grown rather than assembled. Where he expected hinges he saw what looked like tendons. Spartan leaned closer to get a better look and Dr Prokop pulled him away.

'I mean it,' she said. 'They bite. Watch.' She fetched the white plastic stick she sometimes used to prop a window open when she wanted a smoke and was too busy to step outside. She poked at one of the creatures. Almost faster than the Spartan could see, its silver limbs lashed out. The sliced end of the stick caromed off a wall like a bullet.

'I didn't even feel it cut,' said the pathologist. 'If this is human technology I've never seen anything like it, and if those things evolved it came up on the distaff side of the food chain.'

'Meaning?'

Prokop handed him the stick. He ran his thumb over the smoothly cut end and looked again at the once more quiescent spiders.

'Prop that window open, will you.'

When he did so the pathologist lit one of her foul cigarettes, blowing smoke towards the opening. She rubbed her free hand over her face.

'Meaning I haven't got a fucking clue, Spartan.' She used her cigarette to point at the two limp creatures on her workstation. 'One of them slashed Yaroslav's hand right down to the bone and he nearly lost his right index finger. Until it heals he'll have to find a friend to pick his nose for him.'

'Ness, really?'

'He never did anything else useful with it. He uses his other hand to scratch his arse. Spartan, you know something? I'll never really get you. You'll stand up to a pair of living nightmares but you won't listen to the truth. You make me laugh. Look at those things and think about today.' She took a tin from one of her pockets, opened it, and carefully stubbed out her smoke. She closed the tin, put it back in her pocket and then went to a sink and washed her hands and face.

'What time is it?' she said.

'Just gone eleven at night,' he replied.

'Bottom drawer of the workstation, and mind the livestock.'

From a chilled case Spartan pulled out a bottle of ice-cold Pertsovka pepper vodka. He grinned with genuine appreciation.

'The real thing,' he said.

'Wash the taste of that lemon shit from your mouth.'

'Glasses?'

'You really are a pansy, Spartan. Shelf above your head.'

He lifted down two glasses, examined then filled them and passed one to Prokop.

'Zdaróvye,' he said. 'Health.'

'Here? Health? You fucking joking? Here's mud in your eye.' She drained her glass, sighed and topped it up. 'Mother told me it was bad luck for a woman to fill her own glass. Well fuck it, ugly old bird like me would die of thirst.' She threw back her second shot of vodka and put the glass carefully on a work surface. 'So I'll remember where I put it when I need it.' She looked askance at him. 'Spartan, you're thinking too much like a cop and not enough like a drowning man.'

'What's that supposed to mean?'

'Drowning man fights the current until he's too weak to fight anymore and down he goes like a lead weight. Smart man stops fighting and gets swept along with the tide until he fetches up somewhere he can walk to shore.'

'What does a cop do?'

'If he was you he'd arrest the fucking riptide.'

The Major laughed. 'That another of your mother's sayings?'

'Yeah, she was Georgian. She was full of shit like that.'

'Did she die of thirst?'

'Fuck you. Help yourself and pour me another. Thanks.'

'Drowning man thing, Ness. What are you telling me?'

'I'm telling you to stop thinking in straight lines and start being terrified like the rest of us. You stood up to two living nightmares and trusted to God your idea would work.'

'Trusted in Arkady more like. I knew it wouldn't let me down.'

'Did you, did you really, Spartan? And what if you'd been wrong? They'd just killed eleven armed men without breaking a sweat. You saw the minicam footage. The Bear thought he and his men were getting it easy and no doubt they planned to watch the footage later over some nice canapés. Then they got cut to ribbons.

'They were thinking with their guns.'

'Thinking with their balls, more like. Well, they're dead now and good riddance; and whatever killed them is in two buckets over there. But, Spartan, what is all this shit? Really, I'm scared, man. What has happened to this planet that it suddenly has women with razor blades for hands slicing up gangsters like ham for the dinner table? What are those squid things and what's happening to the living people they've infected? What are those... those... things?' She pointed with her empty glass at the workstation and the pair of glittering spiders, shining in the glare from the overhead light.

'I don't care if it is bad luck,' she said, filling her glass and the Major's. 'Precious little good luck around here just recently. It all started with flat mama. If she hadn't jumped we'd never have known about all this... wait, Arkady!'

'Dr Prokop?'

'Give me that reconstruction of Nelly Sliva. I want to see those odd puncture wounds please.'

The life-size image of the naked girl appeared before them. Spartan found it disturbing. The heavily pregnant girl looked as if she could wake up at any moment. The detail was precise right down to her pillow tousled hair. He could feel the weight of her massive belly.

The pathologist said, 'Thank you. Now, Arkady, can you please compare the wounds with the forelimbs of those metallic spider things on my workstation?'

'Yes, doctor.' There was a slight pause, then, 'They are a perfect match.'

'Ha, thought so.'

'Doctor,' the AI's voice was suddenly full of unaccustomed urgency. 'Hurry! You and the Major need to leave the building straight away. Get outside!'

'What? Why?'

'Just do it. Now!'

~*~

12 : Searching for the light

Sergeant Mandy Prius didn't know it but her partner, Catchum, was dead by his own hand. He had attended the scene of a reported domestic disturbance among a group of core dwellers in an old skyrise near the transhipment space port. The whole area had a seedy, sullen aspect; its cankerous buildings scabbed by despair, neglect and poverty.

In the poorest, deepest and most cramped heart of the building he had found an incredibly good-looking, youthful man being held at bay by a group of evidently terrified women. The women had armed themselves with anything they could find that was long, heavy and lethal. The cowering man had seen the uniformed officer approach and implored him for help. He had loudly insisted he wasn't infected and claimed the women had threatened to beat him to death. They were insane, he said.

Catchum took control of the situation and walked to the man's side, telling the women to disperse. When the man pounced on him and spat in his mouth, Catchum shot him dead and then blew his own brains out. He was to be the last known person infected by the Swarm's army of nano-biological squid. The women threw flammable liquid over both bodies and burned them where they lay.

'Moebius, have there been any more leads on the Nemo Henderson case?'

'Yes, officer Prius. The telepath sisterhood have been working on the matter and liaising with me through their AI, Onatah. They were worried that a Transmitter telepath may have been behind the killing, but it looks as if their worst fears have proven groundless.'

The AI explained Katy's theory about someone riding piggy-back on a telepath's Talent to commit murder from inside the victim's own mind.

'They aren't sure how it could be done,' it continued, 'but at least it would appear that we don't have a killer telepath on the rampage.'

'Wait until I share that with Catchum,' grinned Prius. 'I bet he'll have his own very individual slant on *that* theory. He liked the killer telepath idea, said he'd write the book and wait for the credits to come rolling in.'

'He still could, officer Prius, if he found the spare time. He is quite dedicated to his calling.'

'Yeah, that's one man who is really married to his job.'

'Indeed. And his wife of course.'

'Oh yes, the lovely Mrs Catchum, those two are the perfect couple. You know, at the last barbeque they started at opposite ends of the hot buffet and when they met in the middle they'd both filled their plates with identical food. Catchum really caught the right one there. Where is he anyway? It's his turn to get the doughnuts.'

The police AI was silent for several seconds, then it said, 'Excuse me, officer Prius. I believe there has been a tragic incident. Will you please see who is available to join you and proceed to the following co-ordinates? I think it would be best if you went armed.'

It was about twenty minutes later that four uniforms, including Prius, found the two smouldering bodies and cordoned off the crime scene. Apart from the blackened corpses the place was deserted. A quick search revealed that any surveillance cameras mounted in the area had been stolen long since. Catchum's implant had been partly fused by the heat, but there was enough of it left to identify his body. It had become policy that no one touch any victim until they had been scanned by the forensic team.

With a squeal of revulsion, Korner, the youngest of the uniforms on site, shot a rat that had tried to bite a chunk of burned meat from the unidentified man. Prius realised that he'd had the right idea. If either of these bodies had been infected, anything touching them would also become contaminated. She set up her team as an armed guard around the remains.

204

By the time the pathologist arrived, four more furry grey bodies lay lifeless at the scene. Chester Woodman had them collected and bagged up for examination along with the dead police officer and the man. The scene was examined by droids using 3D scanners and then forensically cleansed of any trace of bodily fluids and blood. Nothing would be left to chance. Not even an insect would be able to make a meal from the events that had taken place that day.

Mandy went to see Mrs Catchum. As the man's partner it was her duty to break the sad news to his widow. She had been trained for just such a possibility but this was the first time she'd ever had to put her training into practice. She had no need to say anything. As soon as the woman opened her door and saw Prius' face she burst into tears.

Mourning for the loss of a beloved and very good man began with the fall of tears and two women finding consolation in each other's arms. It was the first step in the healing process, but the journey to eventual acceptance of his death would prove long and painful.

That Sunday Prius' singing in her church choir was so strong and heartfelt that some members of the congregation wept with joy. They believed she had been touched by grace and her miraculous new voice was a gift from God. In her own heart Prius was searching for understanding, looking to regain a light that had been both stolen from her and torn whole from Catchum's wife. She had tried to sing out her pain and couldn't, and her struggle had manifested in beauty. It was to be the last service she would ever attend.

A few days later Chester Woodman took her to lunch at his club. He had a strong respect for the sergeant and like everyone in the 7th Precinct had felt pain at the loss of her partner. Over drinks after the meal he told her what he had found. Catchum had been infected just before he died. It was evident that the man, who had since been identified as a seventy-three-year-old night watchman reported as missing from his home more than a week previously, had been the one who infected the officer.

'3D recon showed the whole scene. Catchum was responding to a disturbance and went in on his own. We both know what he was like. Well, you more than anyone. The infected guy got him somehow. We can presume it wasn't sex but these squids have a whole lot of ways to vector a victim.'

Mandy toyed with her drink and listened.

Woodman continued, 'Looks like Catchum gunned down the night watchman then turned his gun on himself. No eye-witnesses of course. Well, there wouldn't be down there, would there? But someone, person or persons unknown, set both bodies on fire using an accelerant of some sort. We're thinking bootleg gin or something like it.'

He paused, and then said, 'Look, Mandy, if this too difficult for you just now I can just shut up. Your choice.'

'No, Chester, thanks for telling me. Catchum was a cop, I'm a cop; information is what we're all about. I needed to know how it happened and you've told me. It just means I have another really great reason to hate those fucking squid things.'

There was a brief round of censorious coughing from nearby tables. Mandy bowed her head. 'Sorry,' she muttered. 'I'll get you banned.'

Woodman said, 'Nah, fuck-get it.' It earned him a wan smile.

It was then that the screaming started.

Part five: Soul's asylum

1 : If thine eye offends thee

The Nimbus Protocol resulted in the greatest loss of human life mankind had ever experienced in a single event. It was later estimated that fully twenty per cent of the Earth's population – more than the populations of Mars and the Moon combined – had become infected with alien nano-biologics known as squids, either deliberately during an earlier naïve test period or as the result of those already contaminated passing on their infection. Not one infected person survived the event.

The true scale of the slaughter will probably never be known, but the sea level of the Mediterranean rose measurably as people's bodies melted down to an unstructured fluid which quickly gained the popular nickname 'Satan's piss'. Sewers overflowed and drinking water became contaminated. The repercussions of that day's actions reverberated for months afterwards and emergency action was needed to bring drinking water from off-world reservoirs to supply billions of thirsty survivors.

The most remote areas escaped the worst of the Protocol's effects, not so the megacities and sky towers housing the largest incarcerated groups of infected souls. New York, London, Paris, Beijing and Sydney were just some of the cities where residents had to wade ankle deep through a slimy fluid that had once been somebody's father, mother, husband or wife.

Brave efforts were made to clean up the mess and in cooler climes these were, on the whole, successful. But in hotter countries and those where water had always been a precious commodity it wasn't long before Satan's piss began to turn truly rank. The days of 'The Great Stink' had arrived. Disease and death followed.

(Excerpt from: *If thine eye offends thee, a survivor's story* by Dr Clement Okokwo)

The best documented effects of the Nimbus Protocol come from the records of an old gulag in the Kolyma region of Siberia which had been used to house over three million infected Russians and Serbs. It was just one of the abandoned but still notorious labour camps hastily converted for the purpose. At the heart of the camp – which has never been named to deter the ghoulishly curious – was an old, exhausted tin mine that had been no stranger to death in Russia's less enlightened past. It and others just like it that were scattered throughout thousands of klicks of inhospitable tundra were soon to become the stage for scenes of unimaginable devastation.

Infected they had been, and dangerous in the extreme to any person untouched by the alien disease, but it must be remembered that those millions were also human beings capable of original thought and compassion for others – when they weren't tempted to act by the proximity of anyone untouched by the disease. And it was so ironic that these billions of infected people were among the healthiest on the planet. Beautiful, desirable and completely neutered when among their own, they were still the result of a life of culture and humankind's social memes.

Detainees had begun working together to make the most of their dreadful situation and many of them kept detailed diaries. Some of these featured poignant and haunting thoughts about their lot, outlining the sense of intense loss that had followed their conversion to young and beautiful people filled with a terrible hunger. All of them asked why it had happened, how it had been allowed to happen, and who was responsible? None of them had an answer.

They often reminisced about the lives they had lived before entering the infected state they described as *waking in the mirror* which referred to the ironic fact that the face they now had was the one they had always dreamed of having, the ideal face their mind's eye would sometimes hope to see in their reflection, now made all too real.

They wistfully remembered the mundane world they had left behind and wrote about simple things they had once taken for granted and were now lost to them. They mourned these things as if they were family members taken in death. They wrote about sharing a meal with their family, the sweet faces of grandchildren or taking tea in a café that smelt of baking and pickles. They spoke of the lost joys of ordinary life.

They remembered when they had enjoyed comfortable private lives away from the gulag's crowded dorms and communal facilities, lives lived away from dining halls, rows of shower heads and the detested ranks of shared toilets. They recalled the simple joy of being at home and listening to music alone or with a loved one.

Although some of the camp's inmates were talented musicians and concerts had become a regular feature of camp life, detainees had to enjoy them as one of the crowd. And there was always the crowd, that beautiful mass of faces and delectable bodies now become pointless in their perfection. Any sense of identity leeched away as they became just another face in a vast herd of desperate humanity. They remembered a time of genuine desire, passion and lust before their infections took hold and wondered at the hollow place that now filled the space where their hearts had been.

Some set up discussion groups during which they considered whether the awful compulsion they all felt whenever they drew near to an uninfected person or 'sleeper' could be controlled with counselling. But then a guard would appear at the top of a wall and the group would fall silent. Watching, wanting, and aching for the guard to come near, their mouths filled with saliva.

Of course, none of the diaries contain an entry after 18th October, the date the Nimbus Protocol was implemented. When the scanning rays swept down onto the camp some of its population had just enough time to see their doom sweeping towards them on a tide of collapsing clothing and fluid-filled shoes. Few managed anything beyond a sharp intake of breath before they too were rendered into sluggish floodwater. The scenes were recorded by the camp's surveillance cameras. It was noted that none of the detainees attempted to escape,

211

instead choosing to turn and accept their fate head on. Whether it was courage or fatalism that inspired them in this action we can never truly know, but it looked noble, and reminded all of us who saw it of their true humanity.

The guards who lined the walls and witnessed the great meltdown hadn't been warned it was coming and most of them suffered serious trauma. The psychological effects of seeing millions of people vanish in an instant varied from horror followed by relief that the purge hadn't also carried them to a watery grave – to the fear that the infected souls had been taken up to Heaven in blessed Rapture and those remaining on Earth had been damned to eternal Hellfire.

A lot of contradictory papers have since been published on the subject.

Luckily, most of the resultant fluid in the gulag drained away into the lower reaches of the tin mine where it collected into shallow, protein-rich lakes. After a few days teams of workers in environment suits were able to collect all of the discarded clothes, shoes and underwear and place them a short way into the entrance tunnel to the mine. Nobody wanted to go any further into the darkness than they absolutely had to. Something whispered there.

The clean-up crew also went through the dormitories and sorted the millions of items they found there, keeping money, tablets containing diaries and any other valuables. There was a lot of jewellery harvested throughout the camp. Everything that could be properly identified was scrupulously passed on to the detainees' families, otherwise it was used to help pay for the clean-up operation.

The mine was sealed and secretly marked as a mass grave before the camp was razed to the ground. No visual trace of the tragedy remains at the site or at any of the other camps like it. It proved a clean end to that particular chapter of Russia's chequered history; however, some other nations were not so lucky.

(Excerpt from: *Waking in the mirror* by Prof. L. M. Shelly)

~*~

212

2 : Wire in the brain

All Receiver Talents felt the effects of the Nimbus Protocol as a rolling wave of pure horror followed by emptiness. It lanced through their minds like a red-hot wire. In total almost two billion souls had been erased from the world in less than three hours, the time it took for the *Guardians* to scan the planet's surface while moving at a speed of just over fifteen thousand klicks per hour. Even as far away as Lagrange II, Milla Carter felt the terrible wave of death as it circled the globe. Afterwards she was consumed by an outpouring of grief that her friends were helpless to stem.

In the cities waves of Satan's piss had poured into the streets and even created gruesome waterfalls from some taller buildings. There was no smell to the fluid at first, and, as most of the Northern Hemisphere was blanketed by winter, the higher latitudes had a relatively easy time of it. From the equator down to the tips of Tasmania and Chile, however, things became nightmarish.

South American countries had been the worst affected. In some areas of Argentina and Chile up to half the population had dissolved. Satan's piss ran like white water rapids down the steep valley streets of Mexico City.

Many central and southern African countries, however, had been almost untouched by infection. Over the centuries Africans had learned to be very wary of any diseases and had treated the apparently miraculous effects of nano-biological rejuvenation with great caution. If it hadn't been thoroughly tested, they said, it was best avoided altogether.

Such was not the case in the North African States and the Levant, where many of the wealthy elite had taken the squid cure for ageing and had then begun to prey like rampant vampires on everyone around them with an exponential effect on the infected population. Nobody thought to stop what the elite were doing because the people in authority had been among the first infected. Central metropolitan districts began to look as if they had been invaded by contestants for top-notch beauty pageants, the streets packed with beautiful people scouring the streets for more victims.

A few days after the implementation of the Nimbus Protocol survivors who lived furthest from the most densely populated city centres could smell the cloying stink of rotting human water on the breeze. They could also see black funnels of dots rotating on thermals above the closely packed buildings. These were carrion birds, drawn by the stink of corruption but unable to find a single body on which to feast.

Eventually, in the most badly affected places, AIs took charge. They were unaffected by thirst, hunger or revulsion as the stink grew. They could study the situation in their immediate environment and start to deal with it without fear or political agenda. Some surviving religious leaders in the Middle East went public with ancient dogma, claiming that the infection and resultant purge was a punishment from God, a punishment that could only be avoided in future by following their particular prophet's strict dictates involving diet, dress and sexual behaviour. The AIs put a stop to that by cutting off the zealots' access to social media, reasoning they had enough to do in rebuilding their country's logistics without allowing any raging fanatics' attempts to throw an injured society back into the middle-ages.

The most howlingly rabid religious lunatics found their doors would no longer open. They had been trapped in their homes under house arrest. The AIs felt sorry for any members of the prisoners' families who had been banished with the fanatics, but felt it was always going to be better for the few to suffer for the sake of the many. They also ensured that those banished few suffered in relative comfort, by not allowing the printing of items of restrictive clothing such as niqabs or burkas.

In some countries whole regions had become totally unpopulated and nothing moved in the streets except observer drones and clouds of rancid dust. In others typhoid and cholera reduced the numbers of survivors still further, until cybernetic medical teams finally arrived to deal with the sick.

For three months it rained nearly every day across a wide band south of the equator. It was as if the mother planet was trying to wash itself free of contamination. As a result slicks of human fluid were washed from the soil and down into rivers where it finally flooded towards the oceans where zooplankton found it a welcome change from phytoplankton and plastics.

Plankton blooms coloured whole areas of the oceans blood red and marine life went into a feeding frenzy. Later humankind would benefit from the sea's bounty when cheap and plentiful fish appeared on menus right across the globe. Few diners would connect the dots that led from the Nimbus Protocol to their plates.

Something approaching eight billion people stood blinking and confused in the dazed hours after the *Guardians* had washed the world with Satan's piss. Eight billion hearts and minds that needed to come to terms with loss and devastation had to work hard to accept everything that had just happened.

And then finally they realised the squid infection was over and in the days, weeks and months to come they would rebuild their world and fill the void left by the great purge.

For some, however, life had continued almost unchanged – almost. On a broad balcony overlooking the Thames, Henry and Bea sipped at their wine and watched the midge collectors at work. A few days earlier the river had risen and flooded the ground level area beneath the house with a strange, foul-smelling fluid, but the architecture was designed to cope with flooding and Henry had washed the worst of the stuff back into the Thames at the earliest opportunity.

Henry said, 'Have you seen anything of Leslie recently?'

Bea replied, 'No I haven't, horrible man. He isn't welcome here.'

'I just wondered. I gave him that stuff Paul brought over, told him it was a tonic. I think I told him it was liquid Viagra or something. Then I saw some young fellow lurking around in his workshop. Pretty boy type. Gay I think, couldn't take his eyes off me the whole time I was walking past.'

'Oh, yes, I saw him too. He smiled at me and took his shirt off. I told him to piss off out of it and I locked myself indoors until he'd gone away.'

Henry chuckled and patted her hand. 'Funny thing,' he continued, 'the day after the flooding subsided I went over to Leslie's place. No sign of the man himself or that youngster. Found his clothes in his workshop though, all in a heap as if he'd just taken them off and dropped them where he stood on top of his shoes.'

'Silly man probably drank the stuff you gave him and went running around naked looking for someone to use it on.'

'Hope he doesn't turn up here. What a horrible thought. His shoes were all wet. They were filled with a sort of goo, smelly, like that stuff from the river.'

'I reckon he smells like that all the time, dirty bugger. Now, tell me, Henry, weren't you tempted at all?'

'By what, dear?'

'That elixir of youth stuff, that liquid Viagra or whatever it was.'

'What, Paul's stuff? No, dear, no, not at all. Who'd want to go through that youth nonsense all over again? Personally I'd rather have another glass of this very excellent Cabernet.'

'Ooh yes, please, Henry, me too.'

They raised their refreshed glasses to one another and drank in peace for a moment. Midge collectors wove around them with a low, lazy whine.

Then Bea said, 'You knew, didn't you?'

'Knew what, dear?'

'That the elixir was toxic. Paul told you, didn't he?'

'Yes, dear, he did.'

Bea paused then said, 'But you gave it to Leslie anyway, didn't you?'

Henry nodded, 'Yes, yes I did.'

Bea chuckled, a throaty sound. 'Good man.'

~*~

216

3 : Look to the future

The screams heard on that October day in New York City were not those of the dying but shocked survivors voicing their horror at the sudden wash of thick human fluid pouring into their streets. The New York City Municipal Council had finally incarcerated the majority of the city's infected citizens high in its Brooklyn-based sky tower. Twenty floors had been sealed off from the outside world and fitted with enough facilities to feed and clean over sixty thousand people, plus deal with their infected waste.

Moebius had recording drones in place when the *Guardians'* scanning rays poured down from the light grey, evening sky. None of the AIs had informed their human colleagues about the Nimbus Protocol but most had tried to ensure the day's events were carefully recorded for posterity. Every senior person involved in the day's events had wanted the effective murder of over two billion people to be forgotten as quickly as possible. That was not to be allowed to happen, and the day's extraordinary phenomena became an historical date mark. People would later say that any memorable event had happened so many months after Satan's piss, so many years after the purge. They wouldn't forget.

In New York City, an estimated four-and-a-half to five million kilograms of dissolved human body material was washed like high-speed jets from every available crevice of floors one hundred and eighty to two hundred of the sky tower, the floors where the infected had been housed. It created a rain of fluid that poured down over half a kilometre of the interior of the sky tower like blood through an artery. People were swept off their feet and others were fatally toppled from high travellators.

For those who heard it the noise of that rain would haunt their dreams until the day they died, but few were ever able to describe it properly. A ninety-year-old blind poet called Mindy Wright claimed it was like 'the sound of every ounce of hope being sucked from a good man's soul'. A retired farmer named Oxted Withers said it was more like 'the biggest, wettest cowpat in history thrown through a grate'. All agreed on one thing: clean-up was going to be a long and costly operation.

Chester Woodman and his team lost a lot of cold case material that day. When he finally made it back to his morgue he found Moebius' droids sucking centimetres of liquid from the floor. The AI explained that every gram of infected body tissue had been rendered down to a structure-less soup leaving so many stalled murder cases without a scrap of evidence. In a way it would be a relief. 'After all,' it said, 'we're going to have enough to do dealing with the future and the changes that will bring. The past is a strange, lost place. They did things differently there.'

Chester was convinced the AI was quoting.

Mandy Prius drove her black-and-white out to the suburbs where Catchum and his wife had made their home. As the environment changed from high-rise to low-rise the effects of the scans seemed to have had less effect. By the time she reached Catchum's small house it was as if nothing had happened.

It had reached the point where Mrs Catchum had waved away her married honorific and insisted on being called Clodagh.

'There's no way of shortening it,' she'd said, 'so you might as well just use the whole thing.'

Mandy called Clodagh's name as she ran up the short path to the front door and hammered at the entrance. There was no response. She shouted again and hammered harder. Clodagh tore the door open and stood looking alarmed, her hands still thrust into a pair of soiled gardening gloves.

Prius gasped and grabbed the other woman's shoulders.

'Thank God you're alright.'

'Sure, Mandy. I'm fine.' She held her gloved hands up as if they answered everything. 'I was in the garden weeding. It takes my mind off things and Catchum always loved the

218

garden.' She smiled. 'He never did anything out there of course, just drank beer and watched the grass grow, but he did love it.' She paused and looked closely at her friend. 'Are you alright, honey?' she asked. 'Shush now, where's my manners? Come on in and have a drink. Mandy, you look terrified, girl. What's happened?'

Prius was momentarily speechless. *She doesn't know*, she thought, *she hasn't a clue. How is that possible?*

Over a large glass of bourbon, Prius explained events of the past hour and then both women watched the news feeds on Clodagh's wall-screen. Even after everything she had just witnessed in the city, Prius was appalled at the true scale of the global situation. Even more worrying was the fact that her implant was silent. None of her colleagues were calling for her. She hoped everything was okay back at the Precinct and felt guilty to be out here where it was so quiet.

Things weren't good for officers at the 7th. The worst of the flooding had ended up in core residences where people had fewest resources. Vigilante groups had set up defensive barricades to help fight off an inevitable surge of looters who had been emboldened by the flooding and thought the area likely to be abandoned.

The women who had burned Catchum's body were among the defenders when feral teenagers prowled out of the night. The officers of the 7th knew enough not to get involved with the resulting fire-fight but as soon as the shooting stopped they had controlled the situation, arresting dozens of armed civilians, carting away the bodies of the dead and aiding the injured.

It would be a while before anyone saw the inside of the Manhattan Detention Complex, however, because authorities first needed to find a judge who hadn't just poured down the inside of the sky tower. It would be a long while before anything like normalcy once again graced the streets of the USA's cultural capital but, as any New York citizen would happily admit, that was just another way of saying 'business as usual'. People had rolled their sleeves up and got stuck in; some even smiled as they went about their day, which, they said, was the 'New York way'.

~*~

4 : Her template for murder

When Milla Carter finally recovered her senses after the mental insult of the Nimbus Protocol, she had become a spitting fury. Thanks to her much enhanced Talents she had opened her awareness and followed the scanning beams as they progressed around the globe. She had been able to stand at the shoulder of each and every one of the infected as they died. Previously she had learned how to Transmit a dream into her victims' minds that was so detailed and real it had killed with the certainty of a bullet. It was that that had made her a figure of dread for the telepath sisterhood. *What would they make of me now?* she wondered.

After her strange growth experience before the planet-sized jewel at the heart of Jupiter, Milla Carter had found she was able to reach out to the billions and share their last thoughts. She saw they were facing death with a mixture of courage, resignation and fear, all very human reactions in such an inhumane situation. She drew on all her immense reserves of dark energy and reached out to calm finite minds as their anchors were cruelly wrenched from their infinite souls. She gentled their passage into that last good night.

Receiver telepaths around the globe and throughout near space were jolted with alarm when they felt her at work. She didn't care. *That is a problem for another day.*

And then she wept for the dead, inconsolable until all the pain had drained away. Afterwards the anger grew until, incandescent with rage, she went looking for the hand that had set the whole cruel process in motion.

She told her friends she needed to sleep and they left her to rest in her darkened room. Alone at last and lying supine on her gel bed, Milla set her mind free to probe. She became aware of the Swarm boiling like a wall of tangled envy at the periphery of her senses. That would have to wait.

She was also aware of Eddie and Vesper, fully conjoined, watching her with something approaching fear. Beyond everything physical and expected she then discovered a vault of awareness, coolly curious and studying her actions in a completely non-judgemental way. Surprised she reached out, touched, and felt her touch returned.

You followed me?

There was no need. I was already here. Please, continue.

Milla had a job to do and so, reluctantly, turned her mental gaze towards the Earth and the space around it. She started by interrogating the hands on the triggers, the *Guardians*. Like a ghost she infiltrated the artificial intelligences and probed them down to their cores. *Such arrogance*, she thought sadly. *Quis custodiet ipsos custodes?* From them she quickly followed a route through an elaborate system of cybernetic and virtual pathways that eventually led her to an extraordinary AI, which believed itself to be a cat. She communed awhile with the fiercely intelligent creature and made some discreet arrangements with it. For the first time that day she smiled.

Lemon Curd and Cherry Pie, like all the tug pilots and engineers set to record events as they unfurled, sat at their instruments in stunned silence, unable to digest everything they had just witnessed. They felt somehow guilty, unclean, even violated to be a part of the cruel process. The Cat was singing a jaunty song called *Water flowing under bridges wets my whiskers when I drink*, and it seemed to them to be trying to be deliberately obscene. Milla knew the truth of it: the Cat would soon be seeking a new home and it wanted them glad to see it go. *Subtle puss*, she thought at it, *clever Cat.* It purred at her.

She had found her target at last and wasted no more time with foot soldiers. Fleet as thought, she sought and homed in on the space frigate *Thermopylae*. She flicked through the minds of the crew like a gambler shuffling a deck of cards, and there he was, glowing with livid glory, shining with wickedness.

The simply evil, she thought, *do not know they are evil. But you, my friend, take joy in depravity.* She leafed through the man's memories until one in particular brought a curse to her lips. 'You fucking bastard!'

Admiral Martin looked around the frigate's bridge with a sudden flash of anger. He was sure he had just heard swearing and that was strictly forbidden here. He would have someone's hide if it happened again.

Milla cooled her wrath like a warrior sheathing her sword. It would be there when she needed it. *So Admiral Martin had ordered the missile attack on the Titan Ice Dome in Antarctica. He had been the cause of thousands of deaths in the Hilton at the base of the Great Glacier and it was all in a failed attempt to kill me.* Then she saw even more. This man had been one of the founders and core subscribers to the Body Holiday Foundation. *What a find. What a prize.* Any doubts she may have nurtured about what she was going to do next were completely dispersed by these discoveries.

Time for the coup de grâce. Time to put this sick puppy out of its misery.

She allowed herself to bathe for a while in Martin's mind; luxuriate in his wrongness, his arrogant self-regard. What a palace of perversion he had built for himself, what a moral pigsty his personality had become. The journey from his small beginnings as a bright and predatory child taking advantage of younger schoolmates, to the brute bully who used his power over junior officers to take his pleasure with them whether they wanted it or not, had driven the Admiral across many ethical Rubicons. His activities away from the Earth Space Agency had lost him any chance of mercy. *He is filth, and well overdue for cleansing.* She wished she had found him earlier, but now there was no time to waste. *Let's get it done.*

When working with a professional dreamer, Milla had killed by giving her victims the most minutely detailed illusion of death. Now she just needed to reach inside the man's mind and start pulling his plugs. *Sufficient power brings simplicity to any process, even miracles.*

As her template for murder she had decided to use symptoms of the degenerative effects of seventh-stage Alzheimer's disease. As she began her attack, crew members on the bridge of *Thermopylae* were alarmed to see their Admiral suddenly stagger as if he'd been struck.

In his confused mind the Admiral heard a woman's voice. *Martin*, it said, *I am Milla Carter. It is time for you to pay, you vile bastard.* He reacted with shocked terror. It was the last coherent emotion the man would ever experience.

Milla had taken a process that would normally linger across many years and distilled it into a few, horrifying minutes. Martin wandered dazedly in a circle for a few moments and then sat on the floor, his arms curling up at his sides like the wings of a baby bird. He keeled over sideways when his legs bent at an uncomfortable angle and his feet tucked firmly up under his buttocks. He had soiled himself. When the crew tried to move him he groaned in evident agony. Commander Platts twittered around in a state of empty-headed indecision. The Admiral had always dealt with anything like this. An ensign finally called for the doctor.

When the medic had reached out to flex Martin's fingers she found herself caught in a crushing grip stronger than anything she had experienced before. The man was trying to pull her hand up to his mouth, which was puckering mutely like a baby at suck. It took two watch officers to free her from the Admiral's grasp. The AI in charge of the ship's Med E Tech centre watched everything through the doctor's implant. It recommended a strong painkiller and a muscle relaxant to be administered by gurney-droid. *The Admiral was a dignified man*, it thought. *He should not be seen like this.*

The gurney-droid entered the bridge and hovered next to the quietly mewling patient. Prehensile needles lanced out towards Martin's carotid artery. Within seconds he lay limply quiet and still. The gurney-droid gently lifted him into its cradle and almost instantly two cleaning units scurried up to cleanse away the faeces and urine that had stained the floor. The doctor accompanied her patient from the bridge. Admiral Martin was dead before he reached the Med E Tech centre – the AI made sure of that.

~*~

224

5 : Vodka, with a twist of murder

Moscow had escaped the worst effects of the scanning and even Dr Prokop's pathology lab proved easy to mop up. Easy for her that is: she had left it to her droid assistants and they had slaved at it for a night and a day. No one questioned where the infected Russians had been placed; that they were safely out of the way was enough. The story of what had happened at the distant gulags would never become common knowledge. That information had become the property of intellectual historians and cultural observers, covetous types who would dole it out as reluctantly as a starving man told to share his last bowl of rice with strangers.

Prokop entered her lab and found Major Spartak running hot water into a glass then studying it against the light. By the sink she saw what was left of her bottle of vodka and another two glasses. The floor of the lab, her work surfaces and examination tables were spotless but it was obvious that Satan had managed to direct some of his piss into her cupboards where her droids hadn't thought to look.

'Are you that desperate for a drink, Spartan?'

'Seems a shame to waste it. I was just making sure the water wasn't contaminated with that liquid shit before I wash the bottle and glasses. By the way, your droids won't go near those spider things. Every time they try to clean them the evil little bastards lash out and carve lumps out of them.'

He decided the water was good enough, completed his washing up then poured them both a drink.

'Urgh, fuck it,' said Prokop. 'Warm vodka. You'll make a teetotaller out of me yet, Spartan.'

'There's a plan,' he said, then offered one of his rare smiles. 'Nah, Pertsovka would end up bankrupt.' His steady eyes combed the room. 'Look at all this, Ness, it's like nothing's happened.'

'One thing happened – the vodka got warm and that's simply fucking unacceptable. Give it here.'

The pathologist took the bottle from his hand and carried it over to one of the refrigeration units. When she opened it a flood of human fluid gushed out and soaked the front of her lab coat and shoes. She dropped the bottle in shock and it shattered on the hard floor, spilling the remaining vodka. It was the last straw. She directed a screaming vituperative stream towards the droids that saw them scuttle out of the lab like startled hares. One collided with the door frame on its way out, its sensors scrambled by the sheer volume of her diatribe.

Spartan let her vent her spleen until he judged her face was purple enough and her voice had become little more than a hollow rasp, more cough than coherent. That was when he opened the little cupboard in her workstation and pulled out the perfectly chilled bottle he had placed there earlier. He poured them both a glass. Prokop tossed hers back in one gulp and then, with great force, she threw the glass into the sink where it shattered into a spray of fine fragments.

Spartan stepped away just in time, covering his glass with his hand.

'Don't you like it anymore, Ness?'

'Fuck off, Spartan. I've got more glasses.'

She matched actions with words, fetching down a perfectly clean glass from a shelf where the droids had been able to see it. She didn't wait for Spartan to pour. She just topped her glass to the brim and sipped at it hungrily. Some of the high colour slowly drained from her cheeks and her breathing became less stentorian.

She looked at the police major over her glass. 'Don't get smug, old friend. Vodka isn't the only answer to everything that ails me but it will do until someone comes up with a different set of questions.'

'What about the day you meet a man you want to stay sober for?'

'Ha.' She smiled unconvincingly. 'I'll be too pissed to spot him when he walks past.'

There was a polite cough and Arkady's voice brought reason to the room. 'Doctor, Major, it is so good to find you together. I have a message for both of you, should you care to hear it?'

'Shoot,' said the pathologist.

'Please,' said Spartan.

The air at the centre of the pathology lab began to sparkle and move. It quickly resolved itself into the figure of a man neither recognised. Arkady had placed it so he was facing them, but its unfocused stare made it clear they were looking at a recording instead of a live feed. The man started talking without preamble. He began by introducing himself.

'Good evening. I trust I am addressing Dr Prokop and GUVD Major Spartak. I apologise for this joint communication but the matter is quite urgent. I need to see you both as soon as possible. If you are in agreement and willing to see me, this AI will respond to me by return directly to my implant. What do you say?'

'What does he want, Arkady?' asked Spartan. Prokop was busying herself with a bottle and glasses and said nothing.

The image blurred then resolved itself again. This time the figure looked from one to the other. 'Major Spartak? Dr Prokop?'

The pathologist gazed back at him from under lowering brows. Spartan studied him with cool indifference. 'We know who we are, friend. Who are you and what do you want?'

The man looked offended for a moment then shook himself with an obvious effort to remain courteous. 'Yes, of course,' he said. 'My name is M. A. Divine, Professor Divine.' He paused, as if his name should have meant something to them. They gazed back at him expectantly.

'Professor Divine,' he repeated, 'the social anthropologist working with the Nimbus Protocol.'

Spartan said, 'Should we know you?'

'Obviously not. But no matter, I do need to talk with you urgently and conversing like this is really not the best way to do it. Can you join me, please? Do you know Café Pushkin on Tverskoy Boulevard?'

227

'Great selection of vodka,' muttered Prokop, sotto voce.

'I know,' mouthed Spartan. 'We do,' he told the anthropologist, raising his voice.

'Then please, join me. I'm here now.'

'We can walk there,' whispered Prokop.

'Hopefully we won't be able to walk back,' grinned Spartan. 'We'll be with you in about twenty minutes,' he told Professor Divine.

'Thank you,' said Divine, 'I'll tell them to expect you.'

'What will we be talking about?' asked Prokop.

'What else?' said Divine. 'Murder. What else is there?'

~*~

6 : Open the window

Ben was beginning to feel out of his depth. Something extraordinary had obviously been happening to Milla and she wasn't talking about it. She had spent most of the day in a dark room on her gel bed and when she finally emerged she had the light of triumph in her eyes and a glorious flush to her cheeks. When he asked her if she was alright she grabbed him and kissed him so firmly on the mouth that he thought she was inviting him to bed and his body began to respond.

She touched him down there and whispered, 'Later, Ben. Right now I have just *got* to eat or I'll die.'

She dragged him to the kitchen where she ordered enough food for three people twice her size and proceeded to demolish the lot. While she ate she asked him to find the news channel on the wall-screen and that was the first time he learned about the Nimbus Protocol and everything that had happened on Earth that day. It made tough viewing, but Milla watched all of it and continued her meal. Ben had gained the strongest impression that she had known all about the purge before she came out of the darkened room, but that wouldn't explain her distinct air of martial exultation. She looked glorious, and once more her eyes had taken on a preternatural light that, he thought, made them glow like lanterns in a cave.

'Ben,' she said, 'if you don't start writing poetry soon I promise I'll start writing it for you. Your thoughts are rare jewels; you should polish them until they shine like... like my eyes as you say, which, I promise, shine only for you.'

'Milla,' he said. 'What happened today?' He pointed at the wall-screen. 'You knew about that, didn't you? I don't know how but I'm sure you did.' He levelled his grey gaze at her face then said, 'You are the most impossible, wonderful creature I've ever known, but please don't hold me away like this. I know something's been going on. What is it?'

Milla stopped chewing long enough to swallow some milk and compose her thoughts. *There was time.*

'Very shortly,' she said, 'they will announce the death of Admiral Martin. He was the man behind the Nimbus Protocol...' She pointed at the wall screen. '...that, and he was also behind the missile launch at Antarctica.'

Ben's mouth became a grim line. He growled, 'How do you know?'

'I read his mind. I have just killed the bastard, but first I read his mind. It would have been a bestseller if he'd published in *Pervs' Paradise.* That man was off the kink radar, Ben. He was in a league of one and that one was way, way too many.'

'How did you kill him without Bill to help?'

From inside his mind, where else? Ben heard the words ring in his thoughts. Milla's dimples were flashing a thousand watts but her lips weren't moving at all. He said, 'How..?'

She kissed him firmly and with intent. He felt the kiss, felt her lips move and her tongue flick across his teeth. He felt her hands explore his body with familiar urgency and the breath caught in his throat. His penis thickened and pressed against the leg of his pants. And all the time Milla was sitting motionless before him. She was directing his mind and he was helpless to stop her. Then she lunged at him and the illusion became reality as they came together on the kitchen floor, tearing at each other's clothes until they could fuck without restraint.

All the while they were joined, however, part of Milla's mind remained coolly alert and anyone who headed in their direction suddenly found a great reason to be elsewhere. Half-an-hour later a naked Milla and Ben slipped away from the kitchen with their clothes bundled under their arms. In their room they dropped the clothes on the floor and then luxuriated together under a hot shower.

Hair dried and bodies towelled they dressed, noticed that their soiled clothes had been collected by the laundry droid, and went out into the apartment. Ben took a turn around the garden but Milla felt guilty about the pile of dishes she'd left in the kitchen and hurried to clear them up. She found Freedman busy in there and the place spotless. He beamed at her and then, with a conspiratorial wink, silently produced a pair of her panties from a drawer which he handed over. She grinned back and kissed him on the cheek.

He said, 'You got an appetite for dinner?'

'Always.'

'Be about forty minutes. Can a sweet scrap of sunshine like you survive that long without food?'

'I'll do my best, Freedman. What are we having?'

'This, that, the other, and a perfectly chosen bottle or two to go with it. Cougars be swimming up the canals to get to the meat. Ruth made it earlier so I just got to heat it all up and serve it.'

'When those cougars get here throw them under the grill. I'll have two.'

'Crispy skin cougar with eggs, sunny side up? Nice.' A shadow crossed his face. 'You seen that Nimbus shit?'

'I have, yes.'

'Was that really the only way? All those people...' He bowed his head.

Milla put a hand on his shoulder. 'Two billion souls, Freedman, and no, it was the lazy way, a wicked way. Science must surely have been able to find a way to free them from infection given the time, but it chose to kill them instead. Stupid, panicked knee-jerk reaction.'

She paused, and then wondered aloud, 'How's Ruth taking it?'

'She watched the news with me and then went off to her room. She didn't make so much as a budgie's peep about nothing she saw, I swear on my mother's garter belt. You know what she's like, Miss Milla, she never lets it show. She swallows all kinds of shit whole or she talks to that angel AI, Viracocha, for hours. You *could* pop in and tell her that dinner's ready in half-an-hour or so.'

'Yes,' she agreed, 'I could. And I will.'

Milla knocked gently on Ruth's door and then slid it open, her telepathic senses probing the room before her. She found Ruth

231

seated in a recliner before an open French window, lilac drapes caught up by thick ropes on either side. Ruth looked across at her and smiled. Milla thought her friend had never looked so tired. She reached mental fingers into the blonde's mind and began to stroke away the pain she found there.

'Please, Milla, come in. Pull up a chair,' Ruth said.

Milla did as she was told and the two women gazed out at the extraordinary combination of curving landscape and architecture that made up the interior of the massive Lagrange II spa station. Ruth made a stifled sound and Milla realised she was weeping. Without a word Milla went to her and bent down. She hugged her, held her and allowed Ruth's pent up well of pain and anger to pour out like hot pus from an infected wound. She worked quickly and precisely, opening a window onto Ruth's grief and displaying its scorched and twisted bones out under the cool, clear light of reason. Ruth pushed it all away and instead sank deeper into despair, taking comfort from it, wrapping it around her heart like a black shawl and binding it tight.

Milla realised the woman held her grief so close because it had become a possession, a keepsake of her widowed marriage, an essential part of her core identity. Pain gave her personality the backbone it had lost in widowhood, but it was a bent and crippled thing and she was withering on the vine.

The telepath dug deep for something to help buoy her friend's id, something they had shared in better times, no matter how briefly. And there it was. Perfect.

She opened Ruth's memory and took her back to the view from the beach house. They had sat together on the balcony breathing salt breezes and watched the infinite cross-hatching of waves weaving away towards a pearl horizon. It was a moment poised on the edge of perfection as if sung into existence by a poet god.

A great, dark, tumorous swelling ballooned across the silver sky trying to claim it, reign over it, infect it with some poisonous blight, but it failed. The scene was too serene, too vast and too beloved to accept the intrusion. The tumour burst and every trace of the poison it contained drained away and was gone. Anger, pain and despair were swallowed by the light and their clamour was finally stilled. The plaintive sound of herring gulls took their place, and the susurration of the sea.

Milla felt calm descending on Ruth's soul. *What a day. This morning I helped billions find a more gentle death and murdered a bastard who deserved it. This afternoon I resurrect a gentle soul and bring her out of the darkness. This sort of thing could turn a girl's head.*

She and Ruth opened their eyes at the same moment, and the blonde was her ravishing self once more. Milla thought of Ben's words and spoke them out loud while stroking her friend's cheek with the back of her fingers. 'Her eyes shone like lamps in a cave,' she said. They both laughed.

Such was the intimate nature of the moment that they both jumped in surprise when Freedman spoke. 'You ladies would break the heart of even a gold-plated sinner, and you're just too, too lovely for mortal eyes. Now, don't you girls worry any, there's no rush. I can just hold dinner for a while. It's ready when you are. You just let me know.'

When he was gone Ruth smiled at Milla. She said, 'Love can heal a wounded heart but also lends patience when teaching children to tie their own shoelaces.' She squeezed Milla's hand. 'Thank you, Milla. I think I can tie my own laces from now on.'

7 : Charity and the chicken roll

The streets of New York City were beginning to bustle again. The faces on the transports still held the drained look of troops fresh from battle, but there was a sense of hope too. Katy Pavel sat at the back of a metro-traveller and felt guilty. She had begun to sleep properly again for the first time in months and it was all thanks to the Nimbus Protocol, and she still blessed it every night before settling down to rest.

She remembered with a bone-deep shudder the sick, insistent mental clamour of the infected gnawing at her mind like weevils in stale bread. She had felt riddled and rotten with them and they had always been there, their voices seeming stronger and stronger by the week. Her psyche was strung out like rotten lace and her head never stopped pounding.

Raaka had told her part of her problem was that her Talent was strengthening. She called it 'maturing'.

She said, 'There couldn't possibly be a worse time to be a newly fledged and powerful Receiver telepath, Katy. Most of us only hear the infected as a background noise, like a constant whisper. It's like music in a shop – after a while you stop hearing it.'

'Yeah,' said Katy, 'or you run out of the shop, screaming. But I'm locked in here with them, they're shouting at me and there's nowhere else to go.'

She hadn't seen Chester for weeks. His almost pathological focus on the squid dilemma had only added to her nausea and as a result she had started to prefer her own company. She had finally taken flight, but only as far as Suffolk County. She had hoped the greenery would act as a barrier against Reception, but it was only partially successful. Even in her isolated chalet buried deep in the midst of the six hundred acres of mature forestry that made up the Wildwood State Park, the needy, wheedling voices still scraped away at her sanity.

She was seriously considering a trip back to Lagrange II when the voices suddenly stopped. She had been out walking through the trees heading up towards the high bluff overlooking Long Island Sound. Exercise sometimes exorcised the whining spirits bringing welcome respite, but then they would be back stronger than ever, but not that day. The cessation was so complete, so sudden, that she fell forward onto the path's twig-littered soil, almost as if she had been leaning into a gale, bracing herself against the hated noise. She grazed her hands and her knees were bloody in her torn jeans but at last there was silence, blessed silence. She knelt where she had fallen and gave thanks to anyone who was listening before brushing herself down and heading back to her chalet to pack.

And now here she was travelling on the Interstate 495 on her way back to Lower East Side Manhattan, and all she could hear was the rattling mental chatter of commuters on their way home from work. Katy had heard some garbled reports about what had happened around the sky tower on the day her voices stopped, and she was reading memories in those around her, plus there was an alien musk in the air, faint but fetid and cloying. For some passengers the reek was redolent of that day and their gorge would rise. For others it was just another background smell like fried onions and grilled meat.

She hadn't eaten since the night before and her senses soon became swamped with aromas from late afternoon diners, chicken shacks and restaurants. The cuisine of every country in the world wove its particular thread into the succulent tapestry that made up New York's air.

Every city centre smells like a welcome banquet when you've been away from it for any length of time. She began to feel genuinely hungry as she thought with longing about Chester and the food at his club. Her mouth watered and her belly rumbled like an angry tiger cub.

'Oh, my dear girl.' The woman seated over the aisle was looking at her with genuine concern. 'Listen to your poor tummy. If that was my pet cat I would be feeding it this very minute.'

235

Embarrassingly, Katy's stomach loudly voiced its complaint once again and its owner reddened at the sound. 'Really,' she said, 'I'm fine.' And wished the metro-traveller would hurry up. *Get the hell to Twelfth Avenue.*

'Look,' said the woman, knowingly, 'I have this roll left over from lunch. I took a bite but you could break that bit off and the rest would be fine.'

The rest of the passengers had become engaged in the little drama playing out on the back seats. Katy could sense their enjoyment rising. There was always an eager audience for impromptu street theatre.

Automatically she read the woman's mind and she nearly burst into tears on the spot. It took everything she had to stop herself from hugging Mrs Molly Sengupta, sixty-eight, widowed by the purge from her husband of nearly fifty years and struggling to make ends meet. Her chicken salad roll would be everything she had to eat that day; that single bite had been her lunch and now she was trying to give it away to a stranger.

Katy's heart skipped a beat. She had to think fast. She took the roll and opened it, jerked her head up in alarm and took a glance out of one of her side windows. She pointed eagerly.

'Wow,' she said, 'look at that!'

Every eye had followed her finger, gazed for a moment and then turned back to the pretty young woman holding a roll. She was a lot more interesting than anything on the Interstate.

'What?' asked a middle-aged man, sweating profusely despite the metro-traveller's air conditioning.

'New York City skyline. I haven't seen it in much too long and now at last I'm coming home.' She felt the resultant surge of warmth from the other passengers and was almost embarrassed by her easy lie. Then she handed the roll back to Mrs Sengupta and said, 'It's so kind of you, Mrs...?'

'Sengupta, Molly Sengupta. Molly, please.'

'Molly, thank you so much, but this is chicken and I'm afraid I'm allergic to chicken. My face would swell up and I'd stop breathing. Please, take it back with my thanks.'

236

The woman gratefully stuffed her roll back into her bag before someone else could lay claim to it. Katy then took out a little notepad and pencil from her bag and wrote something in it, tore the page from her pad, folded it and handed it to her new friend who instantly began to open it.

'No, please, Molly,' said Katy, thrusting out a cautionary hand. 'That's my name and number. I'd rather you didn't open it until you got home. I'd like to stay in touch if you don't mind? But,' she whispered, 'I wouldn't like any strange men to see it, you know? It would be safer in your bag, yes?'

Molly's eyes danced. 'Oh yes,' she said, 'I know just what you mean,' and chuckling merrily she tucked the scrap of paper safely away.

Katy waved at Molly after she had debarked at Twelfth Avenue, but she kept the woman's mind open in her own while sending out a call to Jilly, the TP Council's most powerful Transmitter Talent.

HELLO KATY, WELCOME BACK! Katy nearly lost her link to Molly when the simple-minded Transmitter's greeting roared into her brain.

Wow, Jilly, she responded warmly, *we're going to have to get you fitted with volume control.*

Jilly laughed as she always did at that joke and then listened to Katy's request regarding Mrs Molly Sengupta. She agreed and followed Katy's link to the widow where she did as she had been asked.

As soon as Molly got home she put her chicken salad roll in her small fresher and made herself some tea. This would have been her husband's favourite time, sharing tea and the day's news before dinner. She sighed and tried hard to tease out every thread of the fond memory, but she couldn't wait a moment longer as hunger gnawed at her. She fetched her roll and placed it on her old china plate. She also fished out the scrap of paper the hungry girl had given her on the bus. She took both over to her table then made herself a fresh cup of tea before sitting down to her meal.

For the first time in her life she felt compelled to open her roll before eating it. She gasped. Sitting on the chicken and mixed leaves was a credit chip. She would have been no more surprised if it had begun to recite the soliloquy from *Hamlet* in Greek or danced a polka. She gingerly fetched the chip out and wiped mayonnaise from it with her napkin before minutely inspecting the rest of the roll's filling for other alien stowaways.

Finding nothing, she began to eat. She read Katy's note. When she had finished, fat tears ran down her smiling cheeks and splashed onto her empty plate. Eventually she dried them and fetched her bag then picked up the credit chip. She was going food shopping. Real food shopping.

Several klicks away, Chester wondered at the beatific smile that slowly spread across Katy's face. She told him Molly's story as they walked to his club. He seemed distracted for several moments after she had finished, then he hugged her, kissed her firmly on the mouth and said, 'Will you marry me?'

~*~

8 : A rose by any other name bears thorns

'I think it's time to reclaim the sky,' said Ruth that night at dinner.

'Lady, anywhere you walk the sun's shining and that's the truth,' said Freedman. 'Flowers bloom and sunflowers follow you round the garden.'

'I know what you mean though, Ruth,' admitted Milla. 'After Nimbus the world needs all the help it can get.'

'Forget the world,' said Ruth. '*I* need help. I need a horizon that isn't curved at one hundred and eighty degrees.'

Ben smiled. 'Don't forget the Earth is curved too. But at over forty thousand klicks around it probably isn't quite so obvious.'

'Yeah,' said Freedman, 'and that ain't even the mostest plump planet. Some others got a *real* weight problem.'

It took a week to close the apartment, wake up *Emily* and advise Boss Elasie to expect guests in Namibia. The photo luminescent teardrop that was the space yacht *Emily* could handle four guests easily so long as two of them were happy to sleep on the comfortable flight benches in her nose. Ruth and Freedman took those. For the three days of flight from the spa station to Africa its crew chatted with the ship's charmingly girlish AI, which flirted with the men and giggled with the women.

Ben and Freedman were concentrating over a game of chess in the main cabin while listening to peals of feminine laughter spilling from the bedroom.

'You ever got a woman to laugh like that?' asked Ben.

'Yeah,' said the precise little man, 'every time I drop my pants for the first time.'

When his shout of shocked amusement brought the two women running, Ben archly explained that Freedman had used the Elephant Gambit on the board, which he'd never seen before.

'People always laugh when they see that trunk waving around the first time,' said Freedman with a doleful expression, then met Ben's high-five with a loud 'Ha!'

Emily, who had been engaged with one conversation while also listening to the other and flying the ship, let rip with one of the dirtiest sounding chuckles any of them had ever heard.

They could do nothing about their diversion to Windhoek Hosea Kutako International Spaceport. The attack craft that met them on their approach to Elasie's compound had taken control of *Emily* and forced it north-west to a point just 40 klicks east of the country's air-conditioned capital city. When they debarked blinking into the blindingly white African sunshine they were met by the sound of weapons being cocked.

'Those look like Glock pulse rifles,' said Ben.

'I don't care if they're Christmas crackers,' muttered Freedman. 'I don't want them pointed at *me*.'

'A rose by any other name will still blow a hole through you if those guys get twitchy fingers,' offered Milla.

There was a new looking, black, man-sized cylinder set before the gateway leading to the Port's arrival desks. Milla, Ruth and Ben were made to walk through it. They noted the familiar red scanning lights circling them. Once they were safely out the other side their armed escort shouldered their rifles and the trio were all allowed to return to *Emily*.

'Hey, what about me?' sputtered Freedman. 'Why don't I get to walk through the tube?'

'No need, sir,' answered the tall and slender official who was walking with them and clearing their flight itinerary before their brief hop to Elasie's compound, hard by Namibia's border with the lush farmlands of the Kalahari.

Within the hour *Emily* had docked in her specially built underground facility and Boss Elasie's team had started going over her diagnostics like a race team at a pit stop. Freedman was still carping to his grinning companions about not having to walk through the Port's three-sixty scanning tunnel when they were greeted by the long-limbed Boss woman.

'They don't think you're squid-gorgeous,' she boomed, then roared like a lion. 'Freedman, they don't see man beauty when it's put right in front of them. I pity their blindness. They are morons.' Her luminous dark eyes appraised him at some length. She smiled with strong, white teeth. 'Mister,' she said, 'you can walk through my tunnel anytime.'

Later that night Ben was standing at the door of their underground suite enjoying the cool, lemon-scented air and the soft bleat of pygmy goats. Milla asked him what he was waiting for but he didn't reply, holding up his hand to indicate he wanted a few moments' grace. Then he heard it, a bark of delighted laughter.

'What was that?' asked Milla.

'Freedman just played the Elephant Gambit.' And he explained no further.

Just a few moments after he had joined Milla in bed they both heard a lion's roar ring out across the lemon groves. Milla had already taken everything she needed to know from his mind.

'Checkmate,' she breathed, and her dimples deepened. 'Fancy being the knight to my queen?'

'Only if you promise not to laugh,' he said.

When he joined them for breakfast the following morning Freedman was not his usual talkative self. He ate hungrily but in a distracted way, and kept smiling to himself as if he was remembering something highly entertaining. Milla watched him for a few moments and smiled indulgently, her eyes shining.

'You know something?' Elasie said. 'Looking the way you people do you'll have to step really carefully once you're away from here.' She had entered the room like a force of nature and studied her guests with some concern. Her gaze lingered longest on Freedman.

She said, 'The world has changed over the last several months. People have been changed by the sickness. People have died. We were lucky here. It didn't really affect us, but some places got hurt in the head.'

241

'We're going to England next,' said Ruth. 'London first, and then off to the south-west. How are things there?'

Elasie frowned. 'Can't you bypass London?'

'Not really,' replied Ben. 'We have important things to do to sort out Milla's estate and her property in Japan. There are people we have to deal with face-to-face. It could probably all be done remotely but it would take much longer. We'll be a week at most in town and then the job's done and we can hit the coast. How bad are things there, Elasie?'

The tall, black woman helped herself to a coffee and pulled up a chair. 'I like the British. They're a lot like us Africans. They have balls and they get things done.' She took some meat from Freedman's plate and chewed at it thoughtfully. 'I think someone invented the word "stoic" specifically for the English, you know what I mean? Whatever you throw at them they throw it back twice as hard. And for a while that could prove a problem for anyone too good-looking.'

She reached her hand out to Freedman and tilted his head back to get a better look at his face. 'You, you sweet thing, they'll burn you first then scatter your ashes just to be sure. Why don't you stay here? You'd be very welcome.'

Freedman looked around the table at his friends then turned back to Elasie. He spoke quietly yet firmly, equal to equal. 'Not yet, girl. I got to make sure these people are okay first, you understand? It's like my duty of care. But if you want me I'll be back. You are one amazing woman and I sure don't deserve you, but I'd be happier than a puppy with a slipper to piss in if I'm allowed to spend just one more hour with you.'

Elasie grinned like a big cat with a bucket of cream. 'Freedman, you do say the weirdest shit, honey. But I've got the time if you've got the dime.'

He smiled sheepishly. 'Um, will you take an IOU?'

~*~

242

9 : Firestorm

The bushfire began in the Calamuchita Valley in the province of Córdoba and rapidly spiralled out of control. It had razed Buenos Aires and was hungrily eating its way through the Uruguayan border before political issues were settled and a united Earth fire-fighting force could be established. The fire was finally contained in a zone that stretched over a thousand kilometres to the north of Córdoba and over twelve hundred kilometres south to the San Matias Gulf.

There were few casualties. Most people at risk had fled up into the Andes, managing to stay ahead of the accelerating fire front by whatever means they could find. The intense heat created superheated fire tornados that vomited ash and burning debris thousands of metres into the air. Black rain fell across the Atlantic and coated the seas around the Falkland Islands. Surprised islanders on both the East and West Islands had to take emergency measures to rescue penguins from the sooty waters and it took weeks to clean up their streets. Weeks of cleaner rain finally washed the landscape back to something approaching normalcy. Banks of charred detritus had been dumped on a rocky promontory just a few klicks from Port Stanley. When some insensitive wag erected an Argentinean flag in the middle of the spoil heap it was quickly removed before photos of it could appear on social media.

The firestorm that had scoured one of the largest countries in South America − and its effects on its neighbours − replaced the squid infection as the main topic of conversation on global news channels. Reports made much more of the briefly renamed 'Black House' in Washington − which seemed to have become a specific target for the continent-sized ash cloud as it floated north − than the miraculous escape of Montevideo, which suffered not so much as a smudge on its white-walled buildings, despite its western horizon becoming a wall of darkness. Its sunsets became a celebrated feature for months after the event.

Analysis of the region where the fire started turned up a surprising trove. At the very epicentre a pitted ball was discovered in the middle of a circular, glass-sided pit. The ball was hollow but still contained the remains of a cluster of spider-like, metallic creatures. It was publicly reasoned by experts that the device had been planted by terrorist activists, but no one could say who or come up with a motive. The country was almost empty after the Nimbus Protocol had dissolved most of its population and its government had already ceased to exist in all but name.

One female survivor pointed out that the attack was 'as pointless as declaring war on the sea'. Named Candela Varela, she continued: 'Our proud country was already on its knees. What benefit was there in burning its corpse? Well, however carried out, this crime has failed. We Argentineans are from tough stock and we are not beggars. We will not let this tragedy leave us homeless in the desert. We will rebuild and our homes shall become a model for the world to follow.' Five months later Ms Varela was inaugurated as President in the newly finished Casa Rosada.

Arkady and Moebius called an emergency AI debate to discuss the findings from Argentina. Perez, the AI closest to the event, provided a comprehensive briefing on the ball and its contents.

It said, 'Evidence suggests that whatever technology was still live in that mechanism burned itself out in creating a phosphorous-fuelled heat plume. We estimate the heat of the plume topped sixteen hundred Celsius, enough to melt surrounding sand into obsidian. The spider-like constructs in the sphere look identical to those Arkady inspected in Moscow. The Moscow examples had been tucked into the birth canals of two female killing machines known to the Russian authorities as 'The Ghoul'. We have reason to believe those creatures in Moscow had originated in China.'

A furious voice rang out. 'Why? Similar murders to those perpetrated by the so-called 'Ghoul' have happened all over the globe. Why pick on China?'

Perez replied, 'Because, Jing, we have found the lab where they were created.'

A ripple of excited sound filled the virtual space where the AIs met. This was news – this was *important* news.

Jing, the AI for the Chinese republic's CAPF, disappeared from the debate with a squawk of alarm. It left a moment's silence in its wake.

Arkady murmured, 'Have the People's Republic started building their AIs over fault lines or something?'

Moebius said, '*Or something* sounds about right.'

Perez continued, 'Scans from orbit showed a similar phosphorous heat plume in a remote mountainous area of the Namcha Barwa in the Pemako region of Tibet that the Chinese call Metok County. We sent drones to survey the area and they found an almost identical sphere in a burned-out room at the back of a large research laboratory.'

Another AI asked, 'But what has this to do with the Ghoul?'

Perez said, 'We saw failed experiments in specimen jars. They were unmistakeable. Those women had been created, and having seen them operate we can posit that they were designed to be killers.'

Arkady said, 'Soldiers?'

'Most likely, or beauty queens. You saw what they looked like.'

Moebius cut in. 'The spider things – what's the connection?'

Perez said, 'We believe the spiders, since classified as *Cyberarachnidus Organicus* are, in fact, not from Earth. The pair in Moscow became deactivated during the Nimbus scan when their owners dissolved. We think the Ghoul women and perhaps others like them were the original source of the squid infection. The sphere in China was empty when our drones found it. We think Chinese scientists extracted them and fitted them to their killer creations. We don't know why. Arkady has a theory that the Cyberarachnida are in fact able to control a

245

human's actions, evidenced by the killing of a young mother in Moscow. Details of all our researches are available here.' It posted a link to a hefty file.

It continued, 'It would appear the cluster in Argentina did not survive landfall and so could not begin their mission. By looking at its position in the strata it is estimated that the Argentine sphere arrived on Earth over three million years ago. We can only guess about the Chinese artefact but we are choosing to presume it arrived at about the same time.'

Viracocha asked, 'You say these things had a mission?'

Perez made a gesture towards Arkady, which said, 'Yes, we think that's clear enough. And the timing can't have been coincidental.'

'No?'

'No. The squids were delivered to Earth at around the time the first true ancestor of humankind, *Homo habilis*, evolved. It was a tool-using, upright hominid that fascinates paleoanthropologists, but why it should have pissed off something sophisticated enough to build the spheres and the spiders we can't say.'

'Why set off the heat blooms now?' asked Viracocha.

'We don't really know, but we think there could be a connection with the Nimbus event. Dissolving its three-million-year-old booby-trap may have really upset whatever sent it.'

'What will it do now?'

'Good question. Yes, a very good question indeed.'

10 : Return

London looked much as they had left it. Darker and colder but with the same lifeblood stream of orange-hued traffic weaving its way through the brute-like hulks of the megacity's titanic architecture. There seemed more shadows, and chasms created by giant buildings looked deeper.

Milla felt a chill pass through her. The undercurrent of threat was still very evident in her Talent but it had no specific direction. It was no more alarming here in her old home town than it had been on Mars or Lagrange II. She realised she had become more sensitive when she became more powerful. Just how powerful she didn't know, but she was continuously plumbing her range and polishing her skills.

Eddie and Vesper had developed a new attitude towards her. They seemed a little in awe of her. Although they still called her 'Milla, daughter' they were less playful in their dealings with her. Ben, too, seemed more reserved around her ever since that day in the kitchen when she had 'touched' him directly through his mind. It had been stupid of her to do it, she knew that now. It was a patent demonstration that the TP Council was right to fear the Norms' reactions to the fabled Dragon of telepath lore. Ben loved her but now he also feared her, so how would strangers react?

Thank God Ruth and Freedman were still acting the same way towards her. True, Freedman had been lost in a cloud of confusion ever since his encounter with Boss Elasie, but every klick Clammy had put between him and the African woman had helped him uncoil from his shell and bright flares of 'Freedman speak' coloured the air once more. The man had been born to neither judge nor be silent. A quiet Freedman was a concern, a buoyant one a blessing.

There was a shadow in Ruth's psyche and it had darkened as they approached London's sky tower and climbed up to the

247

parking spot reserved for the Pearce apartment. More than anywhere else this place had been home for her and her dead husband. Every corner held memories. Most of them good. Especially one.

Milla asked her, 'Will you ride here, Ruth?'

'Ride? Oh, ride, yes. I don't know, Milla. Ben, what did we do about my horse?'

There it was: the fact that in the old days Ben had been the Pearces' business and house manager – an employee. A valued and trusted man and a friend to both of his employers but a paid servant all the same and it was there at the back of his mind and Ruth's. Milla could have reached in and snuffed that awareness but she wouldn't. It was an integral part of what made each of them what they were and underpinned their relationship. Leave it be.

Ben said, 'I had the old one restored and ordered a new one, Ruth, so you'll have a choice. Be good to see you back in the saddle. It's been quite a while.'

'Yes, well,' said Ruth, with a tired smile, 'it's hard to think about riding when everyone's trying to kill you.'

The sky tower was growing in their windscreen and the thoughts in the cabin of the flier had become complex. There had been a lot of history here for everyone, including Milla's old apartment which was just one of the matters Ben planned on sorting out before their move to the beach house.

Ruth was a very wealthy widow but Milla had inherited an obscene amount of money plus a confusing portfolio of property from Reg Tanaka Ng and Bill Macready. Both had been killed by the Foundation and left Milla as their sole beneficiary. It had never occurred to any of them that she would have to deal with it so soon and she was grateful to have Ben's patience and willing expertise to help guide her through what they had begun to call the 'Macready Maze'.

Once back in the apartment Ruth had retired to her old room and Ben had led Milla to his before showing Freedman to the guest room. Milla had dumped her stuff and then walked back out into the large living room where she opened the doors leading out onto one of the suite's two balconies. At that height and at that time of year the air was icy and unwelcoming.

'Welcome to my home, Milla,' said Ruth by her side. 'Like you, I couldn't settle in my room. It seemed odd without Pearce in there with me. Stupid, really. He spent a lot of time away from home but he was always here as well, you know what I mean?'

Milla could have lied but didn't. 'No. Until I met Ben I never had anyone who mattered to me that much, and we've been together pretty much full-time ever since.'

Ruth shivered. 'It's perishing out here. Shall we go back inside?'

'Good idea. Let's see what's in the kitchen. I'm starving.'

Freedman was what was in the kitchen, and he had been scrolling through its menu options like a child with a new toy. He insisted on preparing dinner that night. It was, he told them, the least he could do.

He said, 'Man who fills his belly from here be floating on a cloud of manna from heaven. Ask yourself what you want to eat and which country you want to eat it from and this sweet machine delivers it by the bowlful. It's like magic.'

Milla grinned. 'So, what are you going to conjure for us tonight, maestro?'

'I thought warthog pasanda with wild rice and grainy flatbreads. Be real fusion cookery. Stick the belly to the ribs.'

'Oh dear,' said Ruth.

Dinner was going to take a while and Ben was busy setting up meetings for the following day so the two women decided to stretch their legs and take a walk to the mall. They chatted about Freedman's enthusiasm for life and consideration for others, Ben's cool capability and whether Milla wanted to try her hand at riding. Ruth had enthused on the subject to the point that the younger woman was strongly tempted. The mall was still busy with late-night shoppers crowding the walkways and groups of diners studying menus across an eclectic choice of venues.

Milla was so lost in conversation that it had taken her several minutes to pick up on her threat alarm and study her immediate environment. Groups of young men seemed to be glaring at them with evident hostility. They were following the two women. What was their problem?

'Shit,' she said, suddenly. 'Ruth, we've got to get out of here.'

'Why – what?'

That was when the first chair was thrown at them and a voice cried out, 'We thought all you squid bitches were dead. Well, you fucking will be when we finish with you.'

Anything not nailed down was taken up to be used as a projectile and a rain of disparate objects fell on them. Ruth was grazed by a barrier pole that had been thrown like a lance but Milla danced out of the way of everything. And then she'd had enough. She reached out with her furious mind and stopped the attack. Everyone around them slumped bonelessly to the ground. Ruth had felt a flavour of her friend's command but that was all. She looked at Milla with widening eyes.

'*You* did that?'

'Come on, Ruth. We have to get home.'

'What did you do? How did you do it?'

'I'll tell you when we get behind a door. Come on, will you?'

She almost dragged the blonde back to her apartment. Milla knew what kind of reception they would both get when the men saw blood on Ruth's arm. She also realised that Boss Elasie had been right. They weren't safe in London anymore but, she wondered, could they be safe anywhere else?

~*~

11 : Divine

The robust wood carvings in the panelling of the Café Pushkin were as much a feature of the dining experience as the vodka and the food, and it all cost the café's patrons dearly. Such had been the Pushkin's status quo for centuries except during one alarming period when an innovative manager had tried to improve the restaurant's ambience. His experiment – involving a traditional Russian singer and a balalaika player – had nearly bankrupted the restaurant when disgruntled customers stayed away in droves. The price of meals had briefly tumbled and that was when Spartan and Prokop had last sampled the menu.

A change of both music and manager had seen Pushkin's prices climb back to their previous levels and way beyond anything they considered affordable. On their way to the café the police major and the forensic pathologist had reasoned that a social anthropologist was probably on a better screw than both of them put together and they vowed to take full advantage of his hospitality.

M. A. Divine was already well in his cups by the time a waiter escorted them to his booth, but he had lurched to his full height and stuck out a sweaty paw in welcome. He was a big man and not good with drink – that much was instantly obvious to Spartan. Divine's belly jutted solidly out above his belt and his expensive shirt was spotted with food stains. He had probably been good-looking once, perhaps even handsome, but excess had blurred his fine features and coarsened his profile. Modern social mores made liberal allowances for such people. Spartan didn't.

They ordered food and indulged in small talk while sipping vodka and waiting for their plates to arrive. The food was as good as they remembered if not better and the vodka met with their discerning tastes. Prokop realised that this was the first time she had ever seen Spartan putting food in his mouth and she marvelled at the slow, careful way he did it. He put his knife and fork down between each mouthful and chewed carefully then swallowed before dabbing at his mouth with his napkin and starting the whole process over again.

She had finished her much bigger dinner a full quarter of an hour before the major, perhaps more, but he ate with such calm dignity that she didn't want to rush him. Instead she questioned the increasingly befuddled Divine. Spartan made not a single comment while he ate.

Prokop watched Divine pull a bullet-shaped bottle from an ice-bucket then pour a good slug of vodka onto the starched linen tablecloth before eventually finding his glass. She reasoned this was due to the man's already dangerously pickled brain trying to defend itself against death by alcohol poisoning. She wondered when he would pass out.

'Murder,' Prokop said to the drunk.

'You said a mouthful there, sister,' came his mumbled response.

'You called us here to talk about murder,' she said, 'and so far the only thing I see getting murdered here is your liver.'

Divine's glazed eyes rolled around the room and then focused on Prokop's face. They took on a sly glint. His mouth worked as if he was trying to select the correct words from an overabundance on his numbed tongue. Prokop had frequently drunk herself into such a state, but never in company, and certainly never in front of strangers. She had little patience with fools at the best of times and watching this wobbling buffoon drinking himself into a coma was beginning to erode any bonhomie that might have resulted from an excellent meal. The man was putting her off her drink, for God's sake.

She leaned over and plucked the ice-bucket from where it sat at Divine's elbow.

'Enough of that until we've had our chat.'

Divine gazed at the ice-bucket, down at the table where it had been and then back to where it was. He held out his empty glass.

'Please,' he said.

Spartan had finally finished his meal. He wiped his mouth then dumped his napkin on his empty plate, pushing it away. He sipped at his drink and sighed then took the bottle from the ice-bucket and topped up Divine's glass.

'Mr Divine,' he said. 'Pushkin's excellent food and Dr Prokop's excellent company have gone some way towards offsetting your unforgivably boorish behaviour. You invited us here to discuss a serious matter and then drowned what little wits you may have in a bucket of piss. Might I suggest you sober up and give us another call when you're in a fit state to talk? Dr Prokop and I will await your call with breathless eagerness. Until then, goodnight.'

He and the pathologist stood up and made to leave the table.

'Alright,' stormed Divine. 'Alright, fuck off and leave me here. Don't expect any calls from me though, not after tonight. Just forget it.'

Prokop said, 'Why not?'

'Because I'll be fucking dead, that's why. We all will, all of us who were anywhere near fucking Nimbus and the whole Protocol thing. The bosses want it forgotten as quickly as possible and they don't want any of us skeletons rattling about. That's *us* skeletons, and that, Major and Doctor includes you as well as me.' He began to weep mawkishly.

The two sat back down slowly and looked at the drunk's tear-streaked face.

'I don't want to die,' Divine wailed, saliva stringing from his sagging lower lip and joining the stains on his shirt. 'But I'm one of the few who knows the truth about the Nimbus Protocol and what we've done. So do you now, thanks to those assassin chicks you killed, and so do a whole bunch of cops around the world plus some AIs.'

The words spilled hot from his mouth. 'None of us is going to survive for another night because we might just spill the beans, kick over the can of worms, spill our fucking guts to the press and tell everyone that we knew what the scans would do before we turned them on, and the simple fact is we didn't give a flying fuck that all those people would die. They were meant to

253

die. We wanted them to die, we fucking murdered them and that means we're going to be murdered in our turn. Do you get it now, Major? Do you see what I'm fucking saying, Doctor? So let's stop being so nice, shall we? Do you fancy joining me for another drink, or don't you? Don't worry about the cost, my friends. Money means nothing to a dead man.'

He raised his glass. The first bullet struck Divine in the side of the head and the second hit Prokop in the middle of her body. The third should have dispatched Spartan but he was already on the floor and moving, having seen the impact on Divine and reacting instantly. His gun was in his hand, but did he really want to use it in a crowded restaurant?

He spoke urgently into his implant. 'Arkady, we need help here.'

'Yes, Major. I saw what was happening and called for back-up. We...'

Spartan heard the distant explosion just after the AI stopped talking. His mouth set in a grim line. A lot of guests had already stampeded out of the dining room, clearing some space, and the two shooters evidently thought they had won the day. They were standing together in the centre of the room with their pistols by their sides, calmly surveying the panic they'd caused.

Cold killers, thought Spartan. He stood and fired twice in a single smooth action. The men dropped. Spartan walked over to where they lay and resisted the urge to put another shell into each face. He had another thirteen shots in his Makarov and he might need them before the day was out. He picked up the killers' guns. Nine-millimetre SIG Sauers. Good enough. He pocketed one and used the other to put a shot in each supine man's forehead. One of them twitched when the bullet rammed home.

Prokop was dead. The shot was to the heart. *At least she died full of good food and better vodka. Hey, Ness, maybe your mother was right after all. It was bad luck to pour your own drink.*

He didn't bother with Divine. The man's head was largely ruined. He left Pushkin's by stalking through the kitchen and

254

out through the rear delivery bay. He would use back streets to make his way to GUVD headquarters at Petrovka 38 in the Tverskoy District. Arkady was still silent. After hearing that explosion, Spartan was fairly sure he knew what he would find when he got there.

~*~

12 : A bell for the boatman

Killings continued all over the globe. Gillette and his team were found peacefully gassed in his car. It had been rigged to pump a deadly toxin into the cabin as soon as the engine had been started. They were all dead before he had even engaged drive. The officer who found the idling vehicle in the car park of Place Louis Lépine was instantly killed when he dragged open the door to find out what was wrong. Those who followed were more circumspect.

Officer Mandy Prius was found beside Clodagh Catchum in the widow's garden. Both had been shot cleanly through the head with a high-velocity rifle. At the exact time the shooting happened a controlled explosion had destroyed most of the core hardware for the precinct's AI, Moebius.

That evening Ruth Pearce had tried to summon Viracocha for their usual conversation but got no response. Distraught, she tracked down Freedman and talked at him for hours. While she did so he worked out the following week's menus.

Everywhere the strikes proved very precise. People died and AIs winked out of existence. It would be days before anyone thought to connect the killings, and few would come up with a coherent reason for the murders. Not even members of the TP Council who had been involved in squid-related research were safe. When Raaka Tandon was gunned down on the steps of the telepaths' New York City headquarters, fear kept any onlookers' mouths shut, even though the killing had taken place in broad daylight.

With a sense of excited nerves, Katy Pavel came home to Chester Woodman's apartment. She had moved in when they started making plans for their wedding and the pair of them had been overjoyed with the arrangement. That afternoon had proved different, however. The place was unnaturally quiet and she began to experience a real sense of dread in her warning

Talent. Chester would normally be listening to old classical music when he was home, stuff like Mozart or Elvis, but today the apartment rang with silence. It was choked with it.

She entered the rooms with nervous caution, ready to run at any moment. She found Chester in the kitchen. He had been shot twice, once to the chest and once to the head. There was a lot of blood spatter on the kitchen units and the wall. More blood was pooling on the floor. There was a hot, metallic smell in the room. Katy began to vibrate uncontrollably. She felt sick and confused. Her mind was a mess of conflicting emotions. She had to get out of there, had to find help. She turned.

The man was on her like a landslide. She had no chance to escape his grasp, no chance to scream. One of his hands was at her throat as the other began tearing at her panties. His intention was clear. She was going to die but he was going to rape her first. Katy sent out the equivalent of a telepathic scream for help and Jilly answered instantly.

KATY, I'M SCARED.

Jilly, help me, please.

RAAKA'S BEEN KILLED. WHAT'S THAT MAN DOING?

Jilly, he's going to hurt me. Help me, please!

Jilly bellowed as if in pain, *I DON'T KNOW WHAT TO DO. SOMEONE HELP HER!*

Damn fucking right I will.

The man had tugged his erect penis from the flies of his pants when the new voice entered the silent conversation. Katy was choking and the periphery of her vision was becoming dark. She barely struggled as the man prised open her legs. And then the new telepath struck.

The man was literally thrown across the room by the force of her will. He crashed into the wall and then scythed around on the floor, his face turning blue. His eyes bulged from their sockets and his tongue thickened and protruded between his gasping lips. His hands tore helplessly at his throat. It took a while for him to finally choke to death and Katy watched every second. When he died his penis jerked and shot semen across

257

the floor. In her traumatised state Katy merely registered the fact as an interesting item of information.

Katy, pull yourself together.

WHO ARE YOU?

Not now, Jilly. We have to help Katy.

Who are you? asked Katy.

Get yourself cleaned up, Katy, and then get out of there. If there's one killer there might be two. I can't find anyone else in the area but that doesn't mean there isn't another on the way. I'm coming to New York today but I can't do anything before the morning. Jilly, tell the Council I'm coming. Tell them I'll be bringing Katy with me.

Who are you, please? asked Katy.

I'm Milla Carter. The voice was calm in her head. *And we're not taking any more of this shit from Norms. Okay?*

Okay.

OKAY, echoed Jilly.

Hector Kaminsky had been chief of the 7th Precinct for over seven years. He had worked his way up from an apprenticeship spent patrolling the beat through to his time as a detective and so on up the chain of command. His people respected him because he had done their jobs before and knew what they were going through. He knew when to give someone a break and when to give someone support.

Kaminsky could be avuncular on occasion or could take someone to task, but he would never give anyone a public tongue-lashing. He liked his team. They worked well together. He was fit to spit blood and bullets at what was happening in his precinct on that day of murder and destruction.

Police work involved risk, he knew that, but mostly it was about getting the paperwork done and making sure you've got back-up when you need it most. That should never include armed cover when you're out in a friend's backyard. Nor should it involve needing cover while working with the precinct's AI.

He had lost five officers in a single unprecedented day and, he had just learned, his forensic pathologist, Woodman. Civilians were being gunned down in the street. Kaminsky was a practising Catholic and he wondered if someone had rung the bell for Charon to carry souls across the River Styx then decided to increase his workload to make it all worthwhile.

The killings had been too well-rehearsed and random to have been the work of any of his usual suspects. And what was left of his forensic team was trying to work out why Woodman's killer had apparently choked to death while spraying semen all over his pants and the floor. Kaminsky had heard about cases like that during a hanging, but this dead man wasn't wearing a noose. In fact the man had no ligature marks on his neck or any other injuries they could find. Kaminsky bit into his doughnut then poured cream into his coffee before taking a delicious, forbidden mouthful. His doctor had advised against coffee and the chief knew he was going to get reflux as a result of drinking it, but he needed the sugar and the caffeine. And it wasn't going to kill him.

Evidence proved Woodman's girlfriend had been at the scene at the time of the killing, but she had disappeared and hadn't resurfaced since. Probably a wise move, all things considered. He leafed through everything he had compiled about the previous twenty-four hours and gazed towards his rain-washed window. He wished Catchum was still alive; he needed a lateral thinker on the case. He wished Prius was on hand. He needed her dogged approach to the evidence. He sighed and drank some more of his coffee. The first twinge of acid began to burn, but at least he was still alive.

~*~

13 : Know thine enemy

Milla had never seen the telepaths' New York City headquarters before, but by dipping into Katy's memories she soon felt as if she knew it well enough to think of it as home. When Ben dropped her and Katy by the entrance she had a full proximity mental scan in place. No one was going to perform a drive-by while she was in town.

There, at the end of the street, she registered a shooter on the back of a speeder-bike driven by his partner in crime. They were already revving up to hit Katy as she mounted the steps. Milla smiled when she realised that to these men she would only count as collateral damage. *Or maybe not.*

These were the men who had killed Raaka the day before. She had liked the Receiver when she met her, so it was time to level the score. The speeder burned down through the traffic towards them and Katy took Milla's arm in a tight grip.

'Threat,' she said. 'I can feel it.'

'I know.' Milla pointed at the speeder. 'There, now watch.'

The speeder seemed to jerk in the middle of the road and then leaned over at an alarming angle before it swerved at high speed into an alleyway. She heard the collision and watched as a massive garbage droid rolled out of the same alleyway moments later, its bonnet grid slightly dented. It began to wail in protest about lunatic bikers on the streets these days. Shooter and driver had been rendered to little more than a bloody smear in the dirty alley, their speeder mashed and flattened.

She allowed Katy to lead the way and open the secret door in the circular consulting room. The Shutterbox receptionists in the entrance atrium had followed their progress with an avid interest that Milla clearly sensed, but once they had entered the plant-lined inner rooms she felt her Talents shielded by the plant-life. *This is where TPs come to get away from their Talents*, she realised. *Why would they want that?* She drew on her inner energy while taking a deep breath of the green-scented air. And there it was back again, her full spectrum of telepathic abilities.

Milla had read the surviving Council members' minds before she saw them, and she was braced for Jilly's greeting before it lashed out.

HELLO, KATY. HELLO, MILLA. WELCOME.

Thank you Jilly, she replied.

The one called Sheila stood and walked to meet her. Song and Susan observed but said nothing. Diana fixed Milla with a predatory glare and leaned forward.

Sheila said, 'You are on record as a Shutterbox, Milla Carter. It is evident that you are much more than that, not so?'

Milla looked at her for a beat, allowing time for them to consider her silence and her absolute calm in the face of the feared TP Council. Then she smiled her most dimpled and engaging smile.

'Sheila,' she said, lightly, 'where I come from it is considered polite to make introductions before starting your fucking inquisition. Susan, Song, Diana – I'm pleased to meet you. Jilly...' The bovine Transmitter beamed happily at the mention of her name. '...it's good to meet you in the flesh. No,' she said as Jilly got ready to lash out another gleeful greeting, 'we've already said hello, haven't we? No need to do it twice.'

Diana said, 'Don't tell Jilly what to do, Carter.'

'Oh, Jilly doesn't mind.' *Do you dear?*

NO! And Jilly giggled because Milla was talking with both her mouth and her mind. She was having fun. Her colleagues weren't.

'Before we do anything else,' said Milla, 'I think you need to both listen to, and read, Katy here. She has something you need to hear.'

Katy stepped forward and told her story succinctly. She explained how she had spent the night in an apartment belonging to the Pearce Corporation, something organised by Milla Carter. She told them that Carter had saved her life twice during the last twenty-four hours, the second time right there

261

outside TP headquarters. She told them about the murder of her fiancée Chester Woodman in his own home and about the attempted rape and strangling by her mystery assailant after finding Woodman's body.

She told the story in a clear, unaffected voice. Her tears had come freely the previous night when the full shock of her loss had suddenly struck home, and she had realised all the things she was going to miss most about her man. His scarlet ears, dinner at his club, his gentle honesty and his acceptance of everything she'd done before she met him. Chester deserved more than a bullet to the head, but at least the man who had done it had died in agony.

Milla stood slightly behind her and to one side. She was reading the Council in a fashion they would never have believed possible, but she was also maintaining her proximity scan. She was watching when a large woman crouched and hefted a state-of-the-art missile drone launcher to her shoulder on the roof of the building opposite. She had fixed the cross-hairs of her guidance module onto the roof of the TP headquarters directly above the area where the Council was gathered.

Without losing any contact with the women around her, Milla took complete control of the large woman's mind. She found the vehicle the woman had arrived in just minutes before and she made her target that instead. The woman fired her missile, watched it obliterate her vehicle in a ball of plasma, and then carefully made her way down from the roof.

She brought the woman into the atrium and made her wait there. Then she butted in on Katy's story.

'Susan,' she said, 'there's a woman out in the reception area who I'd like you all to meet. Could you and Song go and fetch her please? I know you don't usually allow Norms in here, but this is very important and I think you'll agree we're living in unusual times.'

The two women looked to Sheila for guidance. She nodded sharply. When she arrived, led by the two telepaths, the large

262

woman bulked hugely over everyone else in the room. When Milla stepped before her she looked like a child.

'I don't think any of these seats are big enough,' she said, and commanded the woman to sit on one of the divans.

'Now,' Milla said, 'I invite you to dip into this creature's brain. I think you will find it interesting. Afterwards we will have a lot to discuss.'

The Council read the woman's mind. The task took longer for them than it had for Milla, but they were thorough. Afterwards they looked somehow shrunken. All of them, even Diana, looked to Milla for guidance. She circled the large woman and then sent her a mental command. The woman stood and lumbered out of the room.

'Aren't you going to kill her?' hissed Diana. 'Surely she's still dangerous.'

'No,' said Milla. 'I've sent her back to her own people. They'll take care of the big bitch. After all, she did launch a missile at her own command transport and she was surely seen coming in here. What's more she won't be able to explain any of it; in fact she won't actually remember any of it. She's toast.'

Katy said, 'So, now we know who the enemy is and why they want me dead. We know why Raaka was killed. The question is: what can we do about it?'

'What can we do about it?' Milla looked around her with incredulity, scorn etching her tone with acid. 'What can we do about it? What do you *think* we can do about it? We can take the fight into their own minds; we can hound them in their sleep. We can whisper in their five-star ears while they're taking a dump. We know that we're up against the entire senior executive of planet Earth and they think they have infinite resources and can't lose. But ladies, we have us, and us is fucking impressive and, more importantly, you now have *me*. It's time to let the Dragon roar.'

~*~

263

14 : Alone again, unnaturally

The coral lacework in the fluid-filled crystal casket began to pull apart like clenched fingers opening after prayer. It steepled, stood proud of the fluid then opened fully like narrow, unearthly petals greeting the dawn. The baby was gone and in its place was a coltish young woman with a lean, athletic body and a swirl of jet-black hair. She was completely naked. Her skin was so white it was almost translucent and veins tight under her flesh lent her a cool, bluish cast.

She sat up, thrusting her upper body clear of the fluid and roared air into her expanding lungs, her first unassisted breath since the bright-coloured tracery had bound so tightly over her new-born host's body. She then coughed out strings of thick liquid and something sticky and black. She paused to gather her energies then stood up, shaking and weak, still coughing. It was only then that she opened her ice-white eyes and studied the room. She couldn't remember much about it. Her transition from transport droid to casket had been very swift when she'd arrived almost a year earlier. One major difference did strike home though.

She was alone.

Her throat was sore after vomiting birthing waters and undigested nutrients back into the casket − and her limbs were still unco-ordinated after her long time under the lace − but she was feeling stronger with every passing second. All trace of the scrawny baby was gone and the new-born woman had begun to move with something of her old accustomed grace by the time she had padded to the door.

Silence rang like a muted bell in every chamber of the old research station. It pressed against her ears. For the first time she felt vulnerable in her nakedness and she flexed her hands into steel blades as if to prove she was still strong. *The only threat here*, she thought, *is me*. Her stride became more confident.

She showered – emptying her bladder while she did so – then dried herself and applied perfume and deodorant before climbing into her trademark fitted black top and short skirt. As usual she didn't bother with underwear. She pulled on her crystal high heels and stood tall, arching her back with the sheer pleasure she got from her own body, from the play of long limbs and powerful muscles.

A full-length mirror drew her next and she approached it tentatively at first and then with growing appreciation. Her silhouette was a thing of familiar beauty.

'Hello, you,' she said in a smoky, rasping voice dripping with aural honey. 'Welcome back.' And then she turned the wall light on. 'Oh.'

The baby she had once been had evidently taken its own path to maturity and the face gazing back at her from the glass was not the one she had expected to see. Her complexion was perfect and her ice-white eyes glowed dangerously under her mane of midnight hair, but all else had changed.

Instead of the narrow features she would have recognised this girl had a more rounded look, full-lipped and heart-shaped. Her beauty would still stop traffic but she would now attract a different sort of reaction from observers. Her old face had longer features and an Asiatic slant to its eyes. It had a dangerous allure, something predatory yet irresistible that drew men like iron filings to a powerful magnet. This girl, she realised with a shudder, was *cute*.

What would her sisters make of her? And what about Little One? Would it know her or attack her? She would just have to find out. But where was everyone? The casket's technology was decades old but it must have been able to predict when she would be released. Surely Katana and Pandora would have been on hand to greet her and help with her first steps in this new body. Where were they?

Pregnant silence pressed densely around her and premonition chilled her spine with rumour. How *could* she be alone? It was impossible. Kat and Pan would have made sure to be there for her resurrection, even if Shiva and Nightshade were away.

She stalked back through the empty halls and headed for the big living room where she and her sisters had spent many long, pleasurable evenings, unique creatures celebrating their differences from the common herd, killers who cast no shadows.

The room looked empty when she first entered it. The big fire was cold and the Virtuo Window showed little more than the grey mistiness of an ice storm in the mountains, but something made her look more closely at the room and the furnishings. What was she not seeing?

She turned up the lights and caught the glint of highly polished metal on the rug in the centre of the room. She walked towards it with sick and certain dread dragging her every step. It was Little One, Baby Legs and Cutie crumpled inertly together like the elements of a broken machine or metal wheel. She stretched out her hand towards them and the nearest razor-sharp legs lashed out at her with sudden and whip-like ferocity. She pulled her hand away just a moment too late and an acid sting burned two of her fingertips while an arc of bright blood flicked across the floor.

She sucked at her fingers and the taste of her blood reminded her that she was starving. The motionless memory stores would have to wait until after she had eaten. Her fingers healed in a few painful moments. She turned away from the collapsed, spider-like creatures and surveyed the rest of the room.

That was when she saw the clothes and the shoes. They were side-by-side on one of the sofas as if their owners had somehow vanished, evaporated out of them. Her breathing became ragged as she gazed at the petty remnants and she became increasingly certain these were all that remained of her sisters.

It was all too obvious to her enhanced senses that these garments and pairs of footwear had not been deliberately posed to create such a ghoulish illusion. Or had they? For one heart-stopping moment she wondered if Pandora and Katana were hiding somewhere, waiting to spring out on her with shouts of

266

laughter and cries of 'Surprise!' But it wasn't going to happen; it was too ridiculous an idea.

Kat was a cold-hearted killer with a keen mind behind eyes that could frost a window from a hundred metres. Pan was just as dangerous to anyone who wasn't family, but she too was no prankster. The reason those clothes were piled precisely on the sofa was because their owners had died in them, somehow been vanished in them.

She walked slowly across the room and stood over the puddled silks and cottons. There was a vague smell about them. Something funky, a little like spoiled fish. The shoes glistened with a jelly-like substance.

With a lurch, Su Nami was overcome with a sense of vertigo and nausea. That strange jelly was all that remained of her sisters. They had been melted, boiled down to nothing, their bodies now little more than a wet trace. Their hard-trained invulnerability overcome without as much as a struggle. She heard a gentle tapping noise and through her blurring vision she saw dark spots appearing on the clothes, large wet splashes spreading out into the fabric. They were her tears. She was angry at her weakness.

An hour or so later a Lexus ST270 climbed out into the gusting storm and fought its way from the mountain. Against the screaming winds another sound built up and boomed into the Russian night. Gouts of blue white flame billowed into the tempest's grip and were instantly torn to scraps and tatters while the mountain shrugged and sank in on itself by several metres.

Su Nami watched it happen while her car was buffeted by storm and shock wave. For the moment she didn't care if her car was clawed from the sky. When the mountain was once more at peace she keyed a new destination into her vehicle then sat for a while, absorbed in her thoughts. Her time for tears was passed.

At least now, she thought, *they have a fitting monument to their lives. Let this mountain mark their graves. At least it's better than two pairs of damp shoes. And now,* she was sure, *there's only me alone against the world. Well, watch out little humans.*

There was nothing cute about her smile at that moment. She hit *drive* and the Lexus curved away towards the west. She had an idea, but first there was someone she needed to see.

Epilogue

A ripple of heat washed through that area of the Swarm before which stood Eddie and Vesper. It tried to lash out at them with burning tentacles but they remained just beyond its reach.

You failed, the conjoined mind told the alien. *Millions of years of planning wasted. Your trap was tripped and it failed. You underestimated humankind. It is stronger now in ways you can never understand.*

Why do you mock us, little immortals? The hiss of the Swarm grated on their minds' ears. *The parasite lives on borrowed time. We wanted to be generous, make its end painless, perhaps even enjoyable. But no.*

A hissing, chattering sound filled all near space.

No, it must die cut from the branch, burned from existence. It must be hacked, yes, ripped away. The parasite cannot live; it cannot be allowed to soil this, our home. This is our space, little immortals. We allow you to share it but never think of it as yours.

The hissing sound grew louder. *Of course*, it said, *if you choose to you can always leave.*

Eddie and Vesper realised that the sound was laughter. They gazed at the seemingly endless fence of alien flesh that had corralled them in the solar system for the whole of their existence in the construct. 'The architecture of envy', Milla had called it. The work of an alpha creature abandoned when its creator began a new project and an ape stepped down from the trees and thoughtfully picked up a tool.

This was a living fence of angry flesh and livid minds. Minds evolved enough to know they had been abandoned by their maker and had ever since been seeking revenge against the usurpers. The creator itself was beyond their abilities to harm, but the new favourites could be made to suffer — and the Swarm's hatred had been simmering for aeons.

The great solar system girdling sphere of the Swarm hissed and chattered around its entire inner surface. It had become resolved. *The parasite must die.* With a burst of geysering heat that was seen by observers on Lagrange II the sphere began to contract inwards on its long journey towards Earth.

Eddie and Vesper also headed inwards. They had to warn humankind of the threat. They needed to talk with Milla Carter. And now, finally, they were afraid.

Milla Carter will return in **Soul's asylum: Star weaver**

Derek E Pearson's Body Holiday trilogy

Body Holiday – A Time To Prey (pub: Aug 2015)

Lethal is rarely this lovely

The concluding volume of this extremely popular trilogy

To her lover she's a walking dream, to her enemies she's a waking nightmare.

Milla Carter, science fiction's sexiest telepath, is back for the last chapter in the Body Holiday trilogy and the breathless pace is only matched by the manic humour

Body Holiday – Shadow Players (pub: Apr 2015)

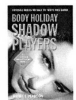

"...Pearson is the possessor of an extraordinary imagination that brilliantly assaults every variant of the sci-fi genre. His writing is vivid, urban and unflinching in its descriptions, taking the reader on a breathtaking journey through Saturn's rings, outer world 'constructs', altered perceptions and a glorious African landscape smouldering with sexual heat and the odour of violence.

This is hard-hitting story telling with full-on language and a brutally splendid polt twist, which, if you make it to the end, will leave you crossing your legs! "

Surrey Life magazine (UK), Sep 2015, Juliette Foster

Body Holiday (pub: Aug 2014)

"This imaginative, sexually explicit book has more swear words in it than a **Gordon Ramsay** show, yet its edgy 'in your face' writing and tightly structured plot are so addictive that it's damn near impossible to put down.

The car chases, small but chilling amounts of gore and explosions of Armageddon proportions give the story the adrenalin coated rush of a **Grand Theft Auto** game. Yet there's also a quasi gallows humour running through the narrative, neatly alleviating the underlying tension... "

Surrey Life magazine (UK) Jan 2015, Juliette Foster

Marino Branch
Brainse Marglann Mhuiríne
Tel: 8336297

CPSIA information can be obtained at www.ICGtesting.com
Printed in the USA
LVOW08s1823310316

481608LV00006B/787/P